FALLEN

BOOK 3 OF THE DJINN WARS

CHRISTINE POPE

Dark Valentine Press

FALLEN

ISBN: 978-0692460788
Copyright © 2015 by Christine Pope
Published by Dark Valentine Press

Cover design and book layout by Indie Author Services.

To learn more about this author, go to
www.christinepope.com.

FALLEN

CHAPTER ONE

Eventually, Lindsay Adarian and I summoned the courage to emerge from the repair shop where we'd been hiding and blink up at the sky. It was still somewhat gray and lowering, but in an ordinary late winter sort of way. No livid clouds the color of a bruise, no circling, angry djinn. Nothing supernatural about it at all.

We knew better, though.

Lindsay stood on the crumbling concrete step outside the shop's main door and shook her head. "It's hard to believe that tiny thing" —and she pointed at the little black box I still held clutched in my cold and shaky fingers— "is holding off an entire army of djinn."

"Well, thank God it is, or we wouldn't be having this conversation right now." I glanced around but saw no one. Not that I'd really expected to; who would have the courage to come outside after that near-attack? The Chosen would be terrified, and the djinn probably not in that much better a frame of mind, their powers now more or less shut down by Miles Odekirk's device.

But then movement down the street caught my eye, and my heart began to beat a little faster. Not from fear, though. Even at this distance, I recognized that purposeful stride, the long black hair blowing in the harsh breeze.

Jace.

As soon as he caught sight of me, he began to walk even faster. I had to wonder where he got the energy, considering how much the box I was holding seemed to steal away the very life force of the djinn, leaving them listless and not much of a danger to anyone.

I didn't have to wonder for much longer, because in the next instant he was there, pulling me into his arms, crushing the device into my sternum. Not that I cared too much; right then it was just good to feel his arms around me, to hear his voice say my name.

"Jessica, so it was you, wasn't it? Zahrias said I shouldn't venture forth to look for you, but I couldn't hide in the resort like a coward, not when you were out here alone."

"Not exactly alone," I told him, pulling away slightly so I could nod in Lindsay's direction. "But considering how we both just got the crap scared out of us, I think I can safely say we're *very* glad to see you."

"That's for damn sure," Lindsay put in as she approached, still shooting those wary glances skyward, as if she expected the djinn to return at any second and rain holy hell down upon us. "Glad to see you're so... mobile."

Jace's mouth twisted. "I suppose that is one thing for which I can thank Captain Margolis and Miles Odekirk. It seems that all those weeks under the influence of that device have made me a bit more able to tolerate its effects than the rest of my people. At any rate, while I am tired and wish more than anything that you could shut it off, I can still function, more or less."

"You're amazing, you know that?" I said, then went up on my toes so I could give him a kiss on the cheek. His skin felt cool beneath my lips, but maybe that was only because of the cold wind blowing on us and not because of the device's influence. Well, I could hope, anyway.

His shoulders lifted a fraction of an inch, as if to brush off the compliment. "I'm not sure about that. There was no way I would wait any longer before coming to make sure you were all right. But now we must get back to the resort. Zahrias wishes to speak to you."

"Good," I said grimly. "Because there are one or two things I'd like to bring up with him as well."

The draining effects of Odekirk's device were a bit more obvious on the djinn leader. Zahrias was paler than I'd ever seen him, and, rather than standing, as he preferred to do during these sorts of convos, he sat in a chair by the hearth, where a fire crackled away. Despite that, the room was fairly chilly, and I didn't bother to take off my coat, but only unbuttoned it. And I could tell from the way Zahrias seemed to shiver beneath his heavy brocade robe that the blazing fire wasn't helping him all that much, although he sat so close to it that I worried a spark might fly out and set fire to his clothing or hair.

Lindsay had gone to check on her own lover, leaving me to attend this briefing with only Jace at my side. Just as well; her usual composure seemed to have deserted her, and I sort of doubted she would have been able to make a very cogent report on what we had seen circling in the skies above Taos. Better that she have some alone time with Rafi while she attempted to restore her frayed nerves, rather than be subjected to Zahrias' questions.

"I suppose I should commend you on your quick thinking," he said, tone wry despite his obvious discomfort. His gaze strayed the side table where I'd placed the device and then moved back to me. "But as it has only made all of us djinn mostly useless...."

"Would you rather be dead?" I asked. Beside me, Jace shifted, although he didn't bother to protest my harsh words. We all knew they were only the truth.

"No, of course not," Zahrias replied. Lips compressing to a hard line, he glanced up at Jasreel. "I see now what you mean. This is very...unpleasant."

"That's one word for it." Jace faced the other djinn squarely, arms crossed over his chest. Unlike Zahrias, he was wearing regular, "mortal" clothes—a dark sweater and faded jeans, motorcycle boots. In different circumstances, I would have found his current attire almost insanely hot. Unfortunately, I had other things occupying my mind at the moment. "But, as Jessica pointed out, it is still better than the alternative."

"And about that," I put in, watching as Zahrias' expression grew shuttered. While he didn't exactly look away, neither did he meet my gaze directly. He knew what was coming next, and didn't want to discuss it...probably because, like the rest of us, he had no answers. But I had to ask anyway. "Just what the *hell* is going on? I thought you had a truce with the other djinn, that they had sworn to leave the One Thousand and their Chosen alone."

"We did—we *do* have a truce."

It was my turn to cross my arms. "Well, it seems like someone on the other side didn't get the memo, because that sure looked like a whole bunch of pissed-off djinn to me. Not that I claim to be an expert. Please, tell me I'm wrong."

"You are not wrong," Jace said, and Zahrias gave him a pained look. Appearing to ignore his leader's glare, Jace went on, "I saw them. Or rather, I felt them coming. We all did. It was the sort of gathering of our kind that is impossible to ignore. As they moved in above us, I tried to call out to them, to ask what they were doing here, but they acted as if they couldn't hear me. Or at least they pretended not to."

"The same way they ignored me as well," Zahrias said. His brow looked positively thunderous, but his voice sounded calm enough as he continued, "From which I gathered that they did not come in peace."

"No kidding," I remarked. "So...what's going on? Why aren't they honoring the truce?"

"I don't know."

Just three words, the syllables ground out from between clenched teeth. I could tell from the dark red flicker in Zahrias' eyes that he was angry, so angry that flames should have been dancing all around him—but they weren't. That manifestation of his abilities must have been tamped down by the device as well. Too bad, as they provided a helpful bellwether for his emotions.

Not that I really needed the extra assistance at the moment. The frown he wore was fearsome enough, and I saw it mirrored in Jace's features as well.

"So they have broken their faith with us," he said, and Zahrias nodded.

"It would seem that way."

"You're awfully calm about it," I told him, and his mouth pulled into the same flat line I'd seen a few moments earlier.

"I have no choice but to be calm," he replied, pushing himself to his feet. He seemed to falter for a second, as if having difficulty maintaining his balance, but then he walked normally enough to the fireplace and leaned back against the mantel of carved juniper.

In doing so, he blocked a good deal of the heat from the fire as well. Then I realized he probably needed it more than I did, or even Jace. My own djinn partner had, as he'd said, far more experience managing the debilitating effects of Miles Odekirk's device.

Zahrias went on, "For the moment, we are protected. I was not indulging in sarcasm when I thanked you for your quick thinking, Jessica, because only a moment more, and all here might have been lost. We are few, and they brought many against us. However, I doubt that any of the djinn living here wish for the current situation to continue indefinitely." He paused, and the shadows beneath his eyes seemed to deepen. "The draining effects are bad enough, but throttled like this, we can no longer use our powers to keep the lights on, the heating systems running. It is going to be a very cold night."

A shiver went through me that didn't have much to do with the temperature in the room. It had been a cold day, but not freezing. But overnight, it would be back in the teens if we were lucky, and possibly colder than that. I hadn't even stopped to think about the way the djinn had been quietly providing everyone here with heat and light...and running water, too, for all I knew. Those were issues that would need to be addressed, and soon.

"At least all the rooms here in the resort have fire-places," Jace said evenly. "We will not want for heat, not in the near term. As for lighting, we can look for candles and oil lamps and such in the shops in town. Luckily, the device will protect us as we move about, since the central part of the town should be mostly protected as well."

"And in the long term?" Zahrias asked. There was very little inflection in his voice that I could detect, but a certain hardness to his jaw told me he didn't expect we'd be able to make do for very much longer.

"We'll figure it out," I told him. No, I didn't like the idea of being without central heat or electricity. However, there had to be something we could do. "I'm sure there are places around here that have generators. Houses with propane tanks for heating and cooking. We can start scavenging for what we need. It'll be all right. There's technology all around us—we just have to figure out how to use it."

"And what about the other djinn? Do you think they'll stay away forever?" Jace asked. We'd been standing next to one another, but right then I felt his hand slide into mine and grip my fingers. His own flesh was cool, and a shiver went through me. He might be managing to give a decent impression of someone coping with the loss of his powers and the associated drain on his vitality, but I knew better. Every hour, every minute, every second that the device operated meant accompanying hours of discomfort, if not outright pain.

One hand went through Zahrias' hair in a nervous gesture I'd never seen him make before. "They will for now, as they assess the situation. For how long?" His shoulders lifted. "I'm not certain. Jessica, will that thing continue to operate once it's been switched on?"

"Yes," I replied. "That is, I can't say for absolutely sure, since I'm no expert, but from what I could tell, it seemed to be pretty much a 'set it and forget it' kind of thing. From what we've been able to find out, it's self-powered. That is, we don't need to recharge it or anything. Beyond that, I don't know much about how to dial it in—that's Lindsay's field of expertise—but I do know it's covering the widest area possible right now. If you want it set up differently—"

"I do not," Zahrias cut in. "I remember you said that it becomes more powerful as the area it 'protects' shrinks. I doubt any of my people would appreciate having its effects intensified. Besides, even though we are gathered here at the resort for safety's sake, it is probably better that as much area here in Taos is shielded as possible."

True, especially if we were going to have to start looting the immediate area for any useful items. I began to nod, then stopped, my free hand going to my mouth.

Jace's fingers tightened on mine. "What is it?" he asked.

"The hunting party," I said. "Aidan and Clay and Martine. They went out a couple of hours ago. Have they come back?"

Zahrias and Jace exchanged a single unreadable look, and Jace shook his head.

"We've heard nothing of them," Jace said quietly. "But I was speaking with Zahrias when the attack began, and so it's possible they returned and we simply heard nothing of it."

"It will be easy enough to find out," Zahrias added. He cocked his head to one side, eyes narrowing, and then his lips pressed together. Something had clearly annoyed him, although I couldn't begin to guess what.

His next statement clarified things a little.

"I cannot call her this way any longer," he said. As my eyebrows went up, he explained, "Lauren. She is not my Chosen, but she is with my brother, and that created a close enough bond between us that in the past I could easily summon her with my mind. Now, though, with my powers suppressed...." The words trailed off, and he gave an eloquent lift of his shoulders.

She's not your lapdog any longer, I thought. But maybe that was a little harsh. After all, I hadn't gotten much indication that Lauren minded being Zahrias' executive assistant, so to speak.

"I'll see if I can find her," I offered. "Actually, I'm kind of surprised that she and a whole lot of other people aren't here already, banging on the door and demanding answers."

That remark earned me a very thin smile. "My people know better than to force their way in where they are not invited."

Well, that was one big difference between humans and djinn. I didn't argue the point, though, but only lifted my own shoulders.

"I'll be back as quickly as I can," I said, then went up on my toes to kiss Jace on the cheek before I let myself out of Zahrias' audience chamber...that is, conference room.

The hallways appeared deserted as I headed out. Maybe no one was going to come and ask Zahrias what the hell was going on, but I knew we mere mortals tended to come together in times of crisis, which meant I had a pretty good idea of where I could find everyone.

A babble of voices echoed down the corridor when I approached the open restaurant area that the Taos group had been using as its communal dining room.

Apparently, even the lush plantings there weren't enough to muffle the noise. To my surprise, I saw Lindsay standing in the middle of a large and agitated group, her hands waving in the air as she appeared to describe what she'd seen less than an hour earlier.

As I hesitated at the edge of the crowd, she seemed to realize I was there, and stopped abruptly. "Ask Jessica," she said. "She was at the shop with me."

Everyone swiveled in my direction, djinn and mortal together. Right then I thought that they'd never appeared more alike, as they all seemed to be wearing similar expressions of worry and dismay. Also, the djinn were clearly struggling with the effects of Odekirk's device—they looked pale and tragic, and more than one of them was clinging to his or her Chosen as if the other person was the only thing holding them up.

Although I felt for them, for the drain on their energy they were currently suffering, I still hated being the center of attention like this. I'd never been the sort of person who liked speaking in front of other people, or doing anything that would attract the notice of others—sexy Halloween costumes notwithstanding. Those had been my friend Elena's idea anyway.

But now? I stood rooted in place, gaze scanning the crowd for Lauren. Damn it, where was she?

Since everyone there was staring at me, obviously expecting an answer, I knew I had to say something. After clearing my throat, I replied, "Well, I don't think what I saw was too different from what Lindsay saw. A dark cloud of djinn. Angry-looking djinn. At least, I think they were angry. It's kind of hard to tell when someone's hovering a thousand feet or so above your head."

"Where's Zahrias?" someone else demanded, a man probably around my age or a year or so younger. He had his arm around the waist of a wan-looking djinn woman. I didn't recognize either one of them, but I'd only been in Taos for a few days, and had spent most my time with Jace or with Lindsay in her make-shift lab. Socializing hadn't been too high on my list of priorities.

"In his room, talking with Jasreel," I said calmly.

"He should be out here with us," the man shot back, blue eyes blazing.

"Maybe he should," I said. "But I'm not his keeper. I'm just looking for Lauren."

The man grumbled something. At the same time, to my relief, I saw Lauren step out of the crowd and come toward me, her djinn partner Dani stumbling along behind her. This was the first time I'd really had a chance to study his features, although I'd met him briefly before. There was something in the shape of his mouth and his brows that recalled Zahrias, although in a gentler, kinder-looking arrangement. This djinn would have been a lot less scary to find on your door-step, telling you that you were his Chosen.

At the moment, though, he just looked ill, eyes shadowed, breathing labored. I hated that they all had to go through this, but, as I'd pointed out to Zahrias, death was a lot worse than discomfort. And more final.

"Zahrias needs me?" Lauren asked.

I stepped closer to her and lowered my voice, since I really didn't want the whole crowd listening in. "Have you heard anything about the group that went out hunting earlier? Aidan and Martine and Clay? They might have been—well, I'm not sure they were close enough for the device to have protected them."

In an echo of my own gesture from a few minutes before, Lauren's hand went to her mouth. "Shit. *Shit.* No, I'd—well, I'd completely forgotten, what with everything that's been happening." She glanced back at Dani, whose shoulders went up infinitesimally. I didn't know if that was all the comment he was willing to make on the subject, or whether he simply didn't have the energy to give a larger shrug. "But they always check in with me when they come back, so I know they're not here."

"Shit" was right. Aidan was the only one of the group I knew beyond attaching a face to a name, but I liked him. And even if I didn't, there had already been enough death, enough people lost. Even three more was too many.

"If we go to look for them—" I began, but Lauren shook her head.

"We can't. It's not safe."

And that was the worst part of it. The best we were able to figure, the device could only protect an area of about one square mile. It had to stay here in Taos where it could do the most good. For all I knew, the rogue djinn were lurking right there on the periphery of its field of effect, just waiting for someone to step over the line.

Jace would never allow me to take such a risk. Aside from that, I knew I wasn't brave enough to attempt that kind of stunt. Anyway, sacrificing myself on a hopeless mission wouldn't help anyone, least of all the people I was trying to save.

"So...what? We just sit here and wait?"

Dani spoke for the first time then. His voice was almost as deep as Zahrias', but softer, not as harsh around the edges. "What else can we do? This demon device you've brought among us is the only thing protecting us. To leave this resort would certainly mean your death."

I was a little startled by the compassion in his voice. True, I'd already noted a number of differences between him and his brother, but even so, I hadn't expected him to be that concerned about a Chosen woman who wasn't his.

"Jace would never let you risk yourself like that," Lauren added.

As much as I wanted to argue with her, I knew she was right. Hell, he hadn't even wanted me to put myself in harm's way while trying to rescue *him*. So no way would he let me go running off to save a group of people I barely knew.

"I hate this," I muttered, and to my surprise, Lauren reached out and laid a hand on my arm.

"I know. We all do. We're all scared, and worried, and—"

Evony's voice cut into the conversation. "I'll go."

Startled, I glanced away from Lauren and Dani to see that Evony had approached us while we were talking, and was standing a foot or so away. Her face was stony, blank, and it was obvious that she had been addressing Lauren, not me.

Lauren seemed to recognize that as well, because she said, "Evony, it's way too dangerous."

A lift of her shoulders. "So what? It's not like I have all that much to live for."

I couldn't help myself, even though I knew I should be staying out of this. "That's not true—"

"Isn't it?" Evony looked back over at Lauren, effectively shutting me down. "Anyway, none of you get to tell me what to do. You're not in charge here."

"No, but I am," said Zahrias, his voice cutting through our conversation. I'd been so focused on Evony that I hadn't even seen him arrive. Jace stood next to him, equally grim-faced.

If I'd had someone like Zahrias staring me down, I didn't think I would have been as openly defiant as Evony. But she merely jammed her hands on her hips and glared up at him.

"In charge of all these poor bastards," she retorted, waving one hand in the general direction of the assembled djinn and Chosen. "But I didn't sign up to have you be the boss of me. You don't get to tell me what to do."

Zahrias stared at her. One muscle in his cheek twitched, and I had the incongruous thought that the twitch had actually come from suppressed amusement, not anger. Maybe he just wasn't used to people standing up to him, let alone some mortal barely more than a girl, someone who didn't even reach his shoulder. "Young woman, since you are now a member of this community, I *do* get to tell you what to do. Just as I will tell everyone else what to do as well."

As she gazed at him, open-mouthed, he swept past her with a passable imitation of his old assurance. God only knows the effort it cost him to stride so strongly, to keep his chin up while Odekirk's device was sucking away at the very essence of his powers.

Everyone else seemed to buy his performance, though, maybe because they were so busy trying to manage their own exhaustion and worry that they didn't have the energy to dissect Zahrias' behavior. He made his way to the front of the group, then raised his hands. All the murmuring that had begun with his arrival ceased.

When he spoke, it was without preamble—no "my friends" or "my fellow djinn" or anything like that. "We have suffered—if not precisely a blow, since the device protecting us now did prevent any sort of actual damage—at least a shock. We thought we were safe here. We thought our fellows would honor the truce and allow us our sanctuary. These two mortals" — he nodded first toward Lindsay, and then toward me—"witnessed the very beginning of what would have been an attack, but we all felt it. We knew our brethren were gathering, although they managed to hide their intent from us, almost until it was too late."

"Why?" asked one djinn, a tall man with dark red hair and amber eyes. "We have done nothing to provoke them."

Zahrias shook his head. "I cannot say why. They have not communicated with me, nor anyone else, so far as I can tell."

"But what of our own missing?" another djinn asked, this one a woman, curvy and dark. I noticed she stood alone, and that her eyes seemed to glitter with unshed tears. Something about her appeared vaguely familiar, and then I realized she was Aidan's partner. Well, that would explain the tears. She must be out of her mind with worry. Or at least, I assumed she must be. Jace would, if their situations had been reversed. Voice shaking, she added, "Are we to do nothing?"

When he replied, Zahrias' tone was gentler than I'd been expecting. "Lilias, I fear there is very little we *can* do. All we can do is hope that the djinn who attempted to attack us were thrown enough off-balance by Jessica's deployment of the device that they had no thought for hunting down any mortals who might have been outside the safe zone."

"That is not much of a hope," Lilias said. One of the tears that had shimmered in her dark eyes finally fought its way free from the tangle of her heavy lashes and began to roll down her cheek.

"But it is still a hope. We cannot allow ourselves to give up. Not this early."

As he spoke, I began to see why Zahrias had been given this post...or had requested it. I wasn't sure which was this case, since I still knew nothing of his history. Maybe soon I'd finally get a chance to ask Jace, but I knew that time wasn't now.

I flickered a glance over at him, wondering why he hadn't come to stand next to me. Then I realized he was rooted in the center of the hallway, arms crossed, as if to block anyone from going out that way.

Not anyone. Evony. He'd heard her outburst, and knew he had to do what he could to prevent her from going out and committing suicide while using the rescue of the hunting group as her excuse.

I love you, I thought at him then.

His mouth curved into a faint smile, quickly disappearing, as if he didn't want anyone else to see it. *And I love you. Because of that, I will do what I can to save your friend from herself.*

It may not be enough, I said sadly.

I know. But if she sacrifices herself, it will be in spite of our efforts, not because of them.

A quick nod, and then I had to return my attention to Zahrias, because he was speaking again.

"This is not the only trial we face, unfortunately. Our powers are gone, and so we no longer have the ability to provide the comforts we've been enjoying here—adequate heat and light, power to run the various electronic devices our Chosen have used."

Another murmur arose from the crowd. I could tell none of them had thought about that—the dining hall had a large fireplace at one end, and it was always kept blazing, possibly for atmosphere more than anything else. But because it had been lit, and because the room was so crowded, it was entirely possible no one had noticed it was a little cooler in here than usual.

Zahrias lifted his hands again, and the mutters subsided a bit. Not all the way, but enough that I could tell they wanted to hear what he had to say next. "I must ask our Chosen to come to our aid now. For tonight, that only means making sure we have enough wood to stock all the fires, and to help us gather bottled water and food so no one goes hungry or thirsty."

"We're going to lose everything in the freezers," Phillip said, his face tight with worry. Since he'd been acting as the community's chef, it made sense that our stockpiles of food were the first thing he'd thought of.

"Not right away," Lindsay replied. She still looked troubled, but now that she had Rafi next to her, his arm looped around her waist, she seemed a bit more composed. "If we keep the freezer doors shut, they'll retain their current temperature for a good while. Especially since we don't have central heat anymore. It's cold enough that they should hang on for longer than you'd think."

"Good," Zahrias said. "One night should suffice, and in the morning, we'll have teams go out to collect generators and fuel."

"Don't forget about solar panels," Lindsay put in. "I'm not a solar engineer, but I interned at a solar design firm a couple of summers ago, and I know enough that I'm pretty sure I can cobble something together for us."

I reflected then that it was a good thing some of the pretty faces the djinn had selected as their Chosen also had some brains behind them. Otherwise, we would have been in far worse shape than we were now.

Apparently, Zahrias seemed to think the same thing, because he nodded, and even managed to smile at Lindsay. "That is a very good idea. I will let you focus on that, and then perhaps Jessica and Jasreel can help coordinate the search for getting us the generators and fuel. If we all work together, then we should be up and running in no time."

Everyone seemed to be in agreement with that sentiment; I saw nods and even a few smiles from the crowd. Amazing how they all seemed to be focused on making life comfortable again. No one was even asking what Zahrias planned to do about the apparent change of heart of the rest of the djinn.

Then again, maybe that was exactly what he'd intended.

CHAPTER TWO

WE DECIDED TO KEEP THE DEVICE RUNNING BEHIND the front desk. From there, it would cover most of the downtown area—not that Taos had exactly what you'd call a downtown, but there was the plaza and the shops clustered around it, and then the commercial businesses along Highway 68, including the all-important Smith's grocery store. Lauren promised to keep an eye on the box, since Lindsay had to assemble a team to help her scrounge whatever solar equipment and supplies might be available in the area.

Not that any of us were too worried about someone touching the innocuous-looking little black box, since at the moment it was the only thing keeping us all alive.

Jace and I commandeered a big Super Duty pickup truck, figuring the bed would be big enough to haul a couple of generators back to the resort. We'd get the fuel on a separate trip. At least the weather was cooperating; the clouds from earlier in the morning had mostly disappeared, and the sky was a pure sapphire blue. The snow on the mountains seemed to positively sparkle in the sunlight.

On a day like this, it was difficult to remember the threat we all faced. But it was out there somewhere, even if that horde of hostile djinn appeared to have gone much farther away than the mile radius the device's field of effect afforded us.

After we'd climbed in the truck and I had pulled out of the resort's parking lot, I asked, "Where did they go?"

Jace didn't pretend to misunderstand. A brief glance out at the clear skies all around us, and then he shrugged. "A djinn doesn't have to be precisely *here*. We have our domains beyond this plane of existence, worlds that exist next to this one, impossibly far away, and yet so close you could reach out and touch them, if only you knew how to pierce the veil that separates them."

That sounded like something right out of science fiction. Then again, he'd already told me that the djinn had come from a different world than ours, a place where the rules of nature weren't exactly the same as they were here. I'd had to believe him, because his people were obviously just as real as anyone else, and yet they weren't human, no matter how much they might appear to be.

"And so when I turned on the device and drove them back—"

"They would have returned to that plane," he said absently, staring out the window. "So it's not as easy as keeping a watch to make sure they're not lurking around somewhere off in the distance. In a sense, they are still here, only in a world that Miles Odekirk's device can't reach."

"Comforting," I remarked dryly. Meaning we didn't dare switch the thing off for even a second, or they would be right on us. But what concerned me even more was the question I had to ask next. "Jace... *why?* You had an agreement with them. What in the world would make the other djinn change their minds about leaving the One Thousand and their Chosen alone?"

"Ace Hardware."

I blinked. "What?"

"There's a hardware store. A good place to look for a generator?"

I supposed so. Having never shopped for one, I had no idea, but I figured we'd better go check. I pulled into the parking lot, which still had a few dusty-looking vehicles sitting in it—older-model sedans and compact cars, all of which apparently were beneath the djinns' notice. Like the Los Alamos survivors, the

Chosen here had gravitated toward late-model SUVs and trucks with four-wheel drive.

We stopped in front of the store, in the fire lane. That was the most convenient spot. Besides, I didn't think the Taos P.D. would be by anytime soon to give me a ticket. Then I said, "You didn't answer me."

His fingers had been resting on the door handle of the truck, but at my remark, Jace let go of it and turned back toward me. Dark eyes met mine, grave and unwavering. "I didn't answer because I have no answer for you. I don't know. As far as I can tell, nothing has changed, or at least, Zahrias has had no indication of an alteration in their intentions."

"I'd say what happened this morning is a pretty good indication."

A small breath escaped Jace's lips, almost too faint to be called a sigh. "Yes, it would appear that way. As frightening as that was, though, it wasn't as if all the djinn who were not part of the Thousand participated."

"How many, then?" I asked. True, nineteen thousand djinn were an awful lot, and I doubted there had been that many swirling in the skies above Taos. Far more than we had in our little community, but still... maybe a couple hundred?

It seemed my guess wasn't too far off, because Jace replied, "I can't say exactly, but more than a hundred, and less than five. It's possible there is a subset of djinn who don't agree with the majority's decision and have attempted to take matters into their own hands."

While I doubted anyone would find such a pronouncement exactly encouraging, it did make me feel a little better. If Jace was right, then that would mean not all the djinn were against us. Not that I knew what we could possibly do to fight off a few hundred rampaging elementals, except keep Odekirk's shield operating and hope for the best. But several hundred was a lot less frightening than nineteen thousand.

"Do you think Zahrias will reach out to the other djinn?" I inquired. "I mean, the ones who probably are keeping the agreement."

Jace's reply was a small, sad smile. "How can he, when his powers are being cut off by the device? And even if they wanted to communicate with him, they would be equally constrained. The field the device projects is invisible to you, but to us djinn looking in from the outside, it is as if everything beyond it is obstructed by dark glass. And...it is painful to go through it. That was another of the experiments Margolis had Odekirk perform on me. They would shut off the device for only a few seconds, not long enough for my powers to return, and have one of their men push me through the edge of the field. It was like receiving electric shocks all over my body. That is why the djinn turned away so quickly. They would have no idea that passing through the field was something they could actually survive."

"My God, Jace." I knew that he'd been through hell, but every revelation like that made me want to go back to Los Alamos and inflict a little torture of my own on the commander.

"It's in the past." Unbelievably, Jace shrugged, as if all the suffering he'd gone through meant very little to him. "In the meantime," he went on, "we should look for that generator. I'm sure Phillip will be relieved if we can get the food protected, if nothing else."

"We'll all be relieved," I said. "Everybody's gotta eat—even djinn."

Jace grinned—a *real* grin, like the kind he used to flash me back when I still thought he was Jason Little River. "That's for sure. So let's make sure we can keep on doing it with minimal difficulty."

We got out of the pickup truck and went into the store. Its windows seemed intact, so I assumed no one had attempted to loot it. Well, Jace had told me there weren't many survivors in Taos, most likely because the town was so small. They'd probably moved on before they could even think about raiding the hardware store, and of course, up until now, the djinn and their Chosen hadn't needed much from it.

Since we'd been on these sorts of scavenging missions before, we'd thought ahead and brought flashlights with us, although we'd decided to get more when and if we found them. Candles would help to light the resort at night, but they weren't inexhaustible.

Flashlights and battery-powered lamps for camping would make a good supplement, depending on what the hardware store had stocked.

The flashlights and spare batteries were easy; we put a dozen flashlights and twice as many packages of batteries in the shopping cart we retrieved from the front of the store. Toward the back, we located the camping section, and gathered up three of the lanterns we found there.

"Good thing the Heat struck in September," I said. "At least the stores hadn't put their camping gear away in the stock room for the winter."

I'd expected Jace to nod, but instead he went still, staring down at me with a sad expression in his dark eyes. "It would have been better if it had never occurred at all, but we were not given that choice, unfortunately."

A protest rose to my lips. At the last second, though, I stopped myself from speaking. I'd wanted to say that if it hadn't happened, then he and I would never have been together. But that was a terrible thing to think. I loved him and couldn't imagine being without him. However, I could never say that our love was worth the deaths of millions of people.

Billions, I corrected myself. *That "B" is pretty damn important.*

Jace seemed, in that way of his, to pick up on what I was thinking. I wouldn't say he was psychic exactly, but very good at reading my expressions, my silences, the things I didn't say clearly just as important as the things I did.

His voice was soft as he said, "Yes, the thought of not having you is not a pleasant one for me, either. I suppose I had a dream of still being with you, of coming to you as those of my kind had done with other mortals from time to time in the past."

"Would that even have been possible?" I asked. I'd wondered about it here and there, mostly because of his somewhat oblique references to other djinn/human pairings. From what I could tell, our relationship—and the relationships of the other elementals in Taos and their Chosen—didn't seem to be unprecedented. If the notion of such relationships had been completely alien to the djinn, then the Thousand would never have tried to save any of us.

"It would have been possible for us to be together. But not easy." He ran his flashlight over the shelves in front of us. "Is there anything else here that would be of use?"

I could tell he didn't really want to talk about the situation. But these were the very subjects we needed to discuss. Yes, we'd spent months together, but it was only at the very end of that period when I'd learned what he really was. Now I felt as if I needed to make up for lost time.

Still, it would be rude not to answer his question, so I quickly looked over the camp stoves and sleeping bags, then shook my head. "I don't think so. They're going to retrofit the ovens to run on propane, and beds and bedding are two things we really don't have to worry about. So let's keep looking for those generators."

Jace seemed relieved that I hadn't pushed the subject, and maneuvered our shopping cart down another aisle as he headed toward the rear of the store. Not looking at me, he said, "There's a question burning in your mind, isn't there?"

"Yes," I replied simply.

"Then ask it."

Well, he had once told me that I could ask him anything. And he'd always been truthful with me, once his djinn heritage had been revealed and he no longer felt he had a terrible secret to hide. It was something, knowing I could trust him in that.

"Would you really still have chosen me if you had the whole world to pick from, instead of only a few Immune?"

At once he let go of the shopping cart and came to me, taking my hands in his and pulling me close. His fingers felt cool against mine, but at least they weren't cold, and his grip was firm enough. I could almost convince myself that nothing was wrong, that Miles Odekirk's device was having very little effect on him after all.

"Beloved, there never would have been anyone but you. I felt the resonance of your soul with mine from the time you came of age, and I mourned, because even then I knew what humanity's fate was to be, that the time of reckoning was only a few scant years off. But then I learned from the creators of the disease that you would be one of the fortunate few who would be immune, and I laid claim to you as soon as I knew."

My heart leapt at those words, and something in me relaxed a little. He had always wanted me, had feared I wouldn't survive the Heat. "How would that have even worked?" I asked. "I mean, it's not as if we're exactly from the same backgrounds. My parents had issues just the few times I dated guys who didn't go to college."

He didn't smile, even though I'd tried to keep my tone light as I asked the question. "Not so very differently from the way we met. That is, I would have approached you as one of your own, made sure you were comfortable with me before I told you the truth."

"And then?"

Bringing one hand to his lips, he kissed my fingers gently before releasing them. "That would have depended on you. Whether you would have accepted what I was telling you, whether you would have made that very great leap."

Would I have? Of course I wanted to think so. I wanted to believe that what he said wouldn't have changed the way I felt about him, that I could have accepted the truth of his heritage, but it's easy to imagine the best of yourself when you're considering a hypothetical situation. "So...would I have gone to your world, if I had made that leap?"

He shook his head. "Such a thing isn't possible. We djinn can live there, but we much prefer it here. And a human being, even one under our protection, granted advanced life and powers of healing, couldn't survive for more than a few hours on the plane where the djinn made their home, once the earth was taken from them. No, we would have lived our lives here, moving on when it began to become obvious to those around us that we weren't aging normally. It isn't the easiest of lives, but there are a few who've managed to do it successfully." Something flickered in his dark eyes, a shadow that I could barely catch because of the bad lighting in the hardware store. But because I knew Jace, I did see it.

"What's wrong?" I asked. It was the first question that popped into my mind, although I couldn't stop myself from also wondering about that reference to having this world taken from them. "Did you—were you with someone like that?"

Another head shake, this one even more emphatic than the last. "No. I wasn't with anyone before you. That is, there were brief...liaisons...from time to time, but that's all. Nothing lasting, nothing important. No, I was thinking of Zahrias."

I could actually feel my eyebrows shooting up. "Zahrias? He was with a...mortal?"

"Yes. For quite a few years. But in the end, she was unable to live with the reality of her existence, that she would go on, and on, and that everyone she knew and loved would die around her, save her djinn lover. So she took her own life. Even though she had the healing abilities that we gift all our partners, if someone is determined enough to kill themselves, they can still succeed. As she did."

"Oh, my God," I whispered. That shocking revelation answered a few questions. Why Zahrias didn't have a Chosen, and possibly why he had come to be the leader of the group in Taos. Maybe he wanted to make sure his fellow djinn had the happy ending he'd been forever denied.

"It was a terrible thing for him." Jace moved closer to me and brushed a strand of hair away from my brow. A simple gesture, but something about it made me want to weep. Maybe it was his way of reassuring himself that I was there, that I certainly had no plans to go anywhere. "I worried that Evangeline's death would make him less likely to look on mortals with any sort of kindness or compassion, but he surprised me. He offered to lead the community here, when no one else seemed inclined to take on the challenge."

"And he's doing a good job of it, too," I said. Strange how your feelings about a person could change so much, once you knew the truth. Yes, Zahrias still seemed far too formidable to me, and I was so very glad that I was Jace's Chosen and not his, but in that moment I realized I wasn't afraid of the djinn leader. Not anymore.

"I'm glad you think so." Something in his expression changed then, and he stepped a pace away from me before aiming his flashlight toward the back of the store. "But we should probably keep looking for those generators. Dark comes quickly at this time of year."

Yes, it did. Too quickly, although I'd begun to notice the gradual lengthening of the days. Spring was coming, even though it was still more than a month away. How long would we have to wait for it here in Taos? I had a feeling it would be slow in arriving, no matter what the calendar might say.

The rear of the store was a jumble of various items that the owners obviously had dumped there because they didn't really fit in anywhere else. That sort of casual chaos would never have flown in Albuquerque, but in Taos, the locals were probably used to it. Chaos or no, we did find two sturdy-looking generators back there, each with multiple outlets.

"Those should help a lot," I said. "At the very least, they'll keep the refrigerators going. But with an output of 5,500 watts, they'll probably do more than that."

"Success," Jace replied, offering me a smile. Something about it looked a little wavery around the edges, though, and I put a hand on his arm just as he was reaching out to take the handle of the generator closest to him.

"Are you okay?" I asked. "Tell me the truth."

For a second he didn't say anything, only watched my face, as if hoping to find some indication there as to how he should reply. Then, "I'm fine, Jessica. Yes, that device is hammering away at me, tiring me, but I can manage. In fact," he added, "I believe that tonight I'll have to prove it to you."

A flicker of heat stirred deep within me. "Oh, really?" I responded, trying to keep my tone light, teasing, just in case he was also teasing me. In the back of my mind had been the fear that the device was taking so much of his energy that he wouldn't have anything left for me, but if he was serious, then apparently that wasn't the issue I'd thought it would be.

"Well, you might have to be on top...." He slanted a sideways glance at me, and despite everything, I couldn't help laughing.

"I'm willing to take that ride," I said, still chuckling, and then he smiled, a real smile, the sort that made a pleasant little shiver run down my spine.

Maybe there was a way we could manage to get through this after all.

We hustled the generators out to the truck, then went back into the store to find a ramp we could use to wheel them up into the bed, since at the moment Jace wasn't strong enough to lift one on his own, and I never would have been strong enough. Luckily, we found what we were looking for on the loading dock. We were just closing up the truck's gate when we heard a voice that was halfway between a whisper and a moan.

"Jessica...."

As one, Jace and I whirled. I couldn't help noticing the way he moved forward, placing himself between me and the owner of that voice, even though I was probably in better shape to take on an adversary at the moment than he was. But then when I saw who was speaking, who it was slumped against the wall of the store, I realized we weren't facing an enemy at all.

The man speaking was Aidan, one of our missing hunters.

CHAPTER THREE

Two hideous gashes marred Aidan's cheeks. Blood still trickled from the wounds, and also stained the camo parka he wore. His long hair had fallen out of its usual ponytail and hung in mud- and blood-spattered strands around his face.

Jace surged forward first, slipping an arm under one of Aidan's shoulders, since it was obvious he had trouble standing, even with the wall to support him. A second later, I went to him as well, sliding under his shoulder and feeling his weight settle on my arm as he slumped against me.

"What happened?" I asked, but even as the words left my mouth, I knew. It had to be the other djinn, the ones whose attack on Taos had been thwarted by Miles Odekirk's device. How Aidan had managed to survive,

I had no idea. And I didn't even want to know what had happened to the other two in the hunting party, Martine and Clay. Judging by Aidan's current condition, it couldn't be anything good.

"They found us," he gasped. Above his head, Jace and I exchanged a knowing glance.

"Yes," Jace said calmly. "Can you walk at all? Our truck is just out in front."

"Yeah."

I had my doubts, but we began shuffling over to the fire lane where we'd parked the truck. Aidan did his best to stumble along, although I'd say his forward motion was probably at least ninety percent our doing. I opened the passenger-side door and pushed him inside as best I could, with Jace lending what little strength he had to spare for the operation. At last Aidan was more or less parked in the center of the bench seat, head lolling to one side.

"I'll hold him up," Jace murmured to me, voice carefully neutral. "You drive."

"Got it." I hurried around to the other side of the truck and climbed into the driver's seat. Obviously, we had to get Aidan back to the resort, but what we'd do with him once we were there, I had no idea. As far as I knew, no one in the Taos community had any sort of medical experience. Yes, I had a few basic first aid skills, thanks to some coaching by my father when I was younger. That didn't mean I knew the first thing about

patching up the sort of horrific wounds Aidan had suffered. I'd just have to hope that they'd heal quickly on
their own. After all, he was one of the Chosen. Lilias,
his djinn, would have given him accelerated healing,
just as Jace had done with me.

I took a quick glance over at him as I maneuvered
the truck down the icy streets. Icy, because the djinn
couldn't keep the roads clear the way they had before
the attack. It would be just our luck to be hit by a major
snowstorm around now on top of everything else.

*Like things aren't bad enough without you borrow-
ing trouble,* I thought grimly. *Worry about that later.
Much later.*

We were all silent as I drove. That is, Aidan didn't
seem to be in much shape for any kind of speech; his
eyes had shut, and I thought he probably would have
fallen over to one side if Jace hadn't maintained a grip
on his arm so he stayed more or less upright.

I ventured, still not completely used to the mental communication we could share, *He'll be all right,
though. I mean, his healing powers should kick in soon
enough.*

Jace's voice in my head sounded grimmer than I'd
ever heard it. *No, they won't.*

What do you mean?

His jaw tightened. *I mean that those powers come
from your djinn partner. With our own powers blocked,
we have no way of sharing them with you. If you're hurt,*

you will heal like any ordinary human. This small power we use now, the way we can speak with one another through our bond...that's all we have. And even that only works when we are in close enough proximity.

Holy crap. I hadn't even stopped to consider that the device would affect our shared powers, since I'd never lost the ability to share this silent speech with Jace, as long as we were in the same building. But of course it made perfect sense that the healing, the long life, would require far more energy. If that was the case, though...if our healing and extended life came solely from our djinn, then....

So...Evony? I asked, pretty sure I knew what Jace's answer would be, even though I hated to hear it.

She has lost Natila, and therefore the protections her djinn lover gave her. She has returned to the way she was...before.

This just kept getting better and better. I wondered if Evony had begun to guess. I hoped not, but she wasn't stupid. All it would take was one scrape, one ragged hangnail to persist when it should have been gone in an hour or so, and she'd know something was wrong.

Even so, we'd have to tell her. That would be fun, considering she wasn't even speaking to me. Much.

But first things first. Despite her protestations that she was just fine with going out and finding the lost hunting party—an expedition that clearly wasn't needed now—as far as I knew, Evony wasn't going anywhere. We had to get Aidan taken care of as best we could, and hope that he'd revive enough to tell us what had happened. I stole a glance over at him. Even under the blood smearing his face, I could tell the wounds he'd suffered would leave a set of horrific scars. And he'd been so handsome. Not my type—even before Jace came along, I'd preferred darker men—but still.

That's the last thing you should be worrying about, I scolded myself. *The important thing is that he's alive, and we've got to do whatever we can to make sure he stays that way.*

Even though the hardware store was only half a mile from the resort at the very most, it still felt as if it took forever to get back there. But at last we were pulling into the parking lot. I drove right up to the front doors—it wasn't as if I'd be preventing any late-arriving tourists from dropping off their luggage—then put the truck in park and hurried around to the passenger side.

Jace was already opening the door. The two of us had more or less wrangled Aidan out of the cab when I heard Lauren's shocked voice.

"Oh, my God. What happened?"

"Two guesses," I said grimly, propping Aidan up as best I could while Jace shut the truck door. "We've got to get him inside. We did find two generators. They're in the bed, so—"

"I'll take care of it." Her worried gaze rested on Aidan's ruined face, and I saw her shiver. "His rooms with Lilias are toward the back of the hotel. There's no way you'll be able to carry him that far."

"Get some of the other Chosen to help," Jace said, his voice tight with strain. I could tell that the exertions of the afternoon were finally beginning to wear on him. "We'll head in that direction, and they can catch up with us."

Lauren nodded, then all but ran into the building. We followed at a much slower pace, more or less holding Aidan up, since somewhere between the hardware store and the parking lot, he seemed to have passed out completely. Maybe that was better. He had to be in a tremendous amount of pain.

Our stumbling little trio hadn't made it much past the lobby when two Chosen I didn't know very well, both tall young men, came hurrying up and took over, slipping their arms around Aidan so Jace and I could finally let go of him. I straightened, rubbing my neck. The next morning, I'd probably be feeling the strain in the muscles of my neck and shoulders.

"You know where to take him?" Jace asked one of them, a lean, good-looking guy with sandy hair and friendly hazel eyes.

"Lauren told us," the man answered. "We can take over from here. You're looking pretty wiped."

Privately, I had to agree. Maybe Jace could hold up under the effects of the device better than most of his fellow djinn, but that didn't mean he was doing well, especially not after expending so much effort just to get Aidan here.

"We'll stay with him," Jace said quietly.

The young man gave the shadows under Jace's eyes and the pinched look around his mouth a dubious glance, and then he shrugged. He didn't quite say, *your funeral,* but I could tell he didn't think Jace had the energy to make it that far.

Nor did I, but somehow he took careful step after careful step, following the two young men all the way back to the suite Aidan and Lilias shared. Just as we approached the door, she came running down the hallway, black hair flying behind her like a dark cloak. Spotting her injured lover, she let out a cry and went to him. Her big dark eyes grew even larger as she took in the ruin of his face.

"What happened?"

Jace sent her a look of mingled weariness and worry. "You know what happened."

Her full lips compressed. "I didn't think they would take it this far."

"Oh, they did."

The two young men carrying Aidan didn't pause for this convo, but took him inside and laid him down on the bed. I briefly noted that the suite seemed to have an Incan motif, with pyramids and lizard-birds in stylized murals on the wall. But then Lilias was going to Aidan and pressing her lips against his forehead.

"It is all right," she murmured. "It is going to be all right."

At least she wasn't recoiling from him. In fact, I saw a fierce tenderness in her features, a determination to make sure he would survive this, no matter what. When she straightened and turned back toward the rest of us, her mouth was set, eyes clear and focused.

"I'll need whatever healing supplies this place might have brought to us here. Are any among you a healer?"

The two young men looked at one another and shrugged. I could tell they'd thought they were beyond needing that sort of help. They probably weren't going to be too thrilled when they found out that all of us Chosen were right back to square one—mortal, vulnerable.

In the meantime, we had to do what we could.

"I have some first aid training," I said. "I'm sure Lauren is looking for someone to help, but I'll do what I can until she can find someone better qualified."

"Thank you," she replied, then glanced over at Jace. "It seems you are even luckier in your Chosen than we all thought."

"Well, I'm no doctor—" I began, and she shushed me.

"Do what you can."

I nodded and hurried into the bathroom. The washcloths and towels appeared clean enough, so I'd start there. Biting my lip, I turned on the tap, wondering if water would even come out. But it did, and it was hot. They must have already gotten the water heaters switched over to propane. As to why the plumbing was working...well, I'd thank my stars for that now and worry about the mechanics of it all later.

After dampening the cloth with hot water, I went back out to the bedroom. The two young men had disappeared, and I looked over at Jace.

"They've gone for supplies."

Of course. I turned back to Aidan and tried not to wince in sympathetic agony as I dabbed at the jagged cut on one of his cheeks with the washcloth I'd prepped. He jerked under these ministrations, but I could tell he was enough out of it that he couldn't sense all of the pain I was probably causing.

I'd just started cleaning the wound on his other cheek when a casually gorgeous Hispanic young man entered the room, carrying a small first aid kit. "I'm Miguel," he told me. "I've had some EMT training, although I ended up not getting my certification after all. Let me take a look at him."

Relieved beyond measure that help more expert than mine had arrived, I handed over the washcloth to Miguel and backed away from the bed. "Why didn't you finish?" I asked as he began to wipe the blood from Aidan's face.

A quick sideways flash of a smile. "Decided to try modeling instead."

Well, I could see the logic in that, with those cheekbones and that smile. I went to take my place next to Jace and twined my fingers in his, glad to feel his touch even if his skin was cool against mine, a sure sign of the havoc the djinn-blocking device was wreaking on his system. Lilias stood on his other side, her hands clenched into fists as she watched Miguel work.

She spoke quietly, pale beneath the usual warm olive of her skin. "What can we do?"

He set the washcloth down on the nightstand and cracked open the first aid kit, then shook his head. "I'll clean the wounds with what we've got here, get some bandages on, but he's going to need something better than that. Butterfly bandages at the very least. Stitches would be better. And antibiotics."

"There's an urgent-care place a few blocks down the road." Lauren's voice came from the doorway, and I turned slightly to see her standing there, pretty features strained, although I could tell from the almost unnatural calm in her voice that she was doing her best to maintain her composure. "I'll send someone over. Just let me know what you need."

As Lauren spoke, Miguel was cleaning Aidan's wounds with alcohol wipes. That must have hurt like a bitch, but he hardly moved, just twitched every so often. Then Miguel laid some gauze first over one wound, then the other, and taped the fabric down as best he could. Without looking up from his work, he said, "I'd better go. I know what to look for. He should be stable enough for now. If it's really only a couple blocks from here, that means the urgent-care facility is close enough that I can go and come back in less than fifteen minutes."

"Are you sure?" Lilias asked. I could tell that she didn't want to run the risk of having the community's only medic too far from his patient.

"Absolutely," Miguel replied, then straightened and turned to face all of us. From the way his gaze flickered down to Aidan and back toward us, I got the feeling something else was bothering him...and I had a good idea what it was.

He said, "He's not healing the way he should be."

"No," Jace returned, tone flat. "And he won't, as long as that device is protecting us from attack by the other djinn."

Miguel glanced at me, dark eyes intent on my face. "You knew." The words weren't exactly an accusation, but they sure felt that way.

"Jace told me on the drive over."

To my surprise, Miguel only shrugged. "Okay. At least now I know what I'm dealing with."

He moved past us and headed out the door, barely squeezing past Lauren. Now her expression was more worried than ever, brows pulled together, jaw tense, but she only said, "Anything else you need here?"

"No," Lilias replied. She went to the table by the window and took one of the chairs, then moved it to Aidan's bedside. I could tell the exertion bothered her—she was breathing hard by the time she was done—but none of us offered to help her. She clearly wanted to do this on her own. "Let Zahrias know what has happened. Jasreel and Jessica can stay here with me."

There was such a tone of command in Lilias' voice that Lauren clearly didn't want to protest. A quick nod, and then she was gone, too, leaving Jace and me alone with the djinn woman and her wounded lover.

An uneasy silence fell. Lilias reached out and wrapped her fingers around Aidan's. Even in his stupor, he seemed to recognize her touch and squeezed faintly, as if to let her know he understood that she was there with him.

Jace and I stood a few feet away, but I could still see the tears shimmering on her cheeks. Without looking at us, she said, "You knew this would happen."

"No," Jace replied gently, "I did not know for certain. I worried that it might. I tried to keep it from happening. But the Los Alamos survivors forced my hand. I could not return to Santa Fe and still keep Jessica safe."

"And now none of us are safe."

For a long, long moment, Jace said nothing, only stood next to me, his hand still in mine. I felt a shudder go through him, and I tightened my grip. I was tempted to reach out to him with my thoughts, but something told me that would be rude, to be holding a silent conversation right under Lilias' nose. Even though I didn't understand all the ramifications of how our communication worked, I guessed that the djinn could only speak in such a way with their partners. Otherwise, that conversation I'd overheard between Zahrias and Jace would have been entirely subvocal, and possibly I would never have discovered his true identity.

Well, except for the part where he'd been floating a few feet above the floor.

At last, Jace spoke. "You think I wanted this?" He didn't sound angry, only tired, and I wished I could take him away from here and back to our rooms, hold him in my arms and let him lay his head against my shoulder. Not even make love, really, only be together, be alone, away from this ongoing nightmare.

But I knew that wasn't going to happen. Lilias had asked for us to stay with her, although at the moment, I couldn't quite understand why. Just so she could upbraid Jace?

She sighed then, and lifted Aidan's hand so she could press it against her cheek. There was such tenderness in the gesture that I found my eyes widening in surprise. I couldn't say why, exactly. It wasn't as if I'd spent much time observing the other djinn with their Chosen, but from what I'd seen so far, they didn't seem all that inclined toward public displays of affection.

Judging by the way her gaze flicked to me, I could tell she'd noticed my reaction. "This startles you?" she asked. "That I would care so much?"

"I—" Helpless, I glanced up at Jace, but he didn't move or say anything. Possibly the slightest lift of his shoulders. Floundering for words, I went on, "I—I'm sorry that he won't be able to heal quickly. I know Miguel will do what he can, but there's bound to be some scarring."

"That matters very little," Lilias replied, and again I found myself surprised. The djinn woman's mouth curled. Then she said, "I suppose you think us all very shallow, with our young and pretty partners...even though you are one of them yourself. It is true that I chose Aidan at first because of his handsome face, but he has been a good companion to me. He is a good man, whether his face is whole or not. And I will let him know that as soon as he awakens."

She pressed her lips against Aidan's hand and then laid it down very gently at his side. Gaze fixed on the young man she loved—and studiously not looking at Jace—she went on, "My apologies, Jasreel. I know none of this is your fault. You cannot be held responsible for the actions of another."

"My thanks, Lilias," he said, his tone strangely formal. When I looked up at him, though, I could see that the solemn way he had addressed her was most likely his way of showing respect for her and her current situation, and not because he was angry. Still, I itched to know what exactly she was talking about. Was this her oblique way of referring to Aldair? It must be.

Jace had told me some of the truth, but I had to wonder right then whether he had told me all of it. That discussion would have to wait, though. For now, Lilias wanted us with her, and I knew Jace would never leave someone in need.

Luckily, Miguel returned only a few minutes after that, laden with cases of supplies he must have pilfered from the urgent-care center. After giving Jace and me a brief nod, he went directly to Aidan's bedside and laid a hand on his forehead.

"Already feeling feverish," he muttered, then rummaged through one of the bags he'd been carrying. "He needs antibiotics, but I couldn't find anything except penicillin-based drugs. Let's all pray he's not allergic."

No kidding. I wondered if someone who hadn't quite finished EMT training would know what to do in the case of a negative drug reaction. Maybe. That was way out of my wheelhouse—I knew enough to clean wounds and bandage them, and even put together a makeshift splint or whatever, but that was about where my first aid knowledge stopped.

We all waited in tense silence as Miguel pushed a capsule between Aidan's dry lips and then coaxed some water down his throat. Of course, if he did end up having a bad reaction, it wasn't as if it would manifest immediately. But for some reason, I kept staring, as if certain the worst was about to happen.

Nothing did happen, of course. Miguel did some more rummaging and produced what looked like high-octane antiseptic, and a packet with a curved needle and a length of pre-cut suture material. At that point he did pause and look over at Lilias. "You may not want to stay to watch this," he said.

She didn't even blink. "I will stay by my Chosen's side."

"Okay." A quick flicker of his gaze up toward us. "But you two—it's probably better if I don't have to do this with a full house. It's been a while since I picked up one of these, you know?"

"Of course," Jace replied immediately. "If that is all right with you, Lilias."

"Yes. Thank you for staying with me. But if Miguel thinks he can do better with only me here, then it's better that you go."

That seemed to be our signal to leave, so we murmured our goodbyes and left the suite. We didn't get very far, however, as Lauren was hovering just around the corner of the hallway.

"How is he?"

"Hard to say," I said. "Miguel said he's already feverish, so he gave him some antibiotics. Now he's starting in with the stitches. He didn't really need us there for that, so...." I trailed off. What else was I supposed to say? None of Aidan's wounds appeared life-threatening, so now it seemed to be a matter of giving him time to heal.

"Got it." Lauren was looking pale, but her voice sounded no-nonsense enough at least. "I'll let Zahrias know. But I also wanted to say thank you for finding those generators. They're already hooked up, and so we don't need to worry about the food spoiling. Lindsay's jury-rigged something with the plumbing—don't ask me to explain how—and we've got running water, at least for now. We could only scavenge enough propane to run four of the hot water heaters, so we'll be taking showers in shifts, I'm afraid."

"That's no problem," I told her, slipping an arm around Jace's waist. "We'll take ours together. In the name of conservation and all that."

She actually did smile at the joke—well, half-joke...I actually thought it was a pretty good idea—but then her expression turned serious again. "Zahrias will want to talk to Aidan when he wakes up. Any idea when that will be?"

Since I had no idea, I could only shrug. "You should ask Miguel about that. But I doubt it'll be before tomorrow morning."

"I was afraid of that." Lauren tucked a piece of blazing red hair behind one ear. "I'll let him know. And you two—well, I suppose you should try to get some rest. Who knows what's going to hit us next."

After delivering that cheerful remark, she gave us a half-wave and then headed off toward the conference room Zahrias had commandeered for his use. Jace took my hand. "Come, beloved. She's right. Aidan is in good hands, and there's nothing else we can do right now. I will confess that I would like to sit down."

Of course he would. Now that I had the luxury to look at him more closely, I could see how shadowed his eyes were, the taut look to his mouth. Lord knows how he'd kept himself going this long.

Giving him what I hoped was an encouraging smile, I said, "We'll go back to our suite, and you can put your feet up for a while. And I'll see about scrounging something to eat, too. Sound good?"

He nodded, and we headed for "home." His steps grew slower and heavier the whole way, and by the time we got to our rooms, it seemed as if he barely had the energy to put one foot in front of the other. Somehow, though, he mustered the strength to bend down and pat Dutchie on the head before finally going to the bed and more or less collapsing on it.

I brought him some water, then murmured that I needed to take the dog for her afternoon walk. And after that, I'd bring him some food.

His words were slurred as he slumped back against the pillows. "Thank you, Jessica. I'm sorry—sorry—"

Pressing my lips against his cut off the unneeded apology. "It's fine. Get your rest. I'll be back before you know it."

Which was only the truth, since his eyes were closing even as I leaned down to clip Dutchie's leash to her collar. As I let myself out, I wondered if my "solution" to the djinn attack had only doomed Jace to a half-life, one in which he would be forever robbed of his true strength.

No. I wouldn't allow myself to believe that. This was a temporary setback, nothing more. And until we could come up with a permanent solution, I would do everything necessary to take care of the man I loved. After all, he'd spent most of the autumn looking after me, making sure I was safe.

The least I could do was return the favor.

CHAPTER FOUR

AIDAN FINALLY WOKE UP LATE THE NEXT MORNING. We didn't see him until that afternoon, though, as he was still very weak. But Zahrias wanted us to be there when Aidan recounted what had happened while he was out on that doomed hunting expedition.

A good night's sleep seemed to have helped Jace a good deal, although the lovemaking we'd teased one another about had never materialized. Instead, I'd spent the night snuggled up against him, hoping I could lend him some of the warmth of my body the way he'd given me his during those cold November nights back in the Santa Fe house. In the darkness, he'd wrapped his arms around me, held me close, and something in that embrace was so tender, so fierce, that I couldn't really regret not having sex. Sometimes, just being next to one another was enough.

I wasn't sure what to expect when we went in to see Aidan. Some mass of horrific Frankenstein-style stitches on his face, I supposed. But while something like that might have been hiding underneath, fresh bandages covered his cheeks, concealing the worst of the damage. His hair appeared to have been brushed and washed, and if he didn't look exactly cheerful, he did seem more or less alert.

Lilias sat next to the bed, her hand still in his. I wondered if she'd stayed there all night, or if she'd dozed on the couch in the sitting area of their suite. Since Aidan lay in more or less the middle of the bed, it didn't appear as if he'd shared it with her.

Several chairs had been brought in; Zahrias was already sitting in one of them, and he gestured for Jace and me to sit down as we entered the room. No protests there. Jace had come to the realization that he couldn't continue to exert himself the way he had the day before, not if he wanted to maintain any kind of usefulness in the long run. That meant sitting whenever possible, and letting me do most of the fetching and carrying. I didn't mind, if that meant he would have a reserve of strength to draw on when he needed it most.

Only a brief nod from Zahrias as Jace and I seated ourselves, and then the djinn leader turned his attention back to Aidan. "How are you feeling today?"

"Like fifty miles of bad road." A hand went up to touch the bandage on his right cheek. "Probably look like it, too. But I'll live. Miguel says the antibiotics knocked my fever right back, so that's something."

"It is, indeed." Zahrias glanced over at Lilias. "Did you sleep at all?"

"Some," she admitted, then added in fiercer tones, "Enough."

That seemed to be sufficient for Zahrias. His shoulders lifted, and he shifted his gaze to the young man lying in the bed. "Tell us what happened."

For a second, Aidan shut his eyes. His lashes were dark brown, much darker than his hair, which had been bleached by the sun. When he lifted his lids again, I was startled by the bright blue of his eyes, which I hadn't really noticed before. Maybe they only looked that bright because of all the bruising around them.

He said, "We went east, toward the hills. Clay said—he was from around here—that we still could find some deer there, maybe pheasant. And he was right. We bagged a buck and a couple of birds, and that filled the ATV we were driving, so we decided to head back." Aidan winced. "That pisses me off. Had to leave a perfectly good buck behind."

"That is not important, dearest," Lilias said gently.

A sigh. "Maybe not. But at least it would have made the whole mess worth something. Anyway, we were headed back into town when all of a sudden the sky darkened overhead, like a cloud passing by. None of us thought much of it, since it was sort of a cloudy day to begin with. But then it was as if that cloud dived down at us, and it got darker and darker, and the Polaris just sort of died on us. And then...*they* were there."

"'They'?" Zahrias asked, although from the brooding expression on his face, I would have said he already knew exactly who "they" were.

"Djinn. Other djinn. I'd never seen them before."

"Any of them?" I cut in, recalling Aldair's blazing blue eyes, how Zahrias had said the air elemental had gone to join those who hunted humans for sport.

Aidan shook his head, then winced. One hand began to move toward the bandages on his left cheek, but he stopped himself and knotted his fingers together on top of the duvet cover, as if worried he'd forget again and reach for his wounded face if he didn't keep his hands in plain sight. "No. There were about ten of them, I think. I mean, there were more, up there, you know?" He lifted a shoulder vaguely skyward, then continued, "But the ones on the ground, the ones who surrounded us...I didn't recognize any of them. Their leader was dark, like you and Jace here. No one ever said his name, though. Anyway, he told us that we were trespassing on land that wasn't ours, and that none of us had any business being here, that our day was over."

In the chair next to mine, Jace shifted, and his fingers clasped the arms, knuckles turning white under the strain. "What did you do?"

A swallow, and I could see Lilias tighten her hold on Aidan's hand, as if to reassure him that she was there, and that he was safe here, no matter what might have happened the day before. He hesitated, the muscles in his throat working. "I—I didn't really do anything at first. It was just—just a shock, I guess. I'd thought we were safe. We'd all been told that we were safe because we were Chosen, you know? But then Clay stepped forward and said as much, that if they had a problem with us being there, they should talk to their leaders, the ones who'd made the agreement in the first place, that we and all the other Chosen like us would be protected. And then—"

Another long pause. I knew whatever it was, it wouldn't be good. Not with Aidan sitting there with his face ripped up, looking like he'd been attacked by a wild animal. Come to think of it, maybe he had.

Voice shaking, he said, "The lead djinn just laughed. And before any of us could even blink, he pulled this long dagger or short sword or whatever from his belt, and drove it right through Clay's gut. Martine screamed. I remember that—her screaming like some chick from a horror movie or something. The lead djinn went for her then."

"He killed her, too?" Zahrias asked. If someone didn't know him very well, they probably would have said he was showing no reaction at all to Aidan's story. But his dark eyes glittered, even though the rest of his features remained still, and I could see the way he was forcing himself to keep from responding. If he'd had the full use of his powers, no doubt he would have been surrounded by a veritable inferno of virtual flames showing his anger.

"No." Aidan shifted on the bed, his head falling backward slightly, as if the strain of sitting up was beginning to take its toll on him. "The djinn grabbed her and threw her over his shoulder. She was still screaming bloody murder and beating on his back, but it didn't seem to faze him at all. He just laughed and said he'd take her as payment for our trespassing. This all happened in less than a minute, you know? I guess I was sort of in shock, but right then I started to yell at him, to tell him to put her down. He just kind of smiled at me, then said, 'Give Lilias my love.' And then that sword came up again, but this time he used it to slice up my face. It hurt like—well, I don't know what it hurt like, because I'd never felt anything like it before. Like fire, I guess."

The second he'd repeated the djinn's words—"give Lilias my love—" she'd gone ramrod stiff, all the color draining from her face. "This djinn," she said faintly. "Did he wear purple? Dark, dark purple?"

Aidan blinked, seeming to consider. "Yeah, I think so. You know who he is?"

In answer, she wrapped both her hands around Aidan's. Although she had looked far more composed this morning than the last time I had seen her, now she wept again, although silently, tears tracing their way down her smooth cheeks. Incongruously, I wondered how she managed to cry without smearing any of the kohl that ringed her big dark eyes.

"I knew him...once," she replied after a noticeable pause. "But that was a long time ago. So long that I had hoped...I'd hoped he'd forgotten."

Forgotten what, I didn't know for sure, although it seemed clear enough to me that Lilias and this vengeful djinn—whoever he was—had some kind of a past together. I glanced over at Jace. He was frowning slightly, but I didn't see anything in his expression that seemed to indicate he knew Lilias' former lover. I supposed that was possible; there were some twenty thousand or so djinn currently alive, and that was a lot of people to keep track of, even if you had many, many lifetimes in which to do it.

Zahrias, however, seemed to know exactly who had killed Clay, mutilated Aidan, and kidnapped Martine. His brows drew together, and his eyes glittered. "Well, it seems Khalim has not forgotten. I suppose I shouldn't be surprised. His was never a very forgiving nature."

At these words, Aidan shifted on the bed, jaw tight with pain. "What...you were together?"

"A long time ago," she said again. With one hand she reached up to wipe away the tears on her cheek. It was a brusque gesture, one made in such a way that I got the impression she was angry with herself for losing control like that in front of everyone. "Long before I chose you, Aidan. You must believe that."

"Oh, I believe it." He leaned his head back against the pillows and shut his eyes. Whether that was from exhaustion at having to recount the story to all of us, or because he didn't want to look at Lilias, I didn't know. Aidan and I had talked, but not about anything personal. Just logistical sorts of things, really. I couldn't claim to know him well, and I had no idea how much Lilias had told him of her life with the djinn before she'd come here to Taos. If I had to guess, I'd say probably not much. Why would she? Those djinn who were of the One Thousand had thrown in their lot with us mortals, and probably thought they'd left their old lives behind for good.

Apparently not. And apparently having a djinn ex-lover could be a hell of a lot worse than having the sort of obsessed human ex who would stalk you on Facebook or loiter around your school or office, hoping to catch sight of you. Not that I knew from personal experience, but my friend Elena had had a couple of doozies. She finally had to get a restraining order for one of them.

Too bad that sort of thing wouldn't really work on a djinn.

"So," I said, because the silence in the room was playing on my already frayed nerves. "Now we know who the bad guys are. Or at least one of them. That's something, right?"

Even though I could tell the effort cost him, Zahrias pushed himself up out of his chair so he could go over to the window and stare at the winter-bare courtyard outside. His hands hung at his sides, as if he didn't have the energy to clench them into fists. "It is very little, actually. I already had my suspicions as to who some of these... troublemakers...might be. I am not at all surprised to find that Khalim actually is one of them."

I hated the flat, defeated tone in Zahrias' voice. He didn't sound at all like himself, but who could blame him? He—like every other djinn in Taos—was trying to function while Miles Odekirk's device continuously sucked away every spare bit of energy he possessed.

"What do you want us to do?" Jace asked then. He appeared calm enough, but there was a faint crease between his brows, one that seemed to indicate he was also troubled by Zahrias' attitude. The djinn community here had only been enduring the effects of Miles's little black box for about a day. That was far too soon for any of them to be giving up, especially their leader.

Zahrias turned away from the window. It was a bright sunny day, the snow in the courtyard retreated to little patches here and there in the shadows. If you only looked at the sky and the evergreens, and not the bare branches of the oaks and sycamores and cottonwood trees, you could almost believe it was springtime.

But we knew better.

His shoulders lifted, and he wouldn't look directly at Jace, or at me. Certainly not at Lilias and her wounded lover. His gaze seemed to be fixed somewhere beyond the walls of this suite. Possibly he was thinking of where the other djinn were hiding, which, according to what Jace had told me, was a very, very long way from here...or just in the next room, depending on how you looked at it.

"Do what you can," Zahrias said at last. "I only fear it will not be enough."

And he moved past us and on to the door, then let himself out. My heart beat once, then again. And again, while the silence grew.

Finally, Jace spoke. "We should go to the lab, Jessica. Let us see how Lindsay is doing."

By "lab" he meant the supply room in the basement of the resort. Lauren had slipped a note under our door to let us know the lab had been moved here from the former auto repair shop we'd been using. I understood the reasoning. The device needed to stay here, close to the people it was protecting. Anyway, Jace had a point.

The key to all this was figuring out a way to have the device shield us from the bad djinn, yet leave our loved ones untouched. Simple, right?

"Okay," I replied, getting up from my chair. Directing my next words at Lilias and Aidan, I asked, "Is there anything we can get you?"

"No," Aidan said. "I mean, Lauren's checking in on us. Go to the lab. We're all right."

I didn't know about that, but I also knew it wasn't my place to argue. Aidan probably wanted Jace and me to get the hell out of there so he could talk to Lilias in private. I would have wanted the same thing, if our positions had been reversed.

"Take care," Jace said quietly as we left the room.

Whether those words had been addressed to Aidan or Lilias, I couldn't be sure.

Unfortunately, Lindsay didn't seem to be doing much of anything when we showed up. She sat at what had probably been the facility manager's desk, the box in front of her. There were tools scattered around, but it didn't look to me as if she'd been using any of them. She was alone, too; maybe her djinn was too exhausted to remain with her, and obviously Aidan wasn't going to be helping anyone out for a while. No sign of Evony, or of Kelli or Randall, the other two who'd volunteered for mad scientist duty.

"That good, huh?" I asked, noting Lindsay's glum expression.

She startled slightly at the sound of my voice; apparently, she'd been very far away. "Worse, probably." With a sigh, she rolled her chair away from the desk and got up. "I've been sitting here and staring at that thing for, like, an hour. I know I need to crack it open if I'm ever going to start figuring it out, but...I just can't." Her big green eyes fastened on mine, worried, helpless. That probably bothered her just as much as anything else. I doubted Lindsay had ever felt helpless in her entire life. Well, at least not until the Heat came along.

"Why can't you?" Jace asked. He stood next to me, regarding her calmly. I knew that it was difficult for him to be in the same room with the device, but you'd never know it to look at him right then.

"Because—well, because it's the only thing keeping us safe right now, isn't it?" With a nervous gesture very unlike her, she shoved a piece of dark blonde hair behind one ear. "If I start fiddling with it, I could break it. And then we'll be even worse off than we are now."

Well, I couldn't argue with her there. For a second I considered making a crack about it being the green wire she needed to cut, and then I realized that would be a very bad idea. Lindsay didn't need lame jokes right now. She needed a way to delve into the device's secrets without destroying it in the process.

Apparently Jace had heard the edge of panic in her voice, because he said, his tone soothing, "Tell us what you have found out about it. Your theories. Then we can go from there."

His words seemed to have some effect, because she let out a small breath and nodded, some of the tension leaving her jaw. "Okay. Well. I can operate it just fine now. The controls aren't that difficult, once you understand how it's supposed to be held. And really, it is sort of a 'set it and forget it' kind of contraption, unless you're actively trying to inflict hurt on the djinn nearby."

Jace winced at that comment. I remembered how Miles Odekirk had been playing with the device when the group from Los Alamos invaded my house. It hadn't been his first field test—that must have occurred when they captured Natila—and so I realized the scientist had been manipulating the box to see what kind of effect the various levels of intensity would have on a djinn, rather than maintaining the device at one particular setting and hoping for the best.

"Sorry," Lindsay said, apparently noticing the pained expression Jace currently wore. "I keep forgetting how rough that must have been for you. I mean, here we've got it set at the lowest level we can use and still have it do anything useful. But they weren't that nice about it in Los Alamos, were they?"

"In general, no." But he gave her a crooked smile as he replied, as if to let her know that he wasn't upset by her remark.

She seemed to get the message, because she smiled a little in return. Then it was gone, her expression serious as she went back to business. "As for how it all works…I can only guess. Like I try to keep telling everyone, I was an engineering student, not a physicist. But I figure, everything in the universe is energy, at its most basic level. All things have their own energy signatures. So my best guess is that the guy who created this thing—"

"Miles Odekirk," I supplied.

"Odekirk. Yeah. I think he must have figured out a way to detect djinn energy, which has got to be very different from the energy signature human beings put out. Once he'd isolated the djinn energy pattern, or whatever you want to call it, then he probably moved on to determining a way he could disrupt that energy pattern." She shrugged. "For all I know, his original intent was to use this device to kill djinn, not just mess with their powers. But once he saw what it could do, he decided that was better than nothing. Obviously, it worked just fine to protect the people in Los Alamos… and now here as well." She stopped then, as if not sure what else she should say.

"I think that's an excellent start, Lindsay," Jace told her.

The compliment didn't seem to improve her mood any. Once again she lifted her shoulders, and then went to the desk so she could pick up the box and shift it from one hand to the other. "It's all just hypotheses. Not-so-educated guesses. Even if I turn out to be right, how much does that help us? It's getting from that idea to whatever's in here"—she tapped one corner of the box, being careful to stay away from the touch screens on any of its sides—"making that happen...that's the important thing. And I don't have a clue how Odekirk even went about doing it."

That made two of us. It was probably asking a lot to expect a grad student in a completely different field of science to decode the secrets of a device only a handful of people in the pre-Dying world would have understood.

Which left us with...what? Finding some way to cope with our new reality? Jace somehow managed that better than the rest of the djinn; maybe he could train them to ignore the effects of the device as best they could. It wouldn't be a very pleasant existence, but it was better than nothing. Or maybe Zahrias could come up with some way to contact the other djinn, those who weren't part of the One Thousand, but who probably weren't working with this Khalim and Aldair and the rest of the thugs. It was possible they didn't even know what was going on. After all, they'd probably made their pact and then gone on their way, not bothering to check in with the dissenters.

No, that didn't make a lot of sense. The djinn, if not all-seeing and all-knowing, still saw a hell of a lot.

True, we were blocked to them now, but they had to have possessed some inkling of what was going on in this little corner of the planet. Obviously they weren't concerned enough to interfere. Which meant we were on our own.

And if we couldn't reverse-engineer this goddamn thing....

...well, then, we'd just have to have the person who'd engineered it in the first place fix it somehow.

My eyes must have lit up, because Lindsay asked, voice sharp with curiosity,

"What is it? You look like you just had the proverbial light bulb go on over your head."

"Yes, Jessica," Jace added. "It seems as if something has just occurred to you."

Oh, it had occurred to me, all right. I drew in a breath, then said, "Lindsay, I know you feel as if you've been beating your head against a brick wall—"

"That's for damn sure."

I grinned. "So how about some expert assistance?"

One of her eyebrows went up. "Assistance?"

From the way Jace crossed his arms, I could tell he didn't like where this was leading. I had a feeling he was going to like it even less in a few seconds.

"If we really want to figure this thing out"—I paused, and decided I'd better just get this over with — "then we'll have to go back to Los Alamos and kidnap Miles Odekirk."

CHAPTER FIVE

BOTH LINDSAY AND JACE WERE STARING AT ME AS if I'd suddenly lost my mind. Maybe I had. But now that I'd thought of it, the solution seemed clear enough. We couldn't expect Lindsay to come up with a solution to our problem. Even if she'd been a graduate student in physics rather than engineering, having her attempt to ferret out the workings of such an arcane device would be like asking me rebuild the solid fuel boosters on a rocket just because I'd helped my father once unclog the fuel-injection system on the car he'd owned before he bought the Cherokee.

At last Jace spoke. "Beloved, such a scheme couldn't possibly work. While I agree that the man who invented this device is the best person to modify it, there is no way we could safely return to Los Alamos, let alone manage to sneak in and abduct Miles Odekirk. Don't you remember how many guards were stationed at the labs there?"

Unfortunately, I remembered all too well. Nothing like the complement of men who'd probably watched over the facility before the Dying had swept away most of the world's population, but still enough that getting in there undetected wouldn't be easy.

Lindsay seemed to find her voice as well. "And it's more than sixty miles from here to Los Alamos. Sixty-plus miles of being completely unprotected against the rogue djinn, since you'd have to leave the device here to make sure everyone else was safe."

"I know," I replied. "But once we're away from here, away from the device, Jace's powers will return. That's got to help us, right?"

Jace shook his head, his expression about one-fourth pride and the rest utter bemusement that I was still pursuing this wild scheme. "I'm gratified by your confidence in me, Jessica, but even at full strength, I am still only one djinn."

"True, but I'm not suggesting that you would be the only one to come with us," I argued. "If the device is protecting Taos, then we don't have to worry about leaving a bunch of people here to keep it safe. We can take a large group—maybe even half—and we'll move quickly. Once we're outside the field of effect, maybe the djinn can 'blink' us—or whatever you call it—from here to Los Alamos. One djinn carrying one mortal. You told me when we escaped Los Alamos that you could have brought me here that way, if you'd only had me to worry about and not Evony and the dog, too."

At first Jace didn't reply, instead cocking his head to one side and pursing his lips slightly, as if considering my plan. That seemed to be Lindsay's cue to cut in.

"You're not seriously thinking about this, are you?" she demanded. "I mean, you do know that it's completely crazy, right?"

"Not completely," he responded. His tone was serious enough, but something about the way one corner of his mouth twitched told me he was willing to entertain the idea. "Believe me, if there were a better alternative, I would gladly pursue it. But I'm fairly certain there isn't."

She folded her arms and glared at both of us. "Okay, I know I haven't been making great progress. But I had to oversee getting the solar panels Jeff and Tony found yesterday hooked up to the resort's grid, and then there was switching over to an electric pump powered by a generator so we'd still have running water, and—"

"We know you've been doing more than your fair share," I said. "And I know everyone appreciates it, even if they haven't said so to your face. But be honest with me—would you be any farther along with the device even if you didn't have to do all that additional stuff?"

A long, long pause. Her eyes wouldn't quite meet mine, and at last she shook her head, defeat clear in the slump of her shoulders. "No. I'm afraid to open it up, Jessica. I can't break it, or we'll all be dead. I was probably glad of all the distractions, just because they gave me an excuse to not work on this thing. In fact, I only came down here a while ago because Lauren more or less told me I had to, that everything else was being handled for now."

"We all can do only what we can," Jace said then. "You included. Jessica's plan may sound insane, but we must move forward somehow, and I know that my fellow djinn will not be content to let the status quo continue for any longer than is strictly necessary. Turning on the device saved us all, and was necessary...but in its present configuration, it will also end up destroying us."

A shiver went through me at his words. I supposed I'd been telling myself that the djinn would learn to manage somehow, would get by until we could discover a better solution, but recalling the way Zahrias had looked earlier made me realize now that we didn't have as much time as we'd thought. He had to be very strong, or he wouldn't have been made the leader here, but his innate strength obviously wasn't enough, not when it was being destroyed in small, soul-crushing increments. Jace's only advantage was that he'd had weeks to get accustomed to the device and its effects on him, had been subjected to it at much higher levels, and therefore had built up a slight tolerance. Even that tolerance wouldn't protect him completely; I'd seen for myself how easily tired he became, how his mouth would go taut with pain when he thought I wasn't looking. No, this couldn't continue. We had to take the risk.

Lindsay seemed to get it as well, because she nodded. "Maybe you're right. I know it's just awful to see Rafi the way he is right now. Maybe that's why, deep down, I've been almost glad that I've been so crazy busy. I can tell him to stay in bed and rest, and then I don't have to see him looking like a shell of himself. That's one devil of an invention that Miles Odekirk cooked up."

"I know," I said grimly. "So maybe it's time to make the devil pay."

Zahrias didn't offer much in the way of protest when we went to him with our scheme. Sitting in his chair, he listened quietly, then said, "If you can find enough djinn and their Chosen to go on this expedition—at least ten of each—then I suppose it is something we should try."

As it turned out, ten of each was a very low estimate.

I couldn't blame the djinn. It was a risky plan, but I got the feeling that most of them were more than willing to take that risk if it meant a few hours or even days of being away from the influence of Miles Odekirk's device. And the Chosen went along with it because they wanted their djinn back the way they'd been before all this began. This post-Dying world was frightening enough without having the person who'd been protecting you the whole time more or less down for the count.

In the end, we had twenty djinn and their Chosen. Because none of the djinn were certain how quickly their powers would bounce back, we made the collective decision to drive to Los Alamos, rather than rely on magic that might or might not fail us at a critical moment. Lauren helped Jace and me with the final selections for the raiding party, just because she knew this group and their strengths and weaknesses far better than I did. Her own Dani was going, since he apparently had been quite a warrior back in the day, before he decided he'd rather be a lover than a fighter. But Lauren would stay behind, since Zahrias needed her.

"Besides," she told me frankly. "I'd be worse than useless on a trip like this. I don't know how to shoot a gun—if a gun even works on a djinn—and I'd just be in the way. Might as well stay here where I can be of some use."

I actually didn't know whether bullets would have any effect on a djinn, either, but I figured I'd find out if I had to.

The person who surprised me was Evony. She confronted Jace and me in the hallway as we were headed back to our suite once the final kidnapping party had been selected. Her arms were crossed, and I could tell from the determined jut of her chin that this was one discussion I wouldn't be able to avoid.

"I'm going, too," she announced, and I blinked, then sent an uncertain glance up at Jace.

Being Jace, he came to my rescue at once. "We appreciate the offer, Evony, but this is going to be a dangerous expedition. Are you a trained warrior?"

"Of course I'm not," she retorted. "I'm a former cocktail waitress who also knows how to wrench on cars. But it's not as if Jessica used to be in Special Forces or something."

I opened my mouth to defend myself, but Jace beat me to it.

"True, but her father was a policeman and trained her how to shoot and fight. Also, she's been inside the Los Alamos labs and can help guide us to where Miles Odekirk might be working."

"I've been there, too—" Evony began.

"In one building, on one occasion. We appreciate what you want to do, but there are important things to do here as well."

"Oh, what?" Her dark eyes were blazing. "Change the oil in one of the trucks? Bring Zahrias his hot chocolate? You can't stop me from going. If you won't give me space in one of the vehicles, I'll just hot-wire one and follow you."

She probably could, too. And would, unless Lauren had a couple of the guys who were staying in Taos hog-tie her and lock her in her suite.

"It's not safe for you," Jace told her.

"And it's safe for the rest of you? Sounds you're all taking a pretty big risk."

His expression was grim, but also sad, as if he knew he was about to tell her something she really didn't want to hear. "Yes, we are, but once we're away from the field that device projects, our powers will return to us. That also means our Chosen will heal more quickly if they are attacked. Evony, you will have no such protection, because Natila is gone. That sort of bond only exists between the djinn and their Chosen. Do you understand why you must remain here?"

While Jace was speaking, Evony had stood very still, her eyes going narrower and narrower. What I didn't see was any sort of surprise or shock in her expression, as if she'd already guessed that with Natila gone, she had none of the supernatural protections the rest of the Chosen enjoyed. And when she spoke, her tone was flat, unyielding. "No. You say your powers will come back, but I saw how wiped out you were after we left Los Alamos. There's no guarantee all you djinn will just bounce back right away once we're out of here. I mean, that's why you're driving instead of just blinking over there, right?"

He gave her the smallest of nods. "You're speaking of my condition as I was after being subjected to the device's effects for weeks and weeks," he replied gently. "The djinn here will have only experienced it for a few days, and those at its lowest viable setting. It is not the same situation at all."

To my own surprise, I found myself cutting in then. "If you're really determined to go, Evony, then you're right—there probably isn't much we can do to stop you. And you do know Los Alamos, which can only help. I guess all I can ask is that you stick close to someone who can help protect you when the shit hits the fan. Maybe Dani. Lauren isn't going with us, so he won't be worrying about her."

"I don't need anyone looking out for me—"

"But you do," Jace interrupted, although his tone was gentle. His voice sounded in my mind.

Are you sure, Jessica?

Yes. She'll come anyway, no matter what we do. At least this way, she'll be with the main group and will stand a better chance. Do you really want to run the risk of her following us to Los Alamos and getting jumped by those same bastards who mutilated Aidan?

The slightest tremor went through him. I doubted that Evony even noticed it, but he was standing right next to me. I could tell my reminder about the fate of the hunting party was not something he wanted to think about. To tell the truth, I really didn't want to think about it, either, but it was important that we always keep in mind what we were up against. And right then I began to suspect that we were up against even more than we'd originally thought. We still had no clues as to what had happened to the Chosen who'd first gone to investigate Los Alamos. Now, though, after seeing what this Khalim and his gang had done, I very much feared that those four had been taken, or killed...or worse.

"You do need someone, Evony," Jace said, his tone a bit firmer. The subvocal back-and-forth he and I had just shared had only taken a second, if even that, and Evony didn't appear to have noticed the slight hesitation. "We all need to look out for one another, because we don't know for sure what we're going to face. We could be attacked the second we're beyond the barrier created by Miles Odekirk's device, or somewhere out on the highway. We could make it all the way to Los Alamos, succeed in taking the scientist...and still be ambushed on the way back here. Many, many things could go wrong. You have never seen the djinn in battle, and I sincerely pray you never will. But if it comes to that...you would do well to have someone looking out for you."

Evony paled slightly. Jace had never raised his voice, had sounded calm and unruffled during this entire speech, but his meaning struck home nonetheless. In fact, it scared me more than I wanted to admit. Unlike Evony, I'd seen with my own eyes the beginnings of one of those attacks—the swirling darkness, the feeling of utter oppression. What it would be like once it got close enough to be personal...well, that was something I'd prefer to avoid.

The group that had attacked Clay and Aidan and Martine had been small, only ten or so, according to Aidan. Our own expedition would have twice that many djinn, and an equal number of us humans. I hoped that would be enough. Because if the djinn came against us with the sort of force I'd seen swirling in the heavens over Taos just the morning before....

It was my turn to shudder.

"Okay," Evony said, her tone quite altered. Now she sounded shaken, as she should be. "I'll talk to Lauren and Dani, see if he's okay with playing babysitter for me. But I'm going either way," she added with a flash of her old defiance.

"As you must," Jace replied. "Although I'm fairly certain Dani will be more than happy to make sure you come to no harm."

Jace was right about that—both Dani and Lauren agreed that if Evony insisted on coming, then he should stand in as her djinn, since Natila was now lost to her. And after that, the preparations moved ahead faster than I would have thought possible.

We'd leave that evening soon after the sun set, since going in under cover of darkness seemed to have a slightly higher chance of success than just strolling in with the sun blazing overhead. Ten vehicles, each with two humans and two djinn, except Dani's SUV, which would also carry Evony. As much firepower as we could scrounge within the mile radius of our current safe zone. That actually turned out to be a lot more than I would have thought, but it seemed as if almost every household we visited had at least a rifle or a shotgun. There was good hunting in the countryside around Taos.

"And will this actually help?" I asked, my tone dubious, as I hefted the shotgun Jace had set aside for me. "I mean, we're not exactly hunting rabbits."

He didn't smile. "Bullets will not kill a djinn, but they can slow them down. Hit them enough times, and they'll be forced to retreat so they can heal. Of course, when they do come back, they'll be angrier than ever, but...."

I got the point. If you were going to pump a djinn full of shotgun shells, you'd better make damn sure you were safely back within range of one of Miles Odekirk's squirrelly little boxes before that djinn came after you, breathing fire.

Literally.

Still, it meant we had more of a fighting chance than I'd originally thought. And it wasn't that far to Los Alamos. An hour and a half, maybe two, depending on the road conditions. Luckily, it hadn't snowed for quite a while now, so the highways should be clear enough. And once we were there....

After Jace and I had loaded our stuff into the big quad-cab truck we were using as the lead vehicle, we went to address the troops.

"There used to be a checkpoint on 502, at the bottom of the hill below Los Alamos," I said, facing the assembled djinn and humans who made up the strike team. We had gathered in the restaurant, since it had the most available space. Even Zahrias' borrowed conference room would have been strained to the gills to hold that many people. "But since we took one of their devices, that means their protected area is smaller, so they would have had to fall back a good deal. Jasreel and I went over the maps, and our best guess is that the first place they can set up an effective barrier is a little farther in, on Trinity Road. But...."

"But we've been analyzing maps of the area, and we've found that there's a better way, one we feel will probably not be as well-guarded," Jace went on. "This is Highway 4, which winds to the south of the labs. In fact, there is a road that cuts off from the highway, one that actually goes straight to the lab facility. We may encounter some resistance there, but probably less than we would on a frontal approach."

Well, that was more or less wishful thinking on both my and Jace's parts, since I hadn't even known about Highway 4—aka Jemez Mountain Road—the entire time I was living in Los Alamos. I'd never heard of anyone getting guard duty out there, but that didn't mean much. The town still kept many of its secrets, chief among them being where exactly Miles Odekirk had his main research lab. I'd spoken to him once in a conference room somewhere on the laboratory campus, and broken Jace out from where he was being held in yet another building, but I'd gotten the impression that the scientist did his main work elsewhere.

Which meant we'd have to do some scouting once we were on the property, and all that scouting would have to be done by the humans in the party, since by that point we'd be in the protected area, and our djinn wouldn't be of much use. Jace had already told me he was coming along, and I didn't bother to protest. He was the most functional of all of them, and he had at least been at the labs. The rest of the djinn would stay with the vehicles, just beyond the perimeter of the Los Alamos safe zone. That is, except for Dani. He, too, insisted on coming along, since Evony was his responsibility. It appeared the djinn took those sorts of things seriously—well, at least the honorable djinn. I doubted whether this Khalim, the elemental who appeared to be the leader of the rogue djinn, would be too concerned about honoring an oath.

"Let them resist," said Evony. Her hand rested on the pistol she now wore in a holster on her hip. "I wouldn't mind a little payback."

A murmur of assent rose from the crowd, and at once Jace lifted his hand.

"This is not about vengeance," he said. "Yes, this Miles Odekirk and the man he works for, Richard Margolis, are responsible for taking one of our own from us. But our true reason for going is to make sure we have the one person in our possession who can alter this device he created, make it so we can live safely here without being robbed of our powers. Understood?"

He looked so stern as he said this that a little thrill went through me. Maybe it was simply that his profile was to me, and so I could admire the fine lines of his strong nose and chin, the way his raven-dark hair flowed back from his brow. But I wasn't sure. This was a side of him he rarely revealed; most of the time, he was gentle, calm. The Jace I watched now—*Jasreel*—he seemed like someone who would put you through a wall without batting an eye.

The message appeared to get through; there was some murmuring, but most of the djinn and their Chosen nodded. After all, it was in their best interests to make sure this all went as smoothly as possible. Otherwise, they'd be doomed to a half-life of hiding here in Taos, suffering as more and more of their strength was taken from them with every passing day.

Even Evony didn't offer any protest, and actually nodded slightly, although I noticed she didn't move her hand, which still rested on the holster at her hip. This was an angle I hadn't even thought of until now—unlike the rest of us, she didn't have any real vested interest in making sure we got Miles Odekirk safely back to Taos. Her djinn lover was gone, and maybe she didn't care one way or another whether the rest of the djinn suffered the effects of the scientist's device or not.

Well, I couldn't think of any graceful way to make her stay behind. Not this late in the game. Dani had already promised Jace and me that he would keep an eye on her. I'd have to hope that "eye" included making sure she didn't cause any sabotage of her own.

Now, though, the sun was almost below the horizon. In less than an hour, we'd be setting out with only some Triple-A maps we'd scrounged from the concierge desk to guide us. No more days of having satellite-guided navigation direct you from Point A to Point B. We'd have to do this on our own.

And it would be dark...very dark. Right then I questioned the wisdom of doing this at night. True, the darkness would prevent the Los Alamos people from seeing us coming, but driving in the dark seemed to be giving the rogue djinn an open invitation to pick us off at their leisure.

I almost began to say something, but then I looked out at the forty people gathered there in the dining room. Human and djinn, with every hair color ranging from jet black to palest blonde, all beautiful in their own way. All tense, yet determined. They were ready to go now. And delaying another night would only weaken our djinn that much more.

Three of the trucks, including the one I would be driving, had those million-candlepower off-road lights mounted on their roofs. Those would do a lot to dispel the darkness. We'd have to turn them off once we crossed from Highway 4 onto Pajarito Road, but in the meantime, they'd be our beacons, our shield against the night.

I looked over at Jace, and he nodded.

"All right," I said. "Let's saddle up and do this thing."

CHAPTER SIX

It still wasn't full dark when we got on the road. The faintest muddy-orange glow lingered on the western horizon, and only the brightest stars had begun to come out. That made me feel a little better, although once we crossed the invisible line that marked the edge of the safe zone and I saw Jace sit up straighter in his seat and let out a harsh breath, I couldn't help shivering a little. Not for his pain; he'd told me it hurt to move through the field, but that only lasted a second, and once he was on the other side of it, he'd be able to bounce back quickly enough. No, my shiver came from the realization that out here, beyond the field, there was nothing to protect us...except each other.

We twisted and turned down Highway 68, taking it easy on the curves, where black ice from the past few days' snow melt might still be lurking. I forced myself to concentrate on the road, on the reflective paint guiding us along the dark highway. If I did that, then I couldn't look up every few seconds, expecting the clear skies to start roiling and hundreds of djinn to rain havoc on us.

Although I'd thought I'd kept myself steady enough, I felt Jace's hand on my knee, then heard his voice in my head.

How are you?

Okay. Scared. Why haven't they attacked us?

A pause. Then he replied, *We may seem all-seeing and all-knowing to you, but in truth, we are not. They may be occupied elsewhere. Or perhaps they're merely waiting for us to reach the flatlands.*

Well, that was reassuring. I pulled in a breath. *Here's hoping it's bingo night in djinn-land, then.*

He chuckled. *Yes, I will hope for that, too.*

In the back seat, our passengers, a djinn named Azael and his Chosen, a guy around my age, Travis Padilla, were silent. Maybe they were having the same sort of mental convo that Jace and I had just shared. Or maybe they were just remaining wary and on guard, Travis with his hands wrapped around the rifle he'd been given when we passed out the weapons. At least he looked as if he knew how to handle it, unlike a few of the Chosen on our team. With any luck, they'd never have to use the guns we'd assigned them.

We came out of the mountain pass that led up to Taos and down into Española. One good thing about the djinn-caused apocalypse and its accompanying population drop; at least we didn't have to stop and wait at every signal as we went through the town. No, we cruised along at a steady forty-five miles an hour, slowing occasionally to avoid vehicles abandoned in the middle of the road. Overall, though, the streets were fairly clear here, and I guessed that was probably the work of the Los Alamos survivors. Española was much closer than either Santa Fe or Taos, and so they must have begun their vehicle-collecting project here once they'd gone through what was available in Los Alamos itself.

Again I tensed. After all, Jace had just mentioned the possibility that the djinn might have been waiting to attack until we got out here. Nothing stopped us, though, and I glanced over at him.

What do you think?

I don't know. His mental voice had been sounding stronger and stronger the farther we got away from Taos, and I could see that he sat up very straight in his seat, his gaze fixed on the road ahead of us. Although he'd never explicitly come out and said it, I'd always gotten the impression that djinn could see better in the dark than us mere mortals. *That is, if they were going to attack, this would be the perfect opportunity. Perhaps they really have been distracted elsewhere.*

I wondered what kind of distraction was required to keep them from pouncing on a group of unprotected humans. Then again, we weren't entirely unprotected. We did have our djinn with us, and now that their powers were no longer being hampered by Odekirk's device, twenty of them did make a fairly formidable force. But it seemed as if it would take more than that to keep the rogue elementals away.

Something I'd wondered about previously resurfaced in my mind. *Jace, is there any sort of government among the djinn? I mean, if the ones who attacked Aidan's hunting party are breaking the agreement, is there anyone who can hold them accountable?*

Not a government as you know it, precisely, he replied. *We have our elders, and there are loose clan affiliations—Zahrias and I are cousins, for example, but—*

Wait, I broke in. *You're cousins?*

Yes, he said, that inner voice tinged with amusement. *That is how we are not precisely what you would call friends, but do know each other very well. This surprises you?*

Um...just a little.

I suppose I can see that. Anyway, some clans are allied with others, while others stand alone, if it suits them. Getting the djinn to agree about the Chosen took a large span of of time, since it required a good deal of individual coaxing. We generally don't like to be told what to do. It's not in our nature. We do have our elders, who pass judgment here or there as necessary. But they generally only step in as a very last resort. If you were imagining some sort of president or parliament or other governing body coming in to make the rogue djinn behave themselves, I'm afraid you're probably out of luck.

The turn-off for Highway 30, the one that would take us toward Los Alamos, was coming up then, so I waited until we were safely on it before replying, *How do you get anything done?*

I might have asked the same of you, considering how well your own Congress was doing right before the Heat struck.

Touché, I said.

A quiet chuckle. *It can be difficult. You mortals had a saying, I believe... "like herding cats." The situation with the djinn is not dissimilar. So the problem now is not that there aren't many djinn who would be angry if they knew what this one faction is up to. It's getting them to do anything about it, once they do know.* He hesitated, then added, *And I fear that most of them will not care overmuch about the deaths of a few more mortals. It's more important—in the minds of my people—that those deaths have resulted from a group of fellow djinn ignoring a solemn treaty that was made and universally agreed upon. They are now oath-breakers, and that, Jessica, is a very important matter.*

I was silent for a moment, digesting what he'd just said. I'd be lying if I said it didn't upset me that the djinn cared more about some agreement being broken than all the death and destruction that resulted from it. But I'd have to put that aside for now. If we got our hands on Miles Odekirk...if he could modify that damned device of his so it still functioned as a shield against the rogue djinn while keeping everyone within its little bubble safe...then maybe we'd have the opportunity to reach out to the djinn who were keeping the pact and have them rein in their treacherous fellows.

Once again, a lot of "if"s. But it would give us some hope. And some was definitely better than none. *I hope you're right,* I told Jace, and he seemed to understand that I wanted to let the matter go for the time being.

We jogged briefly onto Highway 502 so we could pick up the connector that led to Highway 4 and our secret back way into Los Alamos. Even though I knew we wouldn't be on 502 long, I could still feel myself tense. What if Margolis still had some sort of outpost here, despite the danger?

But the road was completely deserted, dark and still under the stars, which by now had fully appeared. A glow off to the east told me the moon, just a few days away from being full, had begun to rise. In a way that was good, since it would provide some helpful illumination. Too much, though, and our risk of detection went way up.

Around here the snow appeared to have mostly melted, just as it had up in Taos. The current warm snap wouldn't last forever, though; it was just the beginning of February, which meant plenty of snow chances still lay ahead of us. I'd be happy if the status quo would hang on just long enough for us to complete this mission and get safely back home. Then it could storm all it wanted.

We passed the turn-off for Jemez Road and kept going. That route would have taken us directly into the heart of Los Alamos, which was the last thing I wanted. No, we had to take the soft-underbelly approach. But as the sign for Jemez flashed briefly in my peripheral vision and then receded into the darkness, I couldn't help wondering about Julia Innes and Dan Lowery. Had Margolis believed their story, or were they now currently occupying the cells that had once held Jace and Evony and me?

I prayed that wasn't the case. This wasn't a rescue mission, but something with a very different purpose. Once we had Miles Odekirk in our custody, maybe then I could ask him about Julia and Dan. In the meantime, I had to push them out of my mind, focus on the dark road in front of me and the man who was the cause of all this trouble.

Well, that wasn't precisely true, or fair. I'd be the first to admit that Dr. Odekirk had caused a lot of misery, but on the other hand, the people in Los Alamos would probably be dead if it weren't for him, not to mention my fellow Chosen in Taos. It just would have been nice if he could have devised a way to protect human survivors without causing so much pain to the djinn into the bargain.

Pajarito Road came up more quickly than I'd expected, and I had to make a hard right turn to avoid passing it by completely. From the back seat, I heard a few muttered curses, but neither Travis nor Azael made any more protest than that. I also heard some squealing rubber behind us as the other vehicles in the caravan made the same hard right turn, and winced. At least I wouldn't have anyone calling up on a walkie-talkie to bitch me out. We'd gone back and forth on the whole walkie-talkie thing, but had eventually decided against it. Too much risk of Margolis and his people sharing the same band and possibly overhearing us, since no one in Taos knew much more about walkie-talkies than how to turn them on.

And then I hit the brakes, because the road was funneling us straight toward a row of guard shacks just like the ones that straddled the front entrance to the Los Alamos labs. The Triple-A maps we'd studied hadn't shown the shacks, naturally. Once again, rubber shrieked behind me, and I even felt a slight shudder go through the truck as the SUV behind us, the one carrying Dani and Evony, kissed our rear bumper.

"Jesus H. Christ!" Travis swore from the back seat.

I ignored him. My heart was going a mile a minute, but as I squinted into the moonlight, I realized all those guard shacks were unoccupied. Of course they would be. We still had to be several miles away from the main part of town, which meant the shacks were well out of the safe zone, the area protected by Miles Odekirk's little boxes.

"Sorry," I said. "False alarm."

There were a couple of grumbles from the back seat, but since none of them were addressed to me directly, I decided to ignore them.

Anyway, I realized there was plenty of room to bypass the shacks on the left side, so that's what I did, driving slowly at first, then picking up speed once we were past them and back out on the main road.

Jace sent me a sideways look.

"Hey, when you come in from the front, the guard shacks there are occupied," I said, adding, since he still didn't look completely convinced, "With people with guns."

"Ah." Then, "I fear that when I was brought to the labs, they placed a bag over my head, so I was in no position to see anything."

I'd forgotten about that...or at least had pushed it to the back of my mind so I wouldn't have to think about it. "I'm sorry."

"It's all right. It wasn't your fault."

Since I didn't know how to respond to his comment, I drove on in grim silence. The landscape to either side of us was covered in scrub juniper, with patches of unmelted snow gleaming here and there in the moonlight. It wasn't very different from much of the terrain you might drive through in northern New Mexico, but what surprised me was how many smaller roads broke off from Pajarito, and how many times I saw small groupings of buildings tucked away from the main road. This all had to be part of the lab complex. I'd had no idea it was anywhere close to this big, and, realizing that, my heart sank a little. Even the part of the campus I'd been to had seemed huge, and now, with all this additional territory it apparently covered, how in the world were we ever supposed to find Miles Odekirk?

"Jessica," Jace said quietly.

I took my eyes off the road for a second so I could look at him. Even in the moonlight he looked pale, and his fingers were grasping the door handle. "What is it?"

"We've passed the barrier."

Shit. I put my foot on the brake, but gradually, so I wouldn't have to worry about the rest of the vehicles in the caravan piling up on us. "How far back?"

"Just a hundred feet or so."

If he was feeling it, then so must the rest of the djinn. I wouldn't have to worry about anyone asking why I was turning the truck around and backtracking down the road. I drove slowly, glancing at Jace from time to time, and after less than a minute, he winced and raised a hand.

"Here."

I pulled off the asphalt and into the shelter provided by a group of juniper trees, bent and gnarled by the wind. One by one, the other vehicles did the same, finding their own cover. It wasn't perfect, but you'd have to be looking pretty hard to find us.

And if we were really lucky, no one would even know we were there.

Everyone got out of their respective trucks and SUVs. One of the vehicles we'd brought with us was a bright yellow Jeep Wrangler—not exactly the same as the Hummer the Los Alamos people used, but at night, if someone wasn't paying close attention, it might pass. We didn't have that much of a choice, since Jace insisted on coming along, and I knew there was no way he could hike a mile-plus uphill while under the influence of the devices operating here in town. No, we'd drive in as close as we could, then ditch the Jeep once we got close to the main part of the campus.

Assuming, of course, that Odekirk kept his own personal laboratory there, and not out in one of these far-flung buildings, far from any prying eyes.

Everyone gathered close by, some of the Chosen shivering in the brisk wind that was blowing down out of the north. The djinn seemed remarkably recovered, now that they were away from any of the boxes. They stood tall and strong, apparently not bothered at all by the twenty-degree temperatures. Well, good. Jace had been right when he'd said they'd bounce back quickly, since they hadn't been influenced by the devices for nearly as long as he had.

"Okay," I said. "You all lie low as best you can. If someone comes along...well, take care of them if you must, but be quiet about it. This is all about not attracting attention, so if someone passes by and doesn't notice you, let them go. The last thing we want is a guard not checking in and then the alarm being raised unless there's absolutely nothing else you can do."

I could tell that wasn't a very popular statement. Despite their apparent agreement back in Taos that this trip was not about revenge, I could tell that some of the djinn—and their Chosen—were just itching to take a piece out of the Los Alamos group. But we had to do everything we could to avoid notice. If someone drove by but didn't see the vehicles more or less hidden here in this forsaken little thicket, then our people would have to let them go.

So I stood there, arms crossed, staring at them all with what I hoped was a close approximation of the flat, dark-eyed stare my father used to level at the low-lifes he dealt with as a cop, and eventually they all looked away. Zahrias had put me in charge, and it seemed the djinn and their partners were willing to follow my lead.

For now, anyway.

Dani stepped forward, Evony a few feet behind him. The last person in the strike team was a young

man named Ethan, and he slipped into place behind
Evony. He'd worked as a bodyguard in the time before,
and had the muscles to prove it. Maybe it would have
made more sense to have them ride with us all along,
but I got the distinct impression that Evony hadn't
wanted to spend any more time in my company than
was strictly necessary, which was why they'd driven
in the SUV directly behind us on the way here. Now,
though, there were no alternatives. It would be the five
of us in that Jeep. I had to hope that was enough.

"Ready?" I asked, more a formality than anything
else. They really didn't have the option to back out this
late in the game.

And they didn't. Both Evony and Dani nodded,
then followed Jace and me over to the Jeep. Standing
by it were a djinn woman I didn't know and a man who
appeared to be pushing the limit of what the djinn
deemed acceptable as a partner—I couldn't guess his
exact age, but he didn't appear to be in the twenty-
five-and-under crowd. Even in the moonlight, there
were visible laugh lines around his eyes, but he was still
movie-star handsome despite that, with black hair and
a good, strong nose.

The unknown man handed me the keys. "Take
good care of her. She got me all the way from Roswell
to Taos."

"I will," I promised, and I meant it. He seemed
attached to the Jeep, and I couldn't really blame him.

I was still mourning the loss of my father's Cherokee. The only thing that reassured me at all was that the Los Alamos people were too respectful of good wheels to have done anything terrible to it. Most likely they'd turned it over to someone else in the community for their private use.

I turned toward Jace and Dani and Evony and Ethan, all of whom waited a few feet away, watching me expectantly. "Let's go."

None of them protested...not that I'd expected them to. I got in the driver's seat, Jace beside me, and Evony and Dani and Ethan climbed into the rear. The controls were laid out a little differently than in the Cherokee I was used to, but not so much that I thought I'd have any trouble piloting the unfamiliar vehicle.

We all buckled ourselves in, and I raised a hand toward the assembled group as we pulled away. That was more bravado than anything else; I was scared shit-less. Scared that we'd be caught. Scared that I might actually have to use the Beretta 9mm strapped to my hip. And, most of all, scared that I wouldn't be able to track down Miles Odekirk and would end up driving around in circles before returning to the waiting group of djinn and Chosen with my tail between my legs.

Jace shifted in his seat so he was more or less facing me. "You have a plan?"

I knew that he spoke aloud so Dani and Evony and Ethan wouldn't feel left out. "Sort of. While it's

possible that Odekirk's lab is in one of these outbuild-
ings, I think it makes more sense that he'd be somewhere toward the center of the facility. Every other
place we met up was near there, not out here in the
middle of nowhere. Say what you want about the guy,
but he was efficient. He didn't seem like the type to be
driving half a mile just to go from one lab to another."

"That does make sense," Dani agreed. He was sitting on the edge of his seat, apparently ignoring the
safety belt. Even though we were now back in the zone
of influence of Miles's devices, Dani didn't seem particularly affected. I remembered then how he'd volunteered to be one of Lindsay's "guinea pigs" during
her tests with our own stolen box. It seemed plausible
enough to me that he'd built up his own tolerance, even
if it wasn't quite as strong as Jace's. "Which building do
you think he'll most likely be in?"

I bit my lip. Definitely not the warehouse where
Jace and Natila had been waterboarded, and where
Natila had met her death. Neither did I think it was
the building where the two djinn had been held captive for a brief period. No, my gut was telling me that
Miles Odekirk had set up his private lab in the same
place where we'd first met, where he'd drilled me about
my presence in Los Alamos, attempting to discover
whether I'd had an ulterior motive. Of course I did,
although he hadn't found that out for several more
weeks. Still, I thought that, busy as he was, he wouldn't

have wanted to waste any more time on me than was strictly necessary, and so he'd interrogated me in the same building as the one where he did all his work.

All right, maybe that was stretching things a bit. But I didn't have any real leads to go on, and, more importantly, I did remember where that building was located, since I'd driven there myself, albeit accompanied by one of Captain Margolis' goons. It seemed the best place to start, and, if we were lucky, anyone hanging around the labs would think, in the moonlit darkness, that the yellow SUV going by was just the Hummer.

Well, unless we were spotted by the people driving the actual Hummer.

Coming in from this angle felt strange. I certainly couldn't claim to know the lab campus all that well, but I did recall how the building where Miles Odekirk had first interrogated me was built in the shape of an "X," and was four stories high. There couldn't be that many structures here with that exact same height and layout, could there?

The answer turned out to be "no." We followed the service road, and after about a half-mile of twists and turns, I saw it, shining there in the moonlight. Even though it was more than three stories tall, the building still looked squat and brooding. Or maybe that was just my mind embellishing what might be going on inside it.

Well, at this hour, I wasn't sure if that would be much of anything, especially now that the resident mad scientist didn't have any djinn to experiment on. I glanced at the clock on the dashboard. Eight forty-five, if the readout was to be trusted. Far past normal working hours, but I had a feeling that Miles Odekirk didn't put in what you'd call your standard nine-to-five.

At least there was no one around that I could see. I drove slowly, circling the parking lot, and spotted a lone vehicle, the same Subaru Forester that I'd seen when I came here the first time. That must be Odekirk's car, although I'd never actually seen him driving it. But that was the only vehicle in the lot, and I let out the smallest breath of relief. It didn't seem as if anyone else was around. Possibly a patrol did pass this way every once in awhile. For now, though, the lot was deserted, except for the Forester.

"That's Odekirk's car," Evony said then. "That piece of shit Subaru."

"How do you know for sure?" I replied, irritated that she hadn't mentioned it before now.

"He brought his car in once to get the brake pads changed."

"Why didn't you tell me?"

A shrug. "You didn't ask."

If she was deliberately trying to piss me off, she was doing a good job. I told myself to let it go, then pulled up next to the building, in the shadows cast by the intersecting wing. If someone got close enough, of course they would see the Jeep, but it wouldn't be immediately obvious to the casual driver making a loop on the service road.

"Okay," I said quietly, although I doubted there was much chance of anyone overhearing me. "When Odekirk interrogated me—"

"He questioned you?" Jace cut in, sounding strained.

That particular convo was something I'd never discussed with him, mostly because I hadn't thought it all that worthy of mention. As far as I could tell, nothing much had come of it. "Sort of. It really wasn't a big deal. He asked me some questions, but it didn't get nasty, if that's what you're wondering about."

"It had better not," Jace responded, a hint of a growl in his tone.

"It didn't," I repeated. I was all for giving the devil his due, but I'd survived that interview unscathed, and I wanted Jace to know that. My reply seemed to be enough to satisfy him, because he nodded. Something about the tight set of his mouth didn't bode well for Dr. Odekirk, though, if he put up too much resistance.

"And you can take it up with him later," Evony remarked, her tone dry. Leather creaked as she moved in her seat. "Right now, the most important thing is locating the asshole, right?"

"Right," Jace said.

"Anyway," I went on, "when Odekirk interrogated me, it was in this wing of the building." I pointed through the windshield, in case anyone had any problems identifying which wing I was talking about. "That was just a standard conference room, but I figure it's probably the best place to start."

"You really think he'd be here at this time of night, and not at home?" Ethan asked.

"Hard to say," I admitted. "But I did get the impression that he was the sort of person who lived for his work, if you know what I mean."

"He has—or had—a house closer to the center of town," Evony added. "But he didn't spend much time there."

I swiveled my head to stare at her in the back seat. "Where'd you hear that?"

"From Shawn, when I was working in the motor pool."

My irritation flared higher. Part of me wanted to snap at her for withholding what could be vital information, but we really didn't have time for that. "Fine. So I'm guessing we have a better-than-average chance that he might be working in this building somewhere. Or I could be be completely off-base, and he could have his actual labs somewhere back down the side of the hill. But we're here now, so we might as well investigate. We'll just start with the most likely scenario and work outward from there."

"Got it," said Ethan, opening the rear door so he could extricate his oversized frame from the back seat. I couldn't really blame him; it had to have been pretty cramped with the three of them back there.

Evony and Dani followed suit, so I got out as well, Jace only a second or two behind me. The wind caught me as soon as I exited the vehicle. Down in that sheltered copse where the rest of the Chosen and djinn waited for us, the night hadn't felt so cold, but up here the wind had a definite bite, even if it wasn't quite as cold as the night I'd approached this building to rescue Jace.

What a boondoggle that had been. I had to hope that history wouldn't repeat itself tonight.

The first time I'd come here, the exterior door had been unlocked. But that had been in full daylight. I couldn't expect the same thing now.

Even so, I experienced a stab of disappointment as Ethan put his hand on the door handle and attempted to push it. "Locked," he said briefly.

A mile down the hill, that wouldn't have been a problem, as either Jace or Dani could have made short work of that lock. Here, though, they were mostly around to lend moral support. Or rather, Jace refused to leave my side, and Dani had been expressly tasked by Lauren to watch out for Evony...so here we were.

But there was Ethan.

Without hesitating, he pulled a pistol from where he had it jammed into the waistband of his pants, then shot at the door handle. It fell onto the ground, leaving a smoking hole behind.

"Someone could have heard that," Evony said severely.

Ethan only shrugged. "Did you have a better idea?"

Of course she didn't, so she settled for sending him a scathing look before pushing the door inward. With her free hand, she pulled out her own pistol. "Let's go," she said in a whispered hiss.

I thought the whisper was sort of unnecessary, considering that Ethan had already shot up the door. But we did need to get moving. I left my pistol in its holster, since I figured Evony and Ethan were doing a decent enough job of providing armed cover. Anyway, while there were guards stationed at this facility, there had never seemed to be more than a few at any given time, except when I'd been caught trying to break Jace out of here.

The place definitely seemed deserted enough tonight. You'd have thought that gunshot would have been enough to bring people running, but we didn't see anyone else as we moved down the corridor, working in tandem to open the doors and make sure that Miles Odekirk wasn't hiding in any of the chambers we passed. Just our good luck that this building didn't have the keypad locks that had been installed in the one where Jace was held captive. That would have stopped us in our tracks. All these doors had regular locks, though, and all of them stood open—mostly because they didn't seem to be hiding anything more sinister than abandoned offices and a couple of storage rooms filled with obsolete computers and banged-up furniture.

Nothing on the ground floor, though, after we'd finished our search, so we located the stairwell and headed upstairs. Our footsteps clanged on the metal stairs, and I winced. Maybe no one was around, but I still couldn't help thinking that we were making ourselves awfully conspicuous. But what did I expect? We were a bunch of civilians...even our djinn. It wasn't as if we were all trained Navy SEALs or something.

"Where do you think all the guards are?" I whispered to Jace.

He lifted his shoulders. I didn't like the tight set of his mouth, which told me he was using sheer will to keep going, despite the draining effect of the devices protecting Los Alamos. Not for the first time, I wished I could have come up with some argument that would have convinced him to stay in Taos, but he wouldn't have heard of it. After our nearly month-long separation, he wasn't about to let me out of his sight.

However, his voice sounded smooth and controlled enough as he replied, "I don't know where they might be. It's possible that once they had no more djinn to guard, they saw no need for regular patrols here. After all, what would they be looking for? Our only desire was to escape, to get back safely to Taos."

That made some sense—if you were dealing with a rational person. But Richard Margolis was far from rational when it came to djinn. He wouldn't see our escape for what it was: a flight to freedom. No, he'd suspect us of leaving so we could regroup, and then come back and mount another assault.

Which, come to think of it, was pretty much exactly what we were doing.

I shook my head. "I think it's probably more likely that he just doesn't have enough people to get any kind of decent coverage when it comes to guard duty. Which is still a good thing, don't get me wrong. It's only—"

My words broke off there, as Ethan opened the door that led into the main corridor of the second floor, and I saw exactly where those missing guards were.

Right in front of us.

I froze, and so did Evony. But Ethan had some kind of experience with this sort of thing—what, I wasn't sure I really wanted to know—and had his pistol out and was firing before the two guys with the bad luck to draw guard duty this evening had a chance to even pull out their own guns. They dropped, silent and unmoving, and I found myself raising my hand to my mouth to prevent myself from making anything except a muf-fled whimper.

"Holy shit," Evony whispered.

"Them or us," Ethan said briefly. His expression was serene, unruffled...about the opposite of how I felt right about then. "Which way?"

She hesitated, then replied, "To the left, I guess."

As we passed the prone bodies of the fallen guards, I couldn't help glancing down. A tiny sigh of relief escaped my lips. I didn't recognize either one of them. For a brief, awful second, I'd worried that Dan Lowery might be one of the men Ethan had shot, but obviously he hadn't been working the night shift this evening. Or at all, I reflected. I still had no idea whether he'd escaped Margolis' wrath after Jace and Evony and I had fled the cells under the Los Alamos justice center.

All the doors we tried were unlocked, opening into offices and meeting rooms and, here and there, what used to be small labs, with banks of tables and comput-ers and oscilloscopes and other equipment I couldn't even identify. Every one of those rooms was empty, and I forced myself not to let out a sigh of frustration.

We doubled back, passing the fallen guards. I hated to look at them, hated that we'd had to resort to violence to keep ourselves safe. All right, grabbing Miles Odekirk and hauling him out of here would be its own form of violence, but our intention wasn't to hurt him, only to get him to help us. Maybe we could have subdued those guards without shooting them. Unfortunately, Ethan hadn't really given us that option, and I didn't have the time or the energy to upbraid him for his impulsive, deadly actions now.

At the far end of the hall was a set of double doors. There had been a similar set on the other side of the building, hiding one of the labs we'd discovered. It was probably too much to ask that Odekirk might be working in the room beyond those doors, but I found myself whispering a little prayer anyway.

Please let this be the one....

Ethan nodded at Evony, and she pushed the door open as he whipped around, gun out. Dani followed, then Jace, with me bringing up the rear.

As in the first lab we'd found, this one was crowded with equipment: multiple computers, their flat screens showing what looked like 3D modeling programs and scrolling banks of code. Oscilloscopes and tables filled with bits and pieces of what looked like junk, but which I guessed must be the components for more devices. Unlike that first lab, however, this one was occupied. Miles Odekirk stood next to one of the worktables, a half-assembled box in one hand. It fell from his fingers as he caught sight of us, hitting the tabletop with a *thunk*.

"Hello, Dr. Odekirk," I said. "You're coming with us."

CHAPTER SEVEN

To his credit, he was only thrown off for a fraction of a second. Then he lunged for the walkie-talkie that had been lying on the worktable amongst the welter of parts and wires and pliers.

But Ethan was too fast for him. In that same instant, he charged forward and knocked the walkie-talkie to the linoleum floor with the hand that wasn't holding the gun. Since the radio was one of those heavy-duty ones with a rubberized casing, it bounced instead of shattering. Still, Miles Odekirk wouldn't be using it anytime soon.

"Hands up," Ethan said, pistol trained on the scientist.

Odekirk seemed to realize there wasn't much use in protesting, so he raised both his hands in the air. "I'm not sure what you think you're going to accomplish with all this," he said, gaze flicking to Jace and Dani, then to Evony and me. He frowned, although I wasn't sure if the scowl resulted from surprise at seeing two djinn functioning more or less normally even in an area protected by the device, or because Evony's and my presence there especially annoyed him for some reason.

In the end, it really didn't matter. "We can discuss that later," I said. "For now, we have to get going. Do you have a coat?"

Apparently surprised by the *non sequitur*, he blinked, then replied, "In the supply closet over there."

"Get it."

He sidled over to the closet in question and Ethan followed, his gun pointed dead in the center of the scientist's back. It was fairly obvious that Ethan didn't trust Miles Odekirk any farther than he could throw him. I didn't trust him, either, but he didn't seem to me like the type to keep a hold-out pistol anywhere around. No, he'd been relying on the two guards patrolling the building to protect him.

Guards who were now dead, thanks to us.

I swallowed uneasily, then watched as Miles pulled out a down coat out of the closet and began shrugging into it.

His tone almost conversational, he said, "Do you really think you're going to get me away from here without being detected?"

Jace smiled grimly. "We got in, didn't we?"

That reply was obviously not what Odekirk wanted to hear; his scowl deepened, but he finished zipping up his coat.

"Okay," Evony said. "That thing you were working on? We want it, and any components you need to finish putting it together."

"I don't see—"

"He's just stalling in the hope that someone will come to rescue him," Dani cut in. He stepped away from Jace and me, located a box, and began piling everything on the worktable into it.

"I had all that organized," Miles protested.

"And you'll organize it all over again once we get where we're going," Evony said. She went to the desk at the far end of the room, where a laptop sat open, then shut it and began gathering up its power cables.

Odekirk's eyes took on a certain glint, as if he'd just deduced what we were up to. "If you think I'm going to provide you with any sort of assistance, you're sadly mistaken."

"We'll see about that," Jace said. His expression was so blank, it might have been carved from stone...that is, unless you happened to take a good look at his eyes. They were colder than a winter night, colder than the dark between the stars.

The scientist swallowed.

"I think we've got it all," Evony announced, glancing over at Dani. He nodded, hefting the box of supplies he'd gathered. I wondered if the djinn would actually have the strength to carry it any distance, but decided I'd wait until he showed obvious signs of fatigue before offering to take it from him.

At that point, I did finally draw my own pistol and point it at Odekirk. "All right," I told him. "Time to go."

He didn't offer any protest, but headed out the door meekly enough. I supposed he probably didn't have much experience with having several guns pointed at him.

"The stairwell," Jace said briefly.

We all headed in that direction, Ethan in the lead, scanning the whole time for signs of any more guards. No one stopped us from getting to the stairs, however, and we hurried down, this time not worrying about stealth. Right then, speed was our objective.

The Jeep still waited for us in the lee of the building, and we herded Odekirk that way. I could hear Dani's labored breathing, so I said, "I can take that box from you."

He shook his head. "No. We're almost there."

I supposed he had a point. It might have taken longer to stop and retrieve his burden from him than it did to stagger the last yard or two to our getaway vehicle. I clicked the remote to unlock it, and Ethan bundled Miles Odekirk into the back seat, with Evony squeezing in next to him. Dani went around to the back and set the box in the cargo area, then got in as well.

Despite everything, I couldn't help but repress a smile at Miles Odekirk's expression, revealed as it was in the moonlight. He didn't look frightened, or even angry. No, he just appeared supremely annoyed, as if being wedged in the back seat of a Jeep Wrangler with a couple of armed human miscreants and a djinn was a huge inconvenience. Well, I supposed in a way it was.

Jace climbed into the passenger seat, and I got in behind the wheel. My foot hit the gas almost the same instant I turned the key in the ignition, and the Jeep leaped forward, tires squealing. Good thing there wasn't any snow or ice in this particular section of the parking lot.

We racketed down the hill. The whole time, I kept stealing glances in the rearview mirror, certain I would see an army of Margolis' goons chasing down Pajarito Road after us, but the asphalt gleamed blank in the moonlight, unoccupied.

"So...what gives?" I asked over my shoulder. "Were those two guards really the only ones in the building? Didn't you have any other kind of surveillance?"

Odekirk's mouth tightened. "Two there, and four more covering the rest of the grounds. Just your good luck that the others were elsewhere. But, as you may have noticed, it is rather a large campus."

His tone was cool, almost disinterested. For all I knew, he'd resigned himself to his fate, whatever that might turn out to be. Or maybe inwardly he hoped our luck was about to run out, and we'd come across those other guards at any moment.

I couldn't help worrying about that, but at the same time, I kept my foot pressed firmly on the accelerator. The farther we got from the labs, the closer we drew to the rest of the group where they waited for us in that stand of juniper. The guards might have been tasked with keeping Miles Odekirk and the facility he now commanded safe, but I wondered if their loyalty to their commander was strong enough that it would lead them to venture beyond the bounds of the safe zone, especially if they were confronted by a group of angry djinn the second they passed over the border.

As soon as we were safely past the area the devices protected, I saw Jace straighten, and from the back seat, Dani let out a tight little sigh. Up ahead I saw the rest of our group, waiting in the cover of the trees. A quick scan of the scene told me they were more or less where we'd left them, although I noticed that some of the djinn had moved toward the road, as if to make sure they'd be the front line of defense in case anyone else came along.

I slowed, then came to a stop. As the waiting group began to move toward the Jeep, I rolled down the window. "I've got him," I said briefly. "Everyone back to their vehicles. We need to get going."

There were no cheers, nothing but a brief murmur among the djinn and their Chosen, and then everyone began to disperse toward the waiting vehicles. I'd handed off the keys of the pickup I'd driven here to Travis, and he and Azael hurried toward the truck, followed by the man whose Jeep I was driving and his djinn companion. In less than a minute, everyone was back inside their respective vehicles and falling in line behind us as we began moving south on Pajarito Road.

That went well, I told Jace.

Almost too well, he responded.

I'd been thinking about the same thing, but I didn't want to admit it. Anyway, the time to be stopped by Margolis' forces was some ways back up the road. My past experience with them had shown that they didn't dare venture beyond the bubble of safety Miles Odekirk's devices provided.

So what would they do when they discovered their resident wizard had been stolen from right under their noses? I honestly had no idea. There were plenty of people in Los Alamos who knew how to operate the little boxes, but that didn't mean they could create any more of them, now that the scientist was gone. If one of the devices malfunctioned, they'd be in a world of hurt.

They're short-staffed, and not all that well-trained, I told Jace after a pause. *Probably they thought they had plenty of people guarding the facility. After all, no one who was a resident would ever think of going in there without an invitation, and no djinn would come any-where close.*

Except those of us who are mad enough to ignore what those devices do to us.

Not mad, I replied. *Brave. The people in Los Alamos are not exactly of a mindset that would believe a djinn capable of personal bravery, or loyalty. So they would never imagine that any of you would willingly come here in order to do what you did.*

What we all did. You and Evony and Dani.

And Ethan, I added. I didn't really like his meth-ods, but I couldn't argue with the results.

And Ethan, Jace conceded. I *hate to see death when it is not needed, but perhaps that was unavoidable. We will just have to do everything we can to make sure there are no more deaths that come about as a result of our actions.*

I wasn't sure that was exactly realistic, but I didn't argue. Like Jace, I thought there had already been far too much death. We should be trying to avoid it. Every life was precious, even the lives of those in Los Alamos, the ones who believed all the djinn were pure evil.

Problem was, some of them actually were. I recalled Aidan's story, how the djinn who'd destroyed his face had laughed and said, "Give my love to Lilias." Surely those were the words and actions of a monster.

But we had no monsters in Taos, only djinn and the mortals they loved. And we had to do everything we could to make sure they could live real lives together, and not suffer endlessly just because some of the djinn had decided to go rogue.

The moon was higher in the sky now, almost directly overhead. It lit the landscape so brightly that we almost didn't need our headlights, although I wasn't foolish enough to try turning them off. This time I didn't miss the turn-off onto Highway 4, and we all slipped onto it with nary a tire screech. From there, just that quick jog on 502, then on through Española, up 68, and back home.

Well, Taos, anyway. In my mind, Santa Fe was still home. And maybe, just maybe, the two of us could come up with a way to get back there. That was what I really wanted—a quiet corner of the world with Jace, a place to love each other and build and grow together.

But first things first.

"Everyone all right back there?" I asked as we passed the last casino in town and began heading out into open territory. That casino might have even been the place where Evony had been holed up with Natila for a while, but I didn't dare ask. Evony's was a wound which had barely begun to heal.

"Just fab," she said in reply to my question. "Although this is probably a little cozier than I wanted to get with the legendary Miles Odekirk."

Dani made a noise that sounded like a muffled laugh, but I could tell the scientist was far from amused.

"I assure you, the feeling is mutual," he said icily.

That made me want to laugh as well. I decided that probably wasn't a good idea, though. It was going to be a tough row to hoe, getting him to help us, and teasing him on top of kidnapping him in the middle of the night almost guaranteed his non-cooperation.

I glanced at the clock on the dashboard. Edging up to eleven. All right, so it wasn't exactly the middle of the night, but late enough that I doubted he'd been expecting company. Did he actually go home, wherever that was, or did he sleep somewhere in the labs, so absorbed in his work that he couldn't bear to be parted from it for even a few hours?

We'd find out soon enough, I supposed. He'd have to be set up in our basement lab, since the auto shop was too far away to be considered safe. Would he stay there, even if given a cozy hotel suite to sleep in?

Just as I was returning my gaze to the road, a wall of fire roared across the highway some fifty yards or so ahead. I let out a scream and hit the brakes, heart pounding, adrenaline bursting along every vein and artery like thousands of firecrackers going off. Behind me, I heard brakes squealing.

"It's them!" Jace shouted, and before I could even blink, he'd undone his seatbelt and was hurrying outside. At the same time, Dani also clambered over a cursing Ethan so he could be out in the open as well.

Gale-force winds blew outward from Jace, causing the wall of flames to waver and dance. As soon as Dani was outside, those winds intensified, shrieking with the voices of a thousand enraged banshees. I wanted to put up my hands to cover my ears, but I wouldn't allow myself to do anything so cowardly. Instead, I pulled out my pistol, thumb on the safety. Right then, I couldn't see anyone except Jace and Dani, but I wasn't foolish enough to think that wall of flames had just appeared out of nowhere.

More of our djinn emerged from their vehicles. Lightning crackled overhead, and the bright moonlight that had guided us along our way disappeared. I knew if I looked up, I'd see more of those same roiling clouds that had accompanied the first attack by the rogue djinn on the people of Taos. But had they been created by the elementals who attacked us now, or our own djinn?

I didn't know. All was chaos and sound and fury, the darkness penetrated by fire and lightning, the wind whipping up dust from all around us. We had twenty djinn—what should have been a formidable number, in most cases. The problem was, I didn't know how many of the enemy confronted us now. They hid in the dark, an inimical presence, one that seemed to weigh on my heart and lungs, to suck all the air out of the surrounding spaces.

We'd brought mainly male djinn with us, but there were also several women. One of them approached Jace now, her pale hair fluttering wildly in the wind like a white banner of surrender. From the way she raised her arms, though, I got the feeling she wasn't planning to capitulate anytime soon. Instead, water flowed out from her, as if she were some sort of latter-day Moses who could not only part the Red Sea, but call it to do her bidding.

The flames the other djinn had conjured flickered, weakened, but only for a moment. Then they surged back up again, brighter than ever. I could see Jace clearly right then, the firelight casting his features into strong relief, his black hair whipping around his head. He was beautiful, but frightening as well. I'd never seen him like this, using his full powers, the winds streaking out around him and beating down that unnatural fire, moving the female djinn's waters forward in a surge as inexorable as a tidal wave.

For the first time, as the water seemed to swallow the fire for a brief second, I could also see one of our adversaries. He stood just beyond the dancing, angry flames. In the uncertain light, I couldn't make out the color of the dark robes he wore, but I could still see his face, hair black as night, features proud and cruel. How could I have ever thought Zahrias' face harsh or unkind? Stern, yes, but there was no evil in his features.

Not like this man—this djinn—who stood there and smiled as the night tore itself apart around him.

In that moment, I couldn't even tell who had the upper hand. The flames would rage forward, and the wind and water would push them back. And we humans could only cower in the vehicles, unsure as to what we should do...except stay inside and hope our champions would eventually emerge the victors in this conflict.

But then I heard Evony mutter, "Fuck this," and push open the door on her side of the Jeep.

To my surprise, I saw Miles Odekirk reach for her, as if to prevent her from participating in this insanity. She was too fast, though, and slipped out into the maelstrom before his fingers could close around her arm.

"Shit!" Ethan cursed, and he, too, was out, leaving me alone in the Jeep. Well, alone with Odekirk. In the rearview mirror, the scientist's eyes caught mine, and then I saw him shake his head slightly. He might have been frightened out of his mind, the same way I felt right about then, but he wasn't so terrified that he intended to leave the safety, however spurious, of the SUV.

Evony was moving fast, running to stand next to Jace. Dark fire glinted off the barrel of her pistol as she pointed it at the black-haired djinn.

There was too much noise from the howling wind for me to hear the gun going off, but I saw the flare from the muzzle, saw her arms jerk from the recoil. Ethan came up beside her and got off another shot, and another.

The flames subsided for a second or two, even while a shrieking filled the air that had nothing to do with the wind Jace and our other djinn had called. I winced, fingers tightening on the grip of my own gun. Had Evony hit our enemy...or enemies? I'd only seen the one, but I knew there had to be many more than that single djinn out there.

An explosion of light—no, fire, this time in concentrated spheres that launched themselves out of the darkness, striking Evony and Ethan so they were thrown to the ground, screaming, then going still.

Another scream echoed in my ears—mine, screaming my denial. My left hand found the door handle, began to pull it.

"Don't," Miles said. "You can't do anything to help them."

Like that mattered. Not when it was Evony lying out there, pistol knocked a yard from her hand, her dark hair fanning out against the asphalt like crumpled silk.

From our own djinn came an answering scream, wind and water and, yes, flame and swirling dust falling on our enemies, a storm so intense, so wild and uncontrolled, that I knew no mere human could hope to survive in it. Maybe no other djinn, either; I stared out into the night, tears rolling down my cheeks, and waited for the counterattack.

It never came. Gradually, the wind's howl died down, and the dust devils subsided, and the water flowed away to nurture the hard winter soil. All that was left were our djinn, faces streaked with dirt, clothing torn. And they knelt by Evony and Ethan, and they wept.

We came into Taos a little after midnight, limping our way to the resort that was our only sanctuary. Jace had held my hand the whole way, fingers tight on mine. Because of that, I knew the precise moment we crossed into the safe zone. His flesh grew cooler, and I knew he no longer had access to his powers.

The powers that had saved most of us, but not all.

I swallowed and fought back the tears. Later, I'd let myself cry, but for now I had to maneuver my borrowed Jeep through the dark streets. No careless energy wasted on lighting the street lamps, not now. Everything we had needed to be used for keeping our food safe, illuminating our one small corner of town.

Evony's limp form lay draped across Dani's and Miles Odekirk's laps. The scientist hadn't made a sound of protest, possibly because he knew we were all poised on a razor's edge, and it wouldn't take much to make any of us snap.

Terrible mixed metaphor, but I wasn't thinking very clearly at the moment.

We didn't have room for Ethan in the Jeep, but he was being brought back to Taos in the bed of one of the pickups. Irrelevantly, I wondered if the ground was even thawed enough for us to bury them properly. It had been warmer than normal the past few days, but still well into the teens at night.

During the whole drive, Jace had been silent. Perhaps he'd only wanted to keep from distracting me; after all, it seemed as if we'd driven off the rogue djinn for the time, but maybe that was only what they wanted us to think. Maybe they'd moved farther on down the road, and were only waiting to pounce on us at the perfect unguarded moment.

That didn't happen, though. It seemed we must have delivered, if not a killing blow, at least a wounding one. All we needed was enough breathing space to get within the device's field of effect, and then we'd be able to regroup.

We got that breathing space, although it was certainly a very solemn caravan that pulled into the parking lot of the El Monte Sagrado. There at last we did see some lights, burning on either side of the front entrance to the resort, and even though it was now past midnight, those doors opened, and Lauren and Zahrias emerged just as Jace and I were getting out of the Jeep.

"Thank God," she began, then apparently saw the stricken look on my face, the way Jace ever so subtly shook his head.

"What happened?" Zahrias asked, dark eyes flickering from Jace to me, and then to Dani as he slid out of the back seat. A second or two later, Miles extricated himself with some difficulty. I saw why at once; he hadn't left Evony behind, but carried her in his arms. It was as if he knew that none of the djinn now had the strength to carry her.

"They attacked your party," Miles said. His face was very pale in the moonlight and the reflected glow from the lights that guarded the front entrance to the resort. In his tone I heard a sort of wonder, as if he still didn't quite know what to make of it all.

Not a muscle moved in Zahrias' face. He stared at Evony, who looked like a broken doll in the scientist's arms. Then he said, "Of course they did. They would have been waiting for an opening."

"But...they were djinn."

"Yes." A grim smile touched the corner of the djinn leader's mouth. "You may find yourself surprised by us, Dr. Odekirk. In the meantime...."

Two Chosen came out of the door then, young men. I recognized David, Aidan's erstwhile partner in guard duty, and I thought the other one's name was Remy, but I couldn't recall for sure. My thoughts kept chasing around one another, unable to settle down. We had succeeded...but we had also failed. We hadn't been able to keep all our people safe.

David moved past Zahrias and Lauren so he could approach Miles Odekirk. "I'll take her," he said quietly, and the scientist startled, then nodded, surrendering Evony's body to one of her own people.

But were we? Some of us were Chosen, as she had been, but I knew she hadn't really felt at home here. Maybe if she had been able to come here with Natila, but....

Now they were both gone.

Tears began to run down my cheeks then, scalding in the cold night air. I felt Jace's touch on my arm.

"Beloved, let us go inside."

"I want to stay with Evony," I said.

No protest. Only a nod, and he replied, "Of course. Let us hold a vigil for her."

I headed over to where David stood with her in his arms, ignoring Miles. Jace came with me, a faithful shadow at my side.

"I know where we can take her," Lauren said, gesturing for us to follow her inside.

As we went, I saw Zahrias approach Miles. "This is not quite the homecoming we had expected, but let me show you the rooms we've prepared for you."

And it seemed Miles could only nod. For myself, I wasn't paying attention after that. I trailed along behind David and Lauren, until at last we came to a large room hung with oil paintings, some abstract, some of what appeared to be local landscapes. In the center of that room were red-upholstered chairs and couches. David went to one of these and laid Evony gently down on it. Her hair slipped over the edge of the cushions, making her look like a sort of latter-day Snow White. Only I knew that no one would be coming along to kiss her awake.

Jace led me to one of the chairs so I could sit down next to her. I took her cold hand in mine and murmured, "I'm so sorry. So, so sorry."

No response, of course. No, I was alone with my grief and my guilt, even though Jace and Lauren and David occupied the room as well.

Beloved, you did nothing wrong.

I shook my head without looking up. *I should have stopped her.*

How? By getting out of the vehicle and endangering yourself as well? We were tasked with retrieving Miles Odekirk, and if you had gone after Evony, you would have left him unprotected. If anything had happened to him, all hope of helping everyone here in Taos would have been lost.

They were sensible words. I even understood them at some level. At the same time, though, I raged at the capriciousness of fate, that Evony should have to endure so much pain and not even have the opportunity to somehow come out on the other side, whole again, if not precisely healed.

Take heart in this, beloved, Jace went on. *Her bullets did hit their target. Khalim was wounded, along with several of his followers. That is why they fled in the end. We were keeping them at bay, but were not strong enough to overcome them all. When Evony and then Ethan fired at them, they gave us the small advantage we needed.*

Hearing this, I felt—well, not exactly cheered, but maybe satisfied. Evony had gone down, but she'd gone down swinging. Since I didn't trust myself to speak, I reached out and took Jace's hand, clinging to it. I didn't even care that his skin was cool against mine, a sure sign that Miles's device was working on him once again.

As I clung to him, I dimly noted that Lauren and David had slipped out of the room. That was all right. I was here with Jace, and that was the important thing.

We would stay here together, and mourn our dead.

CHAPTER EIGHT

THERE ACTUALLY WAS A CEMETERY IN TAOS WITHIN the mile radius of the protective field the device cast, but, as I'd feared, the ground was too hard for a proper burial. I wondered how they'd done it in the time before. With jackhammers and backhoes, I supposed, both of which were in short supply these days. Putting people in the ground was not the djinn way, not all the time, at any rate. Their customs were much more like those of the Vikings—those born of fire went out that way, and those of the air were sent to the afterlife in the same manner. The water elementals were set adrift on the sea, while only the earth elementals took their long sleep in the ground. Since, according to the driver's license I found in the abandoned backpack in Evony's room, she'd been an Aries, a fire sign, it seemed a fitting way to send her off as well. Besides, I had a feeling she would have enjoyed the spectacle.

A group of the Chosen built two pyres in a vacant lot not far from the resort, and the entire colony went to pay their respects. Even Miles Odekirk, who stood off to one side, Lindsay and her djinn not too far away. She'd sort of been assigned to him, since she was the closest thing to a scientist we had. I got the impression neither she nor her partner was too thrilled about the situation. Then again, I doubted Miles was, either.

"I'm surprised a race that can't die has funeral customs," I'd remarked to Jace just the day before the ceremony. We had sat down at a secluded table in the dining room, since our suite had begun to feel like a prison cell. Even taking Dutchie on walks three times a day wasn't enough to throw off that sensation of being trapped.

"No one ever said a djinn cannot die," he said. "It is a much rarer event for us, but it does happen. So the mechanisms must be in place to handle it, one way or another."

Handle it. That was one way to phrase things, I supposed. I didn't think I was handling things all that well, when you got right down to it.

In a way, it was hard for me to even define what my relationship with Evony had been. Friends? Unlikely allies thrown together because of a common goal? And in the end, neither of those things, because Natila had been lost, and Evony had blamed me for her death.

"At any rate," Jace had continued, "we must celebrate your friend's life. She sacrificed herself, and died a warrior. We will all remember her strength and thank her for it."

As for that, I wasn't completely sure. Of course Jace and I would remember, but Evony hadn't really been a member of this community. She hadn't been given the chance. I didn't bother to protest, though. One of the things I loved about Jace was his ability to see the good in people. Whether that made him blind to some of their lesser qualities, well...it was a fault I found easy enough to forgive.

Only a day and a half had passed since our party had returned to Taos. Now the small warm snap seemed to be over, the skies gray and dull, once again threatening snow. I'd heard they could get snow here all the way into June, although that certainly wasn't common. A snowstorm in February, on the other hand, was ordinary enough, but I wanted to scowl up at the leaden heavens. Evony should have had a day as bright and fierce as she was. Also, skies like this now only served to remind me of that first attack by the rogue djinn, and the skin on the back of my neck couldn't help prickling. Never mind that we were safe enough for the moment, surrounded by our invisible shield.

The djinn in attendance looked listless and dull, however, and I noted that not all of them were present. Those who had come, I guessed, were there more for Ethan than Evony. He actually had been a part of the group here. Off to one side, a petite djinn woman with lustrous brown hair leaned against a pale, grim Zahrias and wept. She must have been Ethan's partner.

I wept for Evony, because I knew no one else would.

The flames licked up into the sullen skies. No one spoke, and I wondered, behind my tears, whether I should say something. It felt odd and unnatural to stand there in silence, but perhaps that was how the djinn sent the ones they had lost into the afterlife. Did they believe in such things?

Of course they must. I'd heard Jace speak of God and angels and hell.

Did that mean there was no heaven?

At last it was over, the roaring fires beginning to die down. One by one, the djinn in attendance began to slip away, their Chosen helping them make their way over the uneven ground, since all of the elementals were laboring under the draining effects of Miles's device. And he—well, he stood where he was for a long time, watching the scene with a speculative little frown on his face, as if attempting to reconcile everything he thought he knew about the djinn with what he had just witnessed. At last Lindsay murmured something to him, and they headed back to the resort along with everyone else.

It didn't look as if Miles intended to try to escape anytime soon.

Then again, where would he go?

The next day, Zahrias actually asked me to go check on the progress in the lab. His request startled me somewhat, since I assumed he would have spoken directly with Lindsay if he wanted to know what was going on. Something about the way he phrased that request, however, made me think that he wasn't entirely sure whether he would get an accurate report from her. I liked Lindsay, but I couldn't exactly fault Zahrias for thinking that way; she did have a tendency to inflate her progress, although whether to make herself look good or because she didn't want anyone to give up hope too soon, I didn't know. For obvious reasons, I hoped it was the latter.

Jace didn't accompany me, as Zahrias was having him and Dani and several of the other djinn who'd been on the mission to kidnap Miles Odekirk give a detailed report as to what precisely had happened. I reflected it was just as well that the djinn leader wasn't asking for my input, because even after a day and a half, it was hard for me to remember any exact details. Only a maelstrom of fire and wind and water and dust. Just

Evony and Ethan falling to the ground. All that, and nothing else.

So I headed down into the basement room Lindsay had been using as the lab, not sure exactly what I would find. Miles had appeared subdued enough at Evony's and Ethan's...leave-taking, for want of a better word. It didn't really feel like a funeral—no speeches, no flowers, no girl from the church singing "Ave Maria." But it had been our way of saying goodbye.

But just because the scientist didn't appear to be contemplating a jail break didn't mean he would necessarily cooperate with us. Maybe he was thinking a little civil disobedience was the best way to get back at the people who'd stolen him from Los Alamos.

I didn't have a lot of sympathy. *Well, now you know how it feels, asshole,* I thought as I approached the door to the lab. After all, he'd done the same thing to Jace and Natila, only he'd been given a nice hotel room instead of a jail cell, and gourmet meals from our resident chef rather than whatever odds and ends the Los Alamos people deemed worthy of passing on to their captive djinn. And let's not even get started on the effects of those goddamn devices of his....

As I entered the lab, I noticed immediately that Lindsay and Miles were on opposite sides of the space. She was typing away on a laptop, and he sat at one of the worktables, the pieces of the half-assembled device laid out neatly in front of him.

"How's it going?" I asked, my tone probably too hearty. I'd decided that, no matter what my personal feelings about Miles Odekirk might be, I should do my best to get an accurate report to take back to Zahrias. If that meant playing nice, so be it.

The scientist didn't bother to look up, but Lindsay did stop typing so she could smile at me. Her expression was tentative, though, as if she wasn't quite sure how to act around me so soon after Evony's death.

That was all right. I wasn't entirely sure how to act around me, either.

"I guess...it's going," she said, gaze darting toward Miles and back to me. I was no mind reader, but it wasn't too difficult to figure out that she had roughly a thousand other things she'd rather be doing than being stuck in a basement with Miles Odekirk.

"Any supplies you need?" I inquired, directing the question at him.

So far he'd been ignoring me, but apparently even he thought it would be rude to ignore my query. After setting down a piece of complicated-looking circuit board, he replied, "I highly doubt that this town would have anything I require."

I kind of had my doubts, too. Taos wasn't exactly what you'd call a hub for electronics supply stores. But I decided there was no point in my being rude to him in return. To be fair, he might not have even realized he was being tactless. His social eptness was right up there with Sheldon from *The Big Bang Theory*.

"Well," I said sweetly, "why don't you make a list, and we'll see what we can do. Zahrias wants to make sure there isn't anything holding you back."

At that comment, he pushed himself off the stool where he'd been sitting and stood. Right then, I noticed that he was actually quite tall. Not as tall as the djinn, of course, but tall enough that he made me feel short, which I certainly wasn't. "What's holding me back," he gritted, "is being hauled away from my proper research, stuck in a basement with a hopelessly unqualified graduate student, and being told to produce something from nothing."

I heard Lindsay suck in a breath, but I didn't dare look over at her. No, I needed to keep my attention focused on Miles Odekirk. If I let him intimidate me now, I'd never be able to negotiate with him from a position of strength.

"Lindsay," I said evenly, still holding Odekirk's icy gray stare and thinking he'd been damn lucky that his glasses hadn't gotten broken during the confrontation with the djinn on Highway 68, "would you mind giving Dr. Odekirk and me a few minutes?"

"With pleasure," she replied, then slammed her laptop shut and got up. Her footsteps clanged up the metal stairs.

"All right," I said, after I heard her close the door with a bang, "now that you're done insulting the person who managed to keep the lights on and the freezers running, maybe we can get down to business."

"And what business is that?" I could see one eyebrow arch up above the edge of his rimless glasses, but that was the only alteration in his expression.

I crossed my arms. "Miles, I'm pretty sure you have at least a couple of Ph.D.s. And I know Lindsay and Zahrias were very explicit in what they told you we need you to do for us. So do you really need me to explain it to you all over again?"

No response at first. But after a longish pause, he turned away from me and stared down at the assembled components on the worktable. "No," he said. "But I think none of you understand what you're asking of me."

"Probably not," I told him. "I'll admit that my grasp of quantum mechanics is pretty shaky. If that's even what we're talking about here."

"It is...and it isn't. Your graduate student was correct in one of her assumptions about the device I invented. It does detect the wave signature peculiar to the djinn and disrupt it. My work at the labs already involved that sort of thing, so I—"

"You were looking for djinn?"

At the interruption, his expression turned waspish. "Of course I was not looking for *djinn*. They were a fairytale, a myth. But my work—my classified work, which I will not discuss further—required research into various sorts of wave signatures. Both during and immediately after the Heat struck, my instruments picked up a signal I'd never seen before, and I began tracking it." He hesitated then before turning away from me completely. His back to me, he went on, "I was...preoccupied for a few days there. But the instruments I'd left running continued to take measurements, and after a while, I returned to analyze the data that had been collected."

As he stood there, fiddling with the components on the work table, long clever fingers sorting through the wires and circuit boards, I realized why he didn't want to look at me. Because during those "few days" he'd just mentioned, his wife and child had died. He'd lost everything, and still found it within himself to return to the labs, to the work that took up so much of his life.

Did I dare tell him that I was sorry? Or would he see that as a ploy, my way of trying to show him that I empathized with his losses? Because I did feel sorry for him then, seeing the slump of his shoulders, hearing the slightest tremor in his voice, the one I could tell he was trying so hard to conceal. I'd lost my whole family, true...but I'd never lost a child.

However, I guessed he wouldn't want to hear words of condolences from me. Bad enough that he should be taken captive. Admitting to grief now, in the face of someone he considered an enemy?

I knew he would never do that.

Ignoring the awkward pause, I cleared my throat and said, "So how did you make the leap from finding an energy pattern you didn't recognize to figuring out it was being generated by a race of people who weren't supposed to exist?"

Oddly, my question seemed to have steadied him. He shifted back around then, a circuit board held between thumb and forefinger. Over and over he turned the board, as if he'd never seen such a thing before. Without really looking at me, he replied, "It was, as you say, a leap. But all things of this earth share a certain commonality, and I saw nothing of this wave form in the patterns I was detecting. The way it coincided with the Heat...as a scientist, I can tell you that I don't believe in coincidence. There's a meaning in all patterns, if we only know where to look for it."

"So you figured out it was the djinn?"

"At first, I didn't know what name I should give them. In my mind, I always referred to them as 'the others'—because they certainly were other, whatever else they might be. And that was what I called them when Richard Margolis and his group of survivors came to Los Alamos. It wasn't until I saw one for myself that I realized which name truly belonged to them."

His words puzzled me. I frowned, trying to piece together the chronology. So he hadn't actually known what sort of being Natila was until he saw her in person? But how would he have even known who—or what—he was hunting when he ventured forth, device in hand, to see what it would do?

I asked him as much, and Miles shook his head.

"No. That's not who I mean. I saw one not too long after the Dying, a few days after the commander came to town. This was before I'd perfected the device. I'd already been working on something similar, although it was intended for an entirely different purpose. So I shifted my focus to something that would disrupt the energy signature I'd detected."

"So...where did you see this djinn?" I supposed it was possible one had come poking around Los Alamos before Miles had his device functional; in my mind, I imagined it as a place utterly off-limits to djinn from the beginning, as soon as the Heat had struck, but of course that wasn't true.

"Partway down Pajarito Road," he replied. After setting down the circuit board he'd been fiddling with, he leaned up against the worktable and crossed his arms. Even his glasses couldn't entirely conceal the dark smudges under his eyes. Had he been sleeping much since coming to Taos? It was such a personal question that I didn't dare ask. I could imagine why he wouldn't, but he needed to understand that we meant him no harm. We only needed his help.

Still with his eyes not quite meeting mine, he went on, "I used to walk a good bit...after. It was the only way I could find my focus, and the weather was still good enough then. So I was walking out on Pajarito, getting some fresh air, and I saw a woman. She was a good fifty yards or so away from me, and I began to call out to her—until I realized she was not actually standing on the road, but floating above it."

"So that's why you didn't seem too surprised when I told you that I'd seen Jace and Zahrias doing the same thing." At the time, I'd thought Miles had looked pleased by that particular tidbit just because it was evidence of their djinn natures, but now I realized it was probably more because it had only reinforced something he'd already seen.

"Precisely." He straightened up then and made a minute adjustment to the glasses on his nose. "And although it can be quite windy around here, that day the weather was relatively calm...which was why I couldn't understand why her hair was whipping around as if in a strong breeze."

"Air elemental," I said, and he nodded.

"Apparently. Also, you've lived among them. You know how they look human...but not entirely."

"They're too perfect." By then, I was used to the djinn, to their almost unearthly beauty, but I could only imagine what Miles Odekirk must have thought, seeing that strange woman and her wind-tousled hair, and knowing no human could float off the ground like that, let alone be so uncannily lovely.

"Yes." He was silent then, brows drawn together. When he spoke, he sounded more tired than anything else. "She saw me—I could feel her eyes on me. At that distance, I couldn't tell for certain, but I think she smiled. And then she disappeared."

"Now you see her," I remarked. If that had been me, taking a solitary walk in an attempt to shake off my grief, and I had seen something like that...what would I have done? At least I'd had the opportunity to get to know Jace before discovering what he was. If I'd simply witnessed some strange being floating off the ground and then winking out of existence, I probably would have freaked out.

Miles, however, didn't seem to be the freaking-out type.

"I went back to the lab, noted that another of those strange energy signatures had appeared, this time in extremely close proximity, and realized the woman and the energy pattern had to be connected. Then I went to the library and did some research, trying to match what I had seen with accounts in some of the books there on the supernatural and the occult. And I realized the strange woman must have been a djinn."

"What did she look like?" I asked, curious. She couldn't have been one of the Taos group—Miles Odekirk wasn't exactly Chosen material. Anyway, they were all paired up.

"Beautiful, I suppose. As I said, she was some distance away. Her hair was red, coppery. She wore blue, if I recall correctly, but I don't remember any details, except that the fabric seemed to be filmy and floated easily on the air."

The description could have fit any one of a number of djinn women, but again, she couldn't have been from the Taos group. One of the others, wanting to see the Immune close up? It didn't sound as if she'd made any threatening gestures, or had attempted to harm Miles. So maybe she simply had been curious. I had to remind myself that there were many, many djinn out there—the majority, actually—who weren't part of the One Thousand or one of those opposed to them. Neutral parties. Possibly this djinn woman had been one of them.

Miles shrugged, and went back to sorting the bits and pieces on the worktable. "After that, I finished my first prototype for the device. I'd actually intended it solely as a barrier, something to protect the people in Los Alamos from these beings, these djinn, as we now knew them."

With a lot of people, I would have suspected they were telling me that sort of thing because they thought it was what I would want to hear. *What? I never meant any harm...I just wanted to protect the survivors. The pain and suffering my device causes was only an unfortunate side effect.*

But I didn't think that was the case with Miles. He was brilliant, no doubt about that, but he also didn't seem the type to lie to make himself look better.

"So how did you discover that you were hurting them?" I asked.

His jaw tensed, and I could see the muscles working in his throat. Now that he was in Taos and his own clothes had been left behind, he was dressed like most of the guys here—fleece pullover worn over a T-shirt, jeans, sturdy hiking-style shoes. To me, he looked a lot less intimidating. Funny how a lab coat and a tie could get your hackles up.

"When we captured Natila," he said. Once again, his gaze shifted away from me. "It was Margolis' idea to get her, and Jasreel. He said it was too dangerous to have them in such close proximity to us, away from the rest of their kind. Rogues, he called them. I'll admit I was intrigued by the opportunity to see one of these creatures close at hand."

"They're not creatures," I broke in. "They're people. Different from us, but...."

"I know that now," he said. "I didn't then." Right then, he did look up, and I could see the lines of guilt etched on his face. Voice tight, he went on, "I wasn't expecting Natila to react to my device the way she did. Margolis was...pleased by that. He said it was our new weapon. And when we came to your home to collect Jasreel, he made sure that I kept increasing the intensity. It didn't matter if the size of the field shrank when I did so, as we were only concerned with one djinn at that particular moment." A long pause. "I am sorry about that. And about Natila. At the time, she was only a test subject to me. And now...."

"Now, what?" I demanded. "Hindsight is twenty-twenty, isn't it? If you were so sorry about killing her, then why cut her up afterward? Why not let her have some dignity in death?"

He winced, but I also noticed how he straightened, this time not looking away from me. The gray eyes were fixed on mine, pleading. "Because it was what Margolis wanted, and even I wasn't in a position to gainsay him. Not really. Yes, he needed me to make the devices, but I also needed him to make sure I had the materials and equipment I required at the lab. I know that's not a very good answer, Jessica. But that was my situation."

It would have been easy to hate him. He'd as much as admitted to being bullied by Margolis, and because of his weakness, an innocent woman had died. Maybe even two, if you counted Evony. I sort of doubted she would have been quite as motivated to pull that final kamikaze move of hers if Natila had still been around.

But hate didn't serve much of a purpose, did it? The rogue djinn who'd hurt Aidan and murdered Clay and kidnapped Martine were full of hate, and to what purpose? We hadn't done anything to them, except have the impertinence to be born human...to have djinn who loved us.

"Okay," I said, after a brief, awkward silence. "I'll admit that Margolis is a scary son of a bitch, and maybe there wasn't much you could do to challenge him. But now—right now, there's a lot you can do to help us. We have to come up with some way to have your device repel the djinn who wish us harm, but not affect the ones who are part of our community. The ones we love."

I said that last word deliberately, and with extra emphasis. Miles needed to know that none of us were here because we'd been coerced or frightened into being with our djinn. They were part of us now, and if anything happened to them, I feared we wouldn't be long for this world, either.

He was silent for a long moment, clearly pondering what I'd just told him. How much could he even understand of the bond that connected the djinn and their Chosen?

But he'd loved a woman once, loved her enough to marry her and have a child with her, despite his obvious devotion to his work. Surely he could reach somewhere inside himself, move past his grief, and see that causing more hurt just because he had suffered wasn't the solution.

Then he said, "I don't know if I can do it. What you're proposing—it would require a fundamental modification to how the device works, and even though I'm the one who created it, I still don't completely understand everything about what it does."

His words made my heart sink. Then again, he hadn't said no. He'd only said he wasn't sure. Those were two entirely separate things.

"But you'll try," I told him, my tone firm.

"Yes," he replied. "I will try."

CHAPTER NINE

I bumped into Lindsay as I was leaving the lab and told her that Miles had agreed to do what was necessary to modify his device. Her eyes widened, and she said,

"Seriously? When he's been scowling in there for the past day and a half and telling me it isn't possible?"

"Yes. I mean, he's still not sure exactly what he's going to do or how long it's going to take, but—"

"It's still a start," she cut in. "And better than anything I've been able to accomplish. You must be some kind of miracle worker."

I gave an uneasy laugh. "I don't know about that."

"Well, I do. Too bad they didn't have you working at the United Nations or something."

After delivering that remark, she moved past me and headed down the stairs into the lab, chuckling slightly.

Well, I was glad I could cheer her up, if nothing else. I'd have to see how long her good humor lasted, though. She and Miles didn't exactly get along very well, although maybe now that he really did appear to be focusing on a real solution for us, the tension might ease itself slightly.

I decided that I'd better go see Zahrias and give him a status report. To my surprise, he wasn't in his audience chamber cum conference room, although that was where he'd been last, listening to Jace and Dani and the others give their reports about the raid on the Los Alamos labs. Maybe they'd wrapped it up already; my own convo with Miles Odekirk had taken longer than I'd expected. I knew Zahrias must have his own suite somewhere in the resort, but I'd never been there, and I wasn't sure I wanted to intrude in his private space.

Luckily, I was saved from having to seek him out. Just as I was turning to go back down the corridor, Lauren came around the corner.

"Looking for Zahrias?" she asked.

I nodded. "Is he in his suite?"

"No—since the sun came out, he's been sitting down in the courtyard. He says the sunlight helps his energy levels a bit."

That made sense. On some level, he was a being of fire, and so being exposed to the fires of the sun might help counteract some of the effects of Miles's device.

"Is Jace with him?"

"No," Lauren said. "I think he went to go see how Aidan and Lilias were doing."

It was just like him to check on them once he was done speaking with Zahrias. Aidan still wasn't up and around, since Miguel had apparently told him to take it easy until the antibiotics ran their course. And I had no idea whether many of the other djinn had stopped by, but somehow I doubted it. None of them liked being reminded that their Chosen were now as vulnerable as they were.

The sun seemed to have come out with a vengeance while I was talking to Miles. I blinked at the glare as I emerged into the courtyard. This was the first time I'd actually set foot out here, and my breath caught at the quiet beauty around me. Yes, many of the trees were bare, but their limbs were still graceful, while the evergreens kept the area from appearing too desolate. A small creek chattered through the clearing, burbling over smooth-worn stones. Despite the brightness, the air was still quite chilly, which was why Zahrias had a heavy cloak wrapped around him where he sat under a little pergola, its vines also winter-bare, even as he tilted his face upward to drink in the sun's rays. Leaning up against the stone bench where he sat was a cane.

I tried not to look at that obvious sign of his weakness as I approached him with some diffidence, not sure whether I should be intruding during this time when he was clearly trying to bolster his sagging energy. But his eyes opened immediately as I approached, my hiking boots crunching on the gravel.

"You have spoken with Miles Odekirk." It wasn't a question.

"Yes. He's going to help us...if he can."

"He is uncertain?"

"He claims that even though he created the device, he's still not entirely sure how it works." This confession of Miles might have surprised me more, but after having my mother's spaghetti sauce, which she created out of her head each time and was always amazing, I understood a little bit about putting something together without being entirely clear as to why it worked so well.

My remark earned me a raised eyebrow from Zahrias. On closer inspection, I thought he did look a bit better; some color had returned to his face, and his eyes didn't appear quite as shadowed. "He made this thing, and yet he doesn't know how it works?"

"Not completely. He told me that when he built it, he'd only intended it as something that could block djinn energy, keep it away. It wasn't until he was using it in close proximity to Natila that he realized it had... side effects."

"Hmm." Zahrias pushed himself up from the bench where he'd been sitting and faced me, expression troubled. I noticed that he didn't reach for the cane. "But if he does not fully understand why it does what it does, how can he begin to modify it?"

"He doesn't know yet." As Zahrias began to frown, I went on, "But that doesn't mean much. He's a brilliant man. He'll figure it out eventually."

"Eventually."

What was I supposed to say to that? I could tell that the djinn leader wanted everything fixed yesterday, but you couldn't rush innovation, or inspiration. I guessed now that some of what had occupied Miles at the lab wasn't merely building more devices, but also attempting to learn precisely how the ones he already had actually worked. It had to have been frustrating, to have created a machine and yet not understand all its secrets.

"You can't force these things," I said.

That was clearly not what Zahrias wanted to hear. His lips pressed together, and he replied, "Even though we all must force ourselves to get up each day as our energies become more and more depleted, as we all lose a little more hope. You say we cannot force this Miles Odekirk, and yet we all continue to suffer because of something he created."

The distaste in his voice was clear. If you'd told me even a few hours earlier that I'd be defending the scientist, I probably would have laughed out loud, but right then I found myself saying,

"He understands that. He knows what he's done. And...he's sorry."

"Sorry?" Zahrias repeated, scorn clear in his tone. "I fear I've seen very little remorse from our scientist. But if that's what you wish to believe—"

"I do believe it." Voice hardening, I went on, "Anyway, I'm not trying to say he's blameless. Far from it. But at least he's willing to try to fix things, if he can. Besides, we wouldn't even be in this situation if some of your fellow djinn hadn't reneged on their promise. You might want to keep that in mind."

His shoulders slumped, and then he did turn back slightly toward the bench so he could grasp the cane. It was a plain black thing, obviously scrounged from the local Walgreens, and he grasped it with distaste. I couldn't blame him; if he had to use some kind of support to get around these days, he should have had a cane with a fancy carved handle, something that would have suited the gaudy robes he wore. Unlike many of the other djinn, Zahrias had never stooped to wearing human clothing...or at least, I'd never yet seen him dress that way.

"I do keep that in mind, Jessica," he said. "I keep it in mind every waking moment. But as there is very little I can do about their treachery, I must direct my energies where they will do us all some good. And that means making sure that Miles Odekirk does what we brought him here for."

"He will," I promised.

Zahrias gave me a grim nod, and I fled after that. The whole time, though, I couldn't help thinking about that old saying...the one about making promises you couldn't keep.

That night I ate alone with Jace in our rooms. Maybe it would have been better to go out and mingle with everyone, but I just couldn't find the energy, and Jace made no protest when I told him that I just wanted to take a tray of food to our suite.

Short as it was, that interview with Zahrias had shaken me. I didn't want to see him beaten down and weary, reduced to using a cane to prop himself up. He was the one the rest of us were supposed to look to for guidance, but I could tell he was at a loss as well. We were all trapped in a situation that had no precedent. None of his powers, his age or experience, would do any of us any good now.

At least Jace didn't appear materially weakened. His hadn't been a particularly strenuous day, and that was probably why he was able to smile at me and act more or less naturally. It was only when he thought I wasn't looking that I saw the smile fade, and that taut, strained set I hated so much return to his mouth.

"You're very quiet," he said as I picked up a morsel of chicken and leaned down so I could feed it to Dutchie.

"Am I?" I shrugged, then wiped my fingers on the napkin in my lap. "It's just—I keep thinking there's something else I should be doing, but then when I try to figure out what that is, I keep coming up with nothing."

His dark eyes watched me, careful and sad. "That's because there is nothing you can do. We all have to play a waiting game now."

Waiting for Miles Odekirk to produce a miracle. He'd done it once, so I supposed he could do it again. But this in-between time was positively excruciating.

"I don't know how you can be so calm," I said. "I feel like I'm climbing the walls."

Jace picked up his glass of wine and drank before replying, "I don't have the strength to be anything but calm. Fretting burns up too much energy."

"I'm serious."

"So am I." Eyes still fixed on mine, he went on, "Beloved, I could be pacing the room, crying out against my fate, but what good would that do, except to use up strength I would rather save for you?"

He had a point. We were together, but we hadn't been *together* since the rogue djinn had attempted to attack the colony. As I sat there and gazed at his face, I realized how much I needed him, needed to be with him, if only to prove that we wouldn't allow those other djinn—or the measures we'd taken to protect ourselves—to keep us from one another.

"It wouldn't do any good at all," I said, taking the napkin from my lap and setting it down on the table. I rose from my chair and extended a hand to him. "So please, Jace—lend some of that strength to me now."

He understood, as I'd known he would. After pushing back his own chair and standing up, he took my hand and led me over to the bed. Then, very carefully, he unbuttoned the flannel shirt I wore, each movement of his fingers deliberate, slow. In the past, we'd generally torn each other's clothes off as quickly as we could, and so there was something strange and new and yet oddly erotic about that gradual undoing of my shirt.

His fingers were cool as they slipped the garment off my shoulders, then moved down to the front clasp of my bra. I hardly dared to breathe as he undid it, and then slid it down my arms as well. Trailing in a touch so light I almost could have imagined it, his hands closed over my naked breasts, caressing them. I didn't even care that his skin was cool enough that the sensitive flesh immediately pebbled at his touch. All I wanted was Jace, like this, skin against skin.

When he bent to pull a nipple into his mouth, I cried out, my fingers digging into his hair, which fell like silk over my hands.

"Yes, Jace," I whispered. "Yes."

This was what I wanted—this, but so much more. I pulled away from him slightly, even though it was agony to lose the sensation of his lips on my breast. But I didn't want to tire him out by standing up. We could do so much more with him lying down.

I pushed him against the bed, and he sank down on it, then moved himself into a more comfortable position at its center, a couple of the pillows supporting his head. Good...he knew what I intended to do next.

Off came his pullover and the T-shirt underneath, and then I tugged down his jeans and the briefs he wore under them. In a corner of my mind that I hadn't wanted to acknowledge, I'd secretly worried that he wouldn't have the strength for this, no matter what he might say to the contrary. But as he sprang free of his clothing, obviously hard and ready for me, I allowed myself a little sigh of relief. The device might be weighing on him, sapping his energy, but it hadn't taken enough that he couldn't do this.

I pulled off my own jeans and shoes and socks, then slid in next to him, pressing the length of my body against his, trying to lend him some of my own heat. At the same time, I let my hand slip down to caress him, to begin moving slowly up and down his length.

He moaned, and I increased my speed slightly. Not enough to bring him to climax—I had better plans for that—but it still felt good to hear him respond, to know that he had the energy for this. A few moments later, I shifted so I could take him into my mouth, my tongue moving slowly over his silky skin.

"Jessica...."

My name was more a groan than anything else. Smiling a little, I slowed down even further, moving in languorous sweeps over his flesh.

Another moan, and then he whispered, "Want to taste you...."

"I think I can manage that," I replied, then shifted so I could go to him, let him grasp me by the waist and settle my body right there, his tongue also moving slowly, teasing, as if in payback for the way I'd just tortured him.

Not that I minded. By then, he knew exactly how to pleasure me, how to pull me gently into his mouth so I had to prevent myself from screaming out loud. I grasped the headboard and closed my eyes, letting those shuddering, ecstatic waves move through me, softly at first, and then with such intensity that I did let out a single shocked cry at the end, unable to keep silent any longer.

And then—then I shifted once again, felt his hardness pressing against me, into me, and we were rocking together, his hands reaching up to caress my breasts, the two of us moving in a harmony I'd never experienced with anyone else, each knowing the exact time to push or pull, breaths synchronizing, until at last he thrust into me a final time and I could feel the heat of him within me, filling me.

I didn't move right away. I wanted to stay there, still feeling him inside me, staring down at the perfect sculpted muscles of his body, the way his jet-black hair fanned out over the pillows. His eyes were shut, dark lashes thick and sooty against his high cheekbones.

He was perfection, and even now, I still couldn't quite understand why he wanted me so badly. Maybe the why didn't matter. The important thing was that he did.

At last I climbed off him, then snuggled up against his side, planting a kiss on his neck. He rolled toward me and pulled me close. I'd worried that I might have worn him out, but his heart beat seemed steady enough, slow and strong. By that point I was more or less used to the unnatural coolness of his skin, so I tried my best to ignore it.

"I love you," I whispered, and his arms tightened around me.

"And I love you," he replied. In the candlelight, his dark eyes glinted. "Perhaps now you will believe me when I tell you that I am not so very tired."

"Oh, I'll definitely hold you to that." I took his hand and placed it on my breast. "And this."

A chuckle, and then he was kissing me, his other hand wandering lower, and I thought maybe, just maybe, he and I would get through this all right.

Unfortunately, as the days slipped by, I didn't think I could say the same for our little community in Taos. No one fared as well as Jace, although a few others, like Dani and Lilias, seemed to be managing all right. In Lilias' case, however, it seemed more as if she was driving herself so Aidan wouldn't distract himself from his recovery merely to fret over her. And he was recovering, although at a normal human pace. His face would be forever marred by the scars Khalim's attack had left behind, angry red gashes standing out against his smooth, sun-browned skin. He acted as if it wasn't a big deal, but I wondered how much of that was false cheer for Lilias' sake.

Some of the other djinn, however, were suffering so much under the effects of prolonged exposure to Miles Odekirk's device that they'd taken to their beds, complaining that they simply didn't have the energy to get up. That made life harder for us Chosen, as we had to bring them their meals and any other supplies they might need. But I was glad to see that everyone took on their extra duties without complaint—well, at least without any complaints loud enough for me to hear—and generally did what they could to make a bad situation at least somewhat bearable.

The one person we all wanted to hear from, Miles Odekirk, was conspicuously absent. I suppose it was foolish of us to think that he could make lightning strike on demand, but we were all hoping for a miracle. Lindsay reported that he was working day and night, sometimes only sleeping an hour or two, if that, but as February began to bleed into March, I started to wonder if he would ever find a solution, or whether our djinn would be condemned to this half-life forever.

And from time to time I would go to the outer limit of the shield protecting our little town, and gaze toward the south and west, in the direction of Los Alamos. I couldn't help worrying about Julia and Dan. Yes, we'd done what we could to make it look as if they'd been overpowered during our escape attempt, but what if Margolis had seen right through our admittedly thin deception? If anything had happened to either of them, I knew I'd never forgive myself—even though they had offered their help without being asked.

Then there were the kids. Lord knows what lies they'd been fed about my sudden disappearance. Although I'd been unwillingly drafted as their teacher, that didn't mean I didn't care what happened to them. I tried to reassure myself that Nora Almeida would have simply gone back to tutoring the little group, but I was only partly successful. True, my entire reason for being in Los Alamos had been to rescue Jace. Even so, I hated to think about the damage my precipitous departure might have caused.

I'd been sitting in the courtyard, brooding and ignoring the bright sunshine, the kiss of the fresh air against my skin. It wasn't warm yet, not really, but temperatures had gone up enough that you could sit outside for a while without risking frostbite.

But then I heard voices, angry voices, and I stiffened, glad that I'd chosen a spot hidden behind several thick pine trees. No one would even notice that I was there unless they were specifically looking for me.

The voices belonged to Zahrias and several other djinn, two of whom I only knew by sight, as we hadn't had much interaction. To my surprise, the third was Lindsay's partner, Rafi.

"...has gone on long enough," Rafi was saying. "Do you expect us to cower here forever until our powers fade completely?"

Although I couldn't really see them, save as a blur of color through the branches of the trees, I got the impression that Zahrias stopped at that question. His voice came to me, weary, but still firm. "Your powers will return. They are merely being blocked."

"Blocked, and drained," one of the other djinn said. "Rafi is right. We cannot be expected to endure this any longer. You say that this mortal, this Miles Odekirk, is working on a solution. How do you know this for sure? After all, he is the one who created these devices in the first place. Perhaps he is only stalling because he knows how it makes us suffer."

The djinn seemed to murmur in agreement, but Zahrias' angry tones overrode them. "I know he is working on a solution because your Chosen, Rafi, is also working on it. Lindsay reports to me every day. If Miles truly was dissembling in any way, she would know it."

Some grumbles resulted from that remark, and I wondered if Zahrias had managed to talk them down. After all, he was only telling them the truth. I knew Lindsay came to the djinn leader with regular progress reports because Jace had been there on more than one occasion when she showed up to deliver them.

But apparently that evidence wasn't enough for them, because the djinn who had first spoken then said, "Perhaps that is the case. Perhaps he is doing his best. Obviously, his best is not good enough. And so we should look for other solutions."

"Such as?" Zahrias inquired, tone dry.

A brief pause, and Rafi replied, "We have been discussing this, and we have agreed that the best solution is for several of us to leave—to go beyond the field generated by that hellish device so that our powers will return to us."

Right then I really wished I could have seen Zahrias' face. But of course I couldn't—and I also knew that I needed to stay where I was, hidden, quiet. I didn't want to know what their reaction would be if they caught me eavesdropping.

I heard a low chuckle, and Zahrias said, "And do what, precisely? Although your powers will return to you, that will take time. You would be completely unprotected, vulnerable."

"Not necessarily," Rafi argued. "True, we might be lacking some of our powers, but all we would need is to leave this place and go where we might seek help. Khalim has his followers, but they do not represent all of our kind. If we can enlist the aid of the others, those who would oppose what Khalim is doing if they but knew about it, then we could come back here with assistance. We would not have to live like this any longer."

A silence fell. I hardly dared to breathe, fearing they might overhear even a sigh. That was probably silly, since it was a breezy day, and the wind was soughing through the pines.

At last Zahrias spoke again. "And have you discussed this with your Chosen? Do they agree that it is all very well for you to abandon them to pursue a quest with only a small chance of success?"

"You don't know that for certain," said one of the other djinn, someone who hadn't spoken before this. "Why is it so unlikely that others of our kind would come to lend their assistance?"

"I cannot speak to that," Zahrias replied. "All I am saying is that sending yourselves forth from this world takes more energy than you might think. And drawing on that energy after it has been depleted for weeks and weeks will be difficult at best."

"Perhaps," Rafi said. "Perhaps not. You only have Jasreel's word to go on, and because he is not precisely one of us—"

"We will not go down that road again," Zahrias cut in. His voice was quiet, but I heard the steel in it, and the others must have, too, because after a brief pause, Rafi went on, sounding somewhat chastened,

"And as to our Chosen, we have spoken with them, and they understand the risks. They want us as we were, not as we are now—things with half-lives, hardly worth living. If they agree, who are you to tell us no?"

"Only the one who agreed to lead this group," Zahrias replied. He sounded so tired that I wished I could get up from my hiding place and give him a hug.

Not that he would ever allow such a casual display of affection from a mere human. At the same time, my thoughts skated back to Rafi's remark that Jace wasn't exactly one of them. Just what the hell had he meant by that?

"Lead the group," said the other djinn, the one whose name I couldn't recall. "Offer guidance, and counsel. But not to be our lord and master."

"True. I did not agree to that, nor did you. I cannot hold you here. If you wish to take this risk, then that is your decision."

"Good," Rafi said. "Then it is decided. We will leave this place, and go for help."

"As you will," Zahrias conceded, adding, "And I pray that you will not be the ones in need of help before this is done."

They left, and I sat there on the bench for a long while. I wanted to make sure there was no chance of bumping into any of them before I left—and I also needed that time to gather myself, to process what I'd just heard.

Those djinn were leaving, and Zahrias was letting them go. Worse, their Chosen had agreed to this madness.

As to that remark about Jace...maybe I'd have the courage to ask him about that. Maybe. He'd been so very tired lately, bearing up under the effects of the device, trying to assist Zahrias where he could. Being the lover he knew I wanted, even though our physical intimacies were sapping even more strength, strength he simply didn't have.

Besides, Rafi could have meant anything, including something as simple as Jace not agreeing with those djinn that making a break to get help was a good idea. During my time here in Taos, I'd developed a—well, antipathy was probably too strong a word, but something about Rafi just rubbed me the wrong way. He was clearly displeased by the amount of time Lindsay spent working in the lab with Miles, although I had a hard time figuring out what else she could do that would be of more benefit to the community. What, did her djinn expect her to wait on him hand and foot every second of the day and give him sponge baths or something?

Probably. He was also doing better than some...but maybe he'd been looking around and seeing how some of the more incapacitated djinn didn't have to lift a finger to do anything, and thinking he'd like some of that treatment himself.

Well, Lindsay's domestic issues were her own business. If it turned out that she'd actually agreed to this hare-brained scheme to go off in search of help, then I would just have to keep my mouth shut on the subject.

I headed back to the suite, but Jace wasn't there. That didn't surprise me too much; he'd been spreading himself awfully thin lately, so he could be anywhere from the kitchen, helping Phillip chop vegetables, to assisting with folding sheets and towels in the laundry. The Chosen were mainly the ones who'd been doing that sort of thing, but they weren't above accepting some extra help, especially when they'd had to play nursemaid to a bunch of djinn on top of everything else.

So I glanced at the clock, decided it was late enough to take Dutchie on her afternoon walk, and put on her collar and leash. Of course she was thrilled;

we sometimes let her have the run of the resort, but I didn't want her getting in the way, so she often spent her days sleeping in the suite and waiting for us to take her on a walk.

She danced at the end of her leash as we left the resort grounds and began walking down Kit Carson Road. Off and on I'd contemplated letting her run free, but I worried that she would dart over the edge of the safe zone. Maybe the rogue djinn wouldn't care about a single dog venturing out into unprotected territory. But if she did that, I knew I wouldn't be able to chase after her. I loved that dog, but not enough to risk the kind of bodily mayhem they'd visited on Aidan.

And don't forget about kidnapping, too, I thought, recalling how Aidan had described the way the leader of the rogue djinn had thrown Martine over his shoulder and referred to her as "payment."

I shivered then, but kept walking, letting Dutchie run out to the end of her retractable leash. The fresh breeze blew through my hair, and I pulled in a deep breath. It did feel good to be out here, away from the sense of desperation that hung over the resort we'd made our home.

About a week after Jace and I had returned to Taos, he and Dani had walked the perimeter of the safe zone, marking it as best they could with fluorescent orange paint, the kind that road crews used to label the pavement during construction projects. Because of that, I knew I could go all the way to the plaza while still under the protection of Miles's device. I generally didn't walk the dog quite that far, but today I thought it would feel good to go to the little open square and sit in the gazebo. Just some time alone to gather my thoughts.

Dutchie didn't mind, of course. The longer the walk, the better, in her book. But as I stopped at the corner of Kit Carson and Highway 68, movement caught the corner of my eye. I turned, thinking it was probably one of the other Chosen out on one of their foraging expeditions. There were still some items to be had around town, although the pickings were beginning to get slim. None of us wanted to think about what would happen when we'd completely stripped everything within the safe zone bare.

But this person—this woman, I realized—wasn't moving in any sort of purposeful manner, but rather staggering her way down the road, weaving from one side to the other. In a different world, I might have thought she was drunk.

The breeze caught at her long dark-honey hair, playing with it. My eyes narrowed. None of the Chosen in Taos—or the djinn, for that matter—had hair that color. In fact, I only knew one person who—

I began to run toward her, dragging Dutchie along with me. Since she'd already taken care of business, she was fine with a good run. We pounded down the center of the street, closing the distance between us and the stranger. As we approached, the woman seemed to reach the edge of her endurance, sinking down onto the asphalt. I let go of Dutchie's leash and ran to the woman, trying to grab her before her head smacked into the pavement. As she collapsed into my arms, she stared up at me with wide, frightened gray-blue eyes before passing out completely.

I knew those eyes. I knew her.

The woman I held was Julia Innes.

CHAPTER TEN

I COULDN'T CARRY HER ALL THE WAY BACK TO THE resort. Instead, I told Dutchie to stand guard, then turned and ran up Kit Carson Street as fast as I could, eating up the almost half-mile like someone competing in the Olympics trials. As I pushed my way into the front doors of the main building, I almost collided with Aidan and Lilias, who looked as if they'd just come in from getting their own breath of fresh air. Lilias even had some pink in her cheeks.

"Hey," Aidan said, catching me by the arms before I ran smack into him. "What is it?"

"Yes, Jessica—what's wrong?" Lilias asked.

"J-Julia," I panted, and they exchanged a puzzled glance.

"Julia?" Aidan repeated. "Who's Julia?"

"From—from Los Alamos."

Aidan's eyebrows went up. "What the hell is she doing here?"

"I don't know." By then I'd managed to more or less catch my breath, so I went on, in slightly less frantic tones, "She's passed out in the middle of Highway 68. I left Dutchie with her because I knew I couldn't carry her by myself."

"Show me," he said.

Lilias frowned. "Aidan, that's almost a half-mile from here. Perhaps you should get some help—"

"I can do it," he broke in. Smiling crookedly—a smile that pulled at the half-healed scars on his face— he added, "I'm fine, Lilias. I'm about as better as I'm going to be. In fact, I've been going nuts, trying to take it easy for you. I can do this. I *want* to."

Hesitating, she stared up at him for a few seconds, then at last gave a half-hearted nod. "If you must."

He reached out and touched her cheek, then turned back to me. "Let's go."

Since I didn't want us to be completely worn out by the time we got there, I sort of half-jogged the distance to where I'd left Julia, Aidan keeping up at my side. When we reached the intersection, nothing seemed to have changed. Well, nothing except that Dutchie had taken up a defensive position near Julia's head and was looking up at a crow perched on top of a building that used to be an art gallery. I heard a faint growl coming from my dog's throat, although the crow didn't appear particularly intimidated.

"Good job, Dutchie," I said, bending down to scratch her ears briefly.

At the same time, Aidan knelt next to Julia's limp form. As I turned away from the dog, I realized then how banged up Julia really was—her jeans were torn in multiple places, her jacket was stained, and a bruise marred the lower side of one cheek, down near the jaw line.

"What the hell happened to her?" he asked. Moving with care, he slipped his arms under her so he could lift her from the road. She moaned slightly but didn't open her eyes.

"I have no idea," I replied. I'd witnessed my share of horrors since the Heat had come along, but something about seeing Julia, self-assured, beautiful Julia who never had a hair out of place, battered and dirty and semi-conscious, rocked me to my core. "So let's get her back to the resort and cleaned up, and hopefully then she'll have recovered enough to tell us how she got here."

And why, I thought. I couldn't imagine Julia risking the frightening open spaces between here and Los Alamos without having a damn good reason for making the journey.

With her cradled in Aidan's arms, we made our way back to the resort. It was a much slower trip than the one to retrieve her, but eventually we reached the main doors to the check-in area, where I hurried ahead so I could open them for him. Lilias must have spread the word, because there was quite a crowd waiting for us there, including Lauren, Jace, and Zahrias, as well as a few Chosen who were probably just there to looky-loo.

"I've already gotten a room ready for her," Lauren told me. "It's in the same wing as the room we gave Miles. I thought that might be better, since they know each other already, right?"

She looked a little hesitant, as if uncertain whether she'd done the right thing, and I hurried to say, "That's a great idea. Plus, it's a little closer in, so Aidan won't have to carry her so far."

"Just show me the way," he said, sounding strained. He was a strong guy, but carrying a full-grown woman for a half-mile uphill probably wasn't a picnic for anyone.

"Oh, right. This way."

She led him down the corridor to the right, and we all followed a few feet behind, minus the looky-loos, who decamped after Zahrias gave them a single lifted eyebrow. I unclipped Dutchie's leash so she could tag along in the rear. She was pretty good about not getting underfoot.

"What happened?" Jace asked in an undertone, leaning close to me. He smelled good, of fresh-baked bread, which seemed to prove my hunch that he'd been helping Phillip in the kitchen.

"I don't know," I replied. "I was walking Dutchie, and then I saw someone coming down 68. When I got closer, I realized it was Julia."

He shook his head. "And she was alone?"

"As far as I could tell. Looks like she went through hell to get here, too."

After that, he didn't say anything, but only walked beside me, looking grim. I couldn't blame him. Her appearance had generated about a thousand questions in my head, all of them so far unanswered.

It didn't look as if we'd be getting those answers anytime soon, either. Lauren led us to one of the resort's smaller rooms, not a suite, and Aidan laid Julia down on the bed there. Her head fell against the pillows, but she didn't move.

"I'll go get Miguel," Lauren told Zahrias, who had stopped just inside the doorway and was standing there with his arms crossed. "And some clean things for her."

"Thank you," he said gravely. "And thank you, Aidan, for your assistance here."

His words were clearly a dismissal. Luckily, Aidan didn't seem to take offense at more or less being told to get out. He said easily, "Sure," and then followed Lauren out of the room.

That left Zahrias and Jace and me. "Do you want us to go, too?" I asked. Not that I intended to. I just wanted to know if I'd have to put up a fight.

But Zahrias only said, "No. You should stay, since you knew her. It might be better for her to see a familiar face when she awakes."

He was probably right about that. I moved closer to the bed and reached out to take Julia's hand. Her fingers were cold. Was she in shock of some kind? Or had she merely passed out from exhaustion? She had cuts and bruises and scrapes all over, it seemed, but I couldn't see any wounds severe enough to send her into shock.

Miguel appeared then, carrying a first aid kit he'd lifted from the urgent-care center down Highway 68. Without acknowledging any of us, he went around to the other side of the bed so he could set down the kit. He lifted Julia's wrist, laying his fingers there so he could get her pulse.

"No sign of her waking up?" he asked after gently lowering her arm to the mattress.

"No," I said. "She groaned a little when Aidan lifted her so he could bring her here, but she hasn't made a sound since then."

A nod, and then Miguel was fishing around in his kit. He pulled out the object of his search—a penlight—and bent toward Julia's face, reaching with his free hand to open one of her eyes and shine the light in it. After that he tested her other eye.

"Pupils are responsive," he said after putting the light back in the first aid kit. "I think she's just dehydrated and suffering from exhaustion. We need to get some fluids in her."

"Will she drink when she's like that?" Jace asked.

"I don't know. Let's try it with a little water. If she can't swallow, I'll have to go back to the urgent-care center and see if they have the supplies for me to set up a saline drip."

I swallowed. That sounded a little drastic to me, especially for someone who'd once confessed that he'd never completed his EMT certification. "Do you know how to do that?"

"Yes...in theory."

Zahrias and Jace exchanged a glance.

"Well, let us hope we don't have to take such extreme measures," Zahrias said. Stepping away from the door, he headed to the bathroom, where the original toiletries from before the Dying appeared to still be laid out, including a set of plastic-wrapped glasses. He pulled the plastic off one of them and poured some water from the tap into it—not much, just enough to fill maybe the bottom third of the glass. He handed it to Miguel.

"Here goes," he said, putting it up against her cracked lips. Then he tipped some water into her mouth.

It dribbled down her cheek and onto the stained shirt she wore. I cursed inwardly. But then she seemed to stiffen, and her lips parted slightly. Miguel tilted the glass once again, and this time she drank, greedily gulping at the water until it was gone.

Her eyelids fluttered, just for a second. "More," she whispered.

Thank God. Miguel hurried into the bathroom and poured more water into the glass, and again she drank until it was gone. Then she opened her eyes for real this time, blinking in confusion at Miguel. Of course she wouldn't know who he was. But after that her gaze slid toward me, and she smiled.

"So I made it," she breathed.

"You sure did," I told her. "You're in Taos. You're safe."

She nodded, and her eyes closed.

"She needs to sleep, and she's dehydrated," Miguel said. "But I think she's going to be okay. Someone should stay here with her, though, to give her some more water when she wakes up."

I glanced up at Jace, and he nodded. I would have offered even if he didn't want me to, but that wasn't Jace. He understood that it was more important for me to be with Julia than with him, at least for now.

"I'll have Phillip put together a tray for you," he told me. "Dinnertime isn't that far off now."

"Thanks, Jace." That was all I said aloud, but our eyes met and I added, *We'll need to talk later. There's... stuff...going on.*

You mean about Rafi and Alif and Nizar?

You knew?

*Zahrias came and told me. It's a foolish and danger-
ous errand, but we can't stop them.*

Do you know when they're leaving?

A faint head shake, and then he asked, "Do you
want me to have anything sent up for Julia as well?"

I hesitated. She would be ravenous when she
woke up, no doubt, but that could be hours from now.
"Probably not. I think it's better to wait until she's
really awake. I'll call for you then."

"Of course."

"Probably just soup to start," Miguel warned us.
"We don't know how long it's been since she's had solid
food. Then we'll go from there."

"And in the meantime, we should allow her some
peace and quiet," Zahrias interjected. "The rest will do
her more good than anything else."

It wasn't exactly a command, but it might as well
have been. Miguel and Jace nodded, and stepped out
into the corridor. Zahrias hung back for a moment,
gazing down at Julia's bruised and dirty face.

"I wonder what happened to her," he said, then
ducked out as well, leaving me alone with the sleeping
woman.

I was wondering, too. Leaving aside the question
of what had compelled her to abandon the refuge of
Los Alamos in the first place, how had she survived the

journey here? You'd have thought she'd be easy prey for the rogue djinn.

But she had survived…somehow. And now all I could do was sit and wait, and wonder.

Five or ten minutes after the men had left, Lauren reappeared, poking her head inside the door. In her hands she held several pieces of folded clothing. "I brought these for her," she murmured, then stepped into the room and set the items on top of the dresser.

"Thanks," I said in the same undertone. "I'm hoping that after she sleeps for a while and then gets something to eat, she'll be up for a warm bath."

"It looks like she's earned one," Lauren replied, worried eyes taking in Julia's grimy face. "You really think she walked all the way here?"

"Well, I didn't see a car anywhere," I said grimly. "Or a scooter, or even a bike. She was on foot. Maybe she drove part of the way, but we won't know for sure until she wakes up."

"Damn." Then Lauren seemed to gather herself. "I have to get back, but just send word if there's anything else she needs."

"I will."

She left then, and I folded my hands on my lap, willing myself to be calm and watchful. There wasn't much else I could do, really. The day had been mild enough that no one had bothered to light a fire in the fireplace, although the logs and kindling had already been set up.

I figured that getting the fire going was one task I could perform that would make Julia more comfortable. It would still drop close to freezing tonight, no matter how deceptively pleasant the daytime hours had been.

I got up from my chair and went to the fireplace, then struck a match and held it against the kindling. It caught immediately, the flames catching before licking upward against the pyramidal stack of logs that had been placed there. The warmth moved outward, seeming to caress my face. Maybe it had been colder in the room than I'd first thought.

"That feels good."

At once I turned. Julia was watching me, eyes clear enough, if shadowed.

I hurried over to the bed. "How do you feel?"

"Probably about how I look...like hell. But this bed feels good. And so does that fire." Her voice sounded stronger with every word, and I heaved an inner sigh of relief.

"Do you want some more water?"

"Please."

I took the glass, went to the bathroom, and filled the cup a little more than halfway. Julia reached for it as soon as I approached the bed, so I let her take it from me. If she spilled, well, I'd just mop it up as best I could.

But she didn't. Her hand shook a little, but she was able to raise the glass to her mouth and drink the water without incident. Then she set it down on the nightstand.

"Better."

"Are you hungry?" I asked. If she was up to drinking that much, then it seemed the logical next step was to get some food inside her.

To my surprise, she shook her head. "No. I know I should be, and I probably will be in a little while, but not now." As she looked down at herself, her mouth pursed in distaste. "What I really want is a shower."

"Are you sure you're up to that?" From what I'd seen so far, she certainly didn't look strong enough to stand up for the amount of time a shower would require.

But she nodded. "I think so. And I really—I really just want to wash all that off me."

What she meant by "all that," I didn't know, but if allowing her to take a shower meant the possibility of hearing her story, then I'd help her any way I could. And I'd wait right outside the door in case she ended up needing my assistance.

So I said, "All right," and extended a hand so she could pull herself upright. She wobbled a bit as she stood, but her grip on my hand was surprisingly strong as I guided her inside the bathroom.

"It looks like all the toiletries are still in here," I said, twitching aside the shower curtain so I could put the miniature bottles of shampoo and conditioner and the small bar of soap on the ledge inside the shower stall. "We aren't running on djinn power anymore, though, so try to keep it short if you can. We've all been trying to keep our showers to five minutes, but I think you've earned a little bit more than that."

Julia's eyes seemed to fill with questions at my comment about not having access to djinn power, but she only nodded. After turning on the hot water, I slipped back out to the bedroom and grabbed the stack of clothes Lauren had left behind.

"Here's something to change into," I told Julia, who nodded and took the pile from me. "And now I'll just let myself out."

She managed a tired smile at that, then shut the bathroom door. My chair was all the way on the other side of the room, and I didn't want to be that far in case Julia fell or otherwise needed me to help her out. I supposed I could drag it closer, but then it would be partially blocking the door to the bathroom, since the space really wasn't all that big. Instead, I decided to lean up against the dresser and wait.

Even as exhausted and wrung-out as she obviously was, Julia still managed to be her usual efficient self. The water shut off almost exactly five minutes after I'd propped up myself against the dresser, and a few minutes after that, Julia emerged, now wearing a long-sleeved T-shirt and some yoga pants. She was finger-combing her hair, and I realized that although the bathroom had soap and shampoo and that sort of thing, it wasn't stocked with combs or brushes—or a toothbrush and toothpaste, either. Lauren hadn't left any of those items behind, maybe because she hadn't thought Julia would be up and functioning quite so quickly.

"Sorry there wasn't a comb," I began, but she just shrugged.

"It's okay. This'll do for now." Moving past me, she climbed back into bed and plumped up the pillows behind her. Now that she was clean, I could see how nasty that bruise on the left side of her face actually was. It must have been worse at one time, since it had now faded to a ghastly collection of greens and yellows.

Despite that, it looked suspiciously like someone had plowed his fist into her jaw.

She must have noticed my staring, because she raised one hand and touched her face. "It's getting better," she said quietly. "It used to be blue and purple."

I couldn't keep silent any longer. "Julia, what happened?"

A small sigh escaped her as her fingers played with the edges of the blanket. She'd never been one for nail polish, but her fingernails had always been on the long side, beautifully shaped. Now they were cracked and broken. Without looking at me, she said, "Dan's dead."

"*What?*" The question exploded out of me before I could stop it.

"A little over a week ago. At least, I think that's when it happened." She paused then and tilted her head to one side, frowning, even as her eyes glittered with unshed tears. "I think I lost track of time there for a while."

I needed to sit down. I went back over to my chair and more or less collapsed on it. "I don't understand. What—what happened to Dan?" My throat seemed to be closing up. No, I hadn't ever been with Dan and hadn't wanted to be, but I'd liked him very much. He was one of the good guys, an all-around decent person.

Which seemed to be a sure ticket to an early death these days.

Julia blinked, then swallowed. Hard. "Can—can I have some more water?"

Even though I'd just sat down, I got right back up again, retrieved her glass, then went to the bathroom to refill it. After I handed it to her, she drank half its contents, and nodded.

"Thank you, Jessica." She pulled in a breath, one I could hear hitch in her throat. That made the tears in my eyes sting all the more, but I told myself I needed to keep it together. Julia had survived whatever ordeal she'd been through, so the least I could do was maintain my calm while she related her story.

"Okay," she said, then breathed deeply again. "After—well, after you and Evony escaped with Jace, Margolis lost it. He refused to listen to anything

Dan or I had to say. He was convinced we were connected to your escape. Which we were, of course. I suppose we'd just been hoping that allowing ourselves to be clocked with a gun and knocked out would be enough to convince the commander we were innocent. Unfortunately, it didn't work out that way."

I wasn't sure I wanted to know, but I had to ask. "What did he do?"

"It wasn't that bad at first," she replied. Her fingers kept knotting in the blanket, however, seeming to give the lie to her words. "He locked us both up, but we were expecting that. There really wasn't any evidence, you know, since I'd killed the security feeds, and most of the people in the building were off at Ernie's birthday party. Of course, Margolis thought it was suspicious that the security camera was out—which it was—but again, there wasn't anything to prove that I'd tampered with the system, since it was pretty temperamental anyway."

"But then?"

She glanced away from me, over at the watercolor of the Rio Grande gorge that hung on the opposite wall. "We'd been locked up for about a week, I think, when he came roaring down into the holding cells. I really thought he'd lost his mind—he kept yelling at us, 'How did they do it? Why did they take him?'"

Uh-oh. The sick feeling in my stomach told me who that particular "him" probably was.

Something must have showed in my face, because she said, "So it was you. I figured it must have been someone from Taos who came and took Miles away. But...I guess that's one thing Margolis and I have in common. We both can't figure out...why?"

The last thing I wanted was to interrupt her story with a recounting of everything that had gone wrong in Taos since I got back. Julia needed some context, though, so as quickly as I could, I told her about the rogue djinn and having to use Miles's device here to keep us safe.

"But the djinn can't keep on like this forever," I said. "That's why we took Miles. We desperately need him to modify the device so it can protect us without sapping all their powers."

"And he's actually cooperating?" she asked, expression indicating she didn't think such a thing was possible.

"Yes. But he hasn't had much luck so far."

She seemed to absorb that, leaning against the pillows, her dark finely arched brows drawing together. "It sounds like you might have done Miles a favor in the long run, getting him away from Margolis. I can only hope he figures that out. For a brilliant person, he can be pretty dense sometimes." Her eyes shut, and I wondered if what she'd told me so far had sapped her strength enough that she didn't want to continue. I couldn't bear that. I dreaded hearing what had gone on back in Los Alamos, but I needed to know what had happened to her and Dan.

But she blinked then, and focused her gaze on me. "I'd thought Margolis had lost it before, locking us up like that. But that was nothing. He came in and pulled Dan out of his cell, took him someplace. I don't know where, but I'm guessing up to the labs, since that was where he had his goons torturing your djinn."

I winced, and she added,

"Sorry. I'm just—I'm tired."

"It's all right," I said. Past was past, but we still needed to hear about it so we could formulate our plans for the future.

"No, it's not." A shiver went over her, even though the room was quite warm now that the fire was dancing away happily in the hearth. "Anyway, Dan came back with two black eyes and a broken nose. And there wasn't a damn thing I could do about it, locked up in my own cell the way I was. We couldn't even really talk because of the security camera. All I could do was watch him huddle in a corner and try to stop the bleeding with a piece of fabric he tore off from one of the sheets on his cot."

I almost stopped her there. Hearing the way they'd hurt Dan, someone who'd survived the Dying with his dignity intact, who'd protected Stacy from the more predatory survivors...well, unless you counted Margolis among those predators...it made me want to scream at the injustice of it all. Problem was, I had a good idea that there was far worse news yet to come.

"But they didn't leave it at that," I said, almost in a whisper.

"No. They beat him up for...I'm not sure, but I think it was at least four days in a row. Maybe five. Then Margolis came down and stared at me in that way he has—you know, where your skin wants to crawl right off your body?"

Unfortunately, I knew all too well. And he hadn't even done anything to me, except send a few leers in my direction. He'd been occupied with other things... other women...and so, thank God, he'd never expended too much energy on me. I nodded, but didn't reply.

Julia drew up her knees and clutched them against her body. Staring at the watercolor on the wall, she said, "He told me that Dan had confessed to helping Jace escape, and then to assisting with the kidnapping of Miles. He said that Dan was a traitor, and there was only one thing they did to traitors."

"Execute them," I whispered.

"And that's what they did. I didn't see the execution, of course. No, Margolis wanted to keep me safely locked up. Only his own people were allowed to bring me food and water, keep watch over me. Maybe he thought I might have a few allies in town, so the best way to keep me completely isolated was to only allow the people he trusted implicitly to see me. But Stacy told me later. She didn't go into a lot of detail, but it was enough. I knew anyway, though, even without being told. It's pretty obvious what's happened when your cellmate is taken away and never comes back."

I had no words. Funny, how I'd heard people say that before, but I hadn't really believed it. There was always something you could say. But now—hearing how a good and decent man had been killed because he'd dared to do the right thing, it seemed as if every single word of condolence I'd ever heard had just shrunk up and melted away.

Problem was, I feared that still wasn't the worst of it. Not completely, anyway.

With a shaking hand, Julia reached over for her water glass and drank what remained in it. She stared down at it for a few seconds, then remarked with very little emotion in her voice, "Too bad that wasn't Scotch."

"We have some here at the resort," I said, "but I don't really recommend drinking it on an empty stomach."

The faintest ghost of a smile touched the corners of her mouth. Except for the bruise on her jaw, and the shadowing under her eyes, she really did look much more like the Julia I remembered. But that darkness in her, that thing I couldn't quite figure out until she told me about her abusive fiancé—that darkness seemed magnified now. There was something even more distant, more reserved, in her manner, as if the only way she could deal with any of this was to put up a wall between herself and what had happened.

Still in that same flat voice, Julia went on, "It was the day after Dan was taken away and never came back. Or night, maybe. There aren't any windows down there in the holding area."

I nodded, and she grimaced.

"Sorry. Forgot for a moment that you'd been there, too. So." She stopped then, fingers running through the damp strands of her hair. As it dried, it was taking on a faint wave. I'd remembered it as straight, but she'd probably blow-dried or flat-ironed it. She picked up one lock, holding it between her index and middle finger, then let it fall again. "That night, or afternoon, or whatever. I'd been dozing, probably because I didn't have anything better to do, and it could have been nighttime. But then I opened my eyes and saw Margolis standing there outside my cell. He looked... smug, like he knew a secret that I didn't. And then—"

Her head tilted upward, as if she found something vitally important in the dark wood beams that crossed the ceiling. I knew that probably wasn't it, that she just wanted to avoid looking at me.

A taut silence filled the room. Not sure whether I should say anything, I nonetheless blurted out, "You don't have to tell me. It's okay."

The quiet was so thick, it seemed to throb against my eardrums. "No," she said at last, her tone brittle, calm. "I'm not going to hide from it. I've done too much hiding in my life. He came into my cell and locked it behind him. And then"—she swallowed, and I could see tears shimmering in her eyes — "then he did what he'd come there to do. All in silence. Not one word. He didn't have to tell me why. This was his way of getting revenge. I knew that the whole time. And so I endured it, and didn't say anything, either. I didn't want to give him the satisfaction. And then he got up and left."

My stomach twisted. Right then I was glad I hadn't eaten anything. "Julia, I'm so sorry—"

"It's all right. I lived through it." A blink, and the tears seemed to recede. "I'm not going to give him power over me by dwelling on it. Anyway, that went on for... a couple of days, maybe a week. I started to lose track. The whole time I was wondering whether he planned to keep me down there forever, or whether he was going to kill me, too, once he got tired of me. But then he started working on me, saying he didn't want to keep me a prisoner anymore. All I had to do was confess to helping Dan, and he'd let me out."

"Margolis was just going to let you go?" I couldn't prevent a note of incredulity from entering my voice. He didn't seem the type to simply allow a woman like Julia to slip out of his grasp.

"Well, not exactly. He said he'd have me come live with him, and that after a while maybe he'd let me be his assistant again. Once I'd 'earned back his trust,' in his words."

Shuddering, I asked, "What did you say?"

"I told him I'd think about it. He didn't like that— said I should be grateful to him for giving me a second chance. And I laughed and said I didn't think I should be grateful for the opportunity to be his sex slave and his lackey." Her hand went up to touch the bruise on her jaw. "That's when he hit me. I just took it, of course. It wasn't as if I didn't have some experience with that kind of thing."

"Oh, Julia," I whispered.

"I won't lie—it hurt like a bitch." She shrugged and pulled the blanket up so it was snugged right under her breasts. "But it did feel good to laugh in that bastard's face. He stormed out after that. All I could do was sit there and wait for him to come back. But it wasn't Margolis who showed up the next morning. It was Stacy."

"Stacy?" I asked, bewildered. "Did she—" I broke off there, since I couldn't think of a delicate way to ask if she knew what had been going on between Julia and the commander.

"Oh, she knew. Maybe Margolis bragged, or maybe he talked in his sleep. I didn't ask. But she told me I had to leave. It took me a few seconds to process what she was saying, but then I realized she wanted me to go because she didn't want me interfering with her relationship with Margolis."

"She *what?*" Hearing how Stacy had ended up sleeping with the commander just so she could get a better housing assignment had squicked me out enough. To think she actually was pleased enough with the arrangement that she wanted Julia completely out of the picture...I couldn't help shuddering a little.

"I know." Julia smiled grimly. "But I wasn't about to argue with her personal choices. Not if it meant getting the hell out of there."

"So she broke you out?"

"Basically. She'd heard how I disabled the security system, but she really didn't know how to do it herself, so she wheedled one of the guys—Zach Royce— into doing it in exchange for a blow job. She knew he wouldn't tell anyone because then his head would be on the chopping block along with hers."

I shook my head. "Very resourceful, our Stacy."

"And talented, apparently. So she smuggled me out of there in the back of her SUV, gave me a change of clothes and a jacket, and dumped me right at the edge of the safe zone."

That explained how Julia had gotten out of Los Alamos, but I still couldn't figure out how she'd managed to walk sixty-plus miles from there to here and not be attacked by the rogue djinn. I asked her as much, and she only gave me a fatalistic lift of her shoulders.

"I don't know," she said. "I was terrified the whole time. I kept expecting to have them come swooping out of the sky at me or something. But I didn't see anything. I came into Española and tried to see if I could scrounge some food or bottled water or something, but our people had picked it over pretty well, and I couldn't find anything. I slept there, though, because I was dead tired. And I headed up Highway 68 the next morning, figuring I could make it at least half of the distance between Española and Taos." Pausing then, she gave me a deprecating smile. "I'd forgotten about the part where it was all uphill. Took me a lot longer than I thought it would. I did find some water in a gas station in Dixon, though, and that helped a little. After a point, I suppose I wasn't really thinking of much of anything except putting one foot in front of the other and getting here. I'm not even sure why I chose Taos as my destination, except that you and Jace were here, and maybe you'd take me in." Another one of those weary little shrugs, and she said simply, "I didn't have anyplace to go."

"Yes, you did," I said, my tone a little fiercer than I'd intended. "You had here."

She didn't respond at first. But as I watched her, a certain tension seemed to leave her body, and she slumped back against the pillows, as if she was finally allowing herself to relax. Then, "Did I hear someone talking about soup?"

A rush of relief went through me. She had a long way to go before she healed, but I thought she'd just taken the first step. "Coming right up," I told her.

She smiled.

CHAPTER ELEVEN

MIGUEL BROUGHT THE SOUP HIMSELF, AND SEEMED a little astonished at how quickly Julia had recovered. "You should sleep for real after you eat," he told her in stern tones. "I don't want you to overdo things."

"No worries," she replied. "I think I'll probably sleep for a week or two after this."

That seemed to satisfy him, and he left the hotel room soon afterward. Almost as if they'd decided to take turns, Lauren came in only a minute or so later, bringing with her a little care package of a new toothbrush and some toothpaste, and a comb and a brush.

"And if you need anything else, be sure to let me know," she said, flashing the two of us a smile before she went back out again.

"Is she always so cheerful?" Julia asked.

"Basically, yes," I replied.

"Impressive."

But I could tell she was getting tired; her head was drooping to one side, and she kept blinking. It was time for me to go.

"Rest now, okay?" I said quietly. "You're safe here."

Julia didn't even answer, but gave a bob of her head that might have been a nod. I took the water glass from the nightstand and refilled it, then set it down next to her. That way it would be there if she woke up in the middle of the night and was thirsty.

After that, I banked the fire and turned off all the lights, except the small one on the dresser. I didn't want to her to feel completely disoriented at being in a strange place if she ended up not sleeping through the night. Finally, I slipped out and shut the door behind me.

Jace, I called out.

Beloved. Is everything all right? I was beginning to worry.

We're both fine. Julia woke up and wanted to talk, and then Miguel brought her some soup. She's sleeping now. I hesitated, then added, *Can we eat alone in our rooms tonight? I don't really feel like being around people right now.*

I left it at that, but he seemed to understand that Julia's story had rattled me, because he said, *Of course. I've already walked Dutchie, so I'll go to the dining room and pick up some food. You go back to the suite and rest.*

That sounded like a fabulous idea, so I did as I was told and headed back to our rooms, glad that everyone else seemed to be at dinner, and so I wouldn't be forced to answer questions about Julia and her condition. Maybe the truth would come out at some point, but I really didn't want to be the one to be spreading her story all over the place.

Dutchie was curled up by the fireplace and gave me a tail thump as I entered the suite, but otherwise she didn't seem too inclined to move from her comfortable position. I leaned down and patted her on the head, then added another log to the fire to keep things going.

Perfect timing, as Jace came in just a minute or two later, pushing a room service cart ahead of him. "Handy things," he said, indicating the cart.

"Well, there are definite perks to holing up in a resort," I said, glad that we were both keeping things light for the moment. I knew they would take a definite turn to the dark side once I started relating what Julia had told me.

For a few minutes, though, we were both quiet as we moved the food from the cart to the table. Jace had also brought a bottle of wine, and he opened it, then poured a healthy measure into both our glasses. I would have asked him how he'd figured out that I needed it, but there really was no point. When it came to me, Jace just *knew*.

We were partway through our chicken tortilla soup when he asked gently, "Do you want to talk about it?"

"Not really," I replied. "But I probably should."

So I told him what Julia had told me, punctuating the story with sips of wine and wondering if one bottle would be enough to get through all this. As I spoke, Jace was silent, expression turning more and more grave with each revelation.

Because I could see the pity filling his eyes—and because I knew Julia would hate being the object of such an emotion—I brushed past all that as quickly as I could, then asked, "Jace, how was she able to make it all the way here without being intercepted? I mean, I know you told me once that the djinn weren't all-seeing and all-knowing, but it seems as if they're pretty good at tracking down wandering humans. So how did Julia escape?"

His brows knitted together as he considered my question. "I can't say for certain. It does seem, from what she herself said about other groups of survivors disappearing, that the djinn who went hunting humans preferred going after larger groups. Perhaps they simply didn't see the sport in running down a lone woman. They could have decided to leave her for later, after the big groups were gone."

I supposed that was possible. And after our last foray to Los Alamos, no one had ventured out at all. If there had been any other djinn lurking in the area, they might have gotten bored and gone off in search of better amusement. I wouldn't flatter myself into thinking that we'd dealt them a serious enough blow that they'd disappeared entirely. True, Evony and Ethan had done some damage, and the djinn on our team that much more, but it shouldn't have been enough to deter the rogue djinn indefinitely.

"Maybe," I said, my tone uncertain at best. I picked up my wine glass and swirled the pale liquid within, watching it catch glints of gold from the flames dancing in the hearth. It was entirely possible that we'd never know exactly how Julia had been lucky enough to walk sixty-plus miles to get to Taos and never face any kind of attack.

"Jessica, isn't the important thing that she got here safely?"

"Maybe," I said again. This time I drank some wine, then set the glass down. My relief that Julia was still alive had begun to be replaced by a low, slow-burning anger. She shouldn't have had to go through all that in the first place. Hadn't she suffered enough, even in the days before the Heat came along and changed everything? And then there was Dan. He was dead because of us. No, we hadn't pulled the trigger, but he'd risked everything to help us escape and had paid the ultimate price.

And what of all the other nameless dead, the ones who had no one left to mourn for them?

"I want to know," I began, then paused, watching as Jace regarded me with increasing concern in his dark eyes. I must have been broadcasting my roiling emotions without even realizing it. This was a conversation I'd wanted to have for some time, but had also avoided it, simply because I wasn't sure I wanted to hear the answers Jace might give. Now, though, as I rode the crest of my anger, I couldn't hold back any longer.

Ask me, beloved.

I sat up straighter and said simply, "I want to know how God could let this happen. You've spoken of God before, so I know you believe in Him."

"It's not a question of believing, Jessica. We djinn know He exists."

Such an earth-shattering comment, uttered in such calm, reasonable tones. Okay, fine. If God really did exist, then we'd start from there.

"All right, then. If God created this world and everything in it, then how could He let it all be destroyed? How can He let good people like Julia and Dan suffer when horrible men like Margolis seem to get away with whatever they want?"

Jace didn't really sigh, but he did let out a small breath as he leaned back in his chair. "You ask questions that men have been asking since the dawn of time."

"I know they have. But I want answers."

A half-eaten roll lay at the edge of his plate. He picked it up and broke off a piece, then chewed it slowly. Stalling, or just attempting to get his thoughts in order?

It seemed to be the latter, because he said, once he was done chewing, "God did not let everything in the world be destroyed. It's all still here—the animals and the trees and the flowers and the insects. Only mankind is gone."

"'Only mankind'?" I repeated, incredulous. "You say it like it doesn't matter!"

His expression softened. "It was a great tragedy—one that I and the others here in Taos and many more of my people tried to stop. But the course had been decided upon. And yes, God let it happen. Do you forget that He wiped the slate clean once before, with a great flood?"

"That's just a myth," I protested, and Jace lifted an eyebrow.

"It is no myth. It happened, although not precisely as it was described in your writings. And there were those among my people who saw how this planet was being slowly destroyed, how that damage might be irreversible in a generation or two, and so they devised a way to stop that destruction. Killing off mankind seemed a reasonable trade-off to them. As to why God did not stop them...well, I can't say for sure, except that perhaps He thought He had given you your chance, and you had squandered it." A pause, and he added softly, "I mean that as the general 'you,' of course."

So many objections to this statement rose in my mind, I wasn't sure which one I should utter first. All right, I had to begin somewhere. "I'll admit that I'm not all that knowledgeable on the topic—my family wasn't very religious—but I was sort of under the impression that all that Old Testament wrath of God stuff wasn't really how He operated anymore."

Jace shook his head. His forefinger was resting on the base of his wine glass, drawing swirling patterns there. "I'm not one to pretend to understand all His motivations. All I know is that the djinn weren't stopped. They devised the means of mankind's undoing, plotted how to release it. At no time did He intervene." A pause, and then he added, "Well, I heard a rumor that word had come from somewhere that there was to be as little suffering as possible, and so the effects of the Heat were modified somewhat, but—"

"'Little suffering'?" I burst out. "God must have a pretty cockeyed idea of what suffering is. I saw my whole family die from the disease, and they sure as hell suffered!"

Right then I couldn't begin to read Jace's expression. Sadness because of the way I'd had to lose my family members one by one, but also...perhaps...a bit of frustration. With me, or with his inability to convince me of God's—and the djinns'—side of things? I had no idea, and right then I could feel the awful crushing pressure of it all over again, of trying to help and knowing it would do no good, of standing by as not just my family, but the whole world died around me.

"Jessica," Jace said. He pushed back from the table a bit—not to stand up, I realized, but to give himself a little breathing room. His eyes sought mine, as if willing me to understand. "It looked like suffering to you, but really, it wasn't. Once the Heat took hold, they could no longer sense what was happening to them. And death came swiftly, relatively speaking. I've seen the great plagues sweep over mankind, witnessed so much death...and believe me, those people suffered. Day after day of fevers, of coughing, of having their very blood turn to poison—"

I slammed my hands down on the table and clung to its edge, as if that was the only thing keeping me from running away. Maybe it was.

"All right," I said bitterly. "I get it. You djinn made a nice, neat, clean disease that would wipe out mankind and leave no messy corpses behind, and God was okay with that."

"*Some* of the djinn made that disease," Jace corrected me. His tone was very gentle, and in a way, I
hated his forbearance, his calm. I wanted him to get
angry and raise his voice so we could have a real fight
over this. If we did that, if we lost control in a way we
never had before, then I might finally have the chance
to scream out my anger and frustration and despair,
even though I knew he wasn't the person I was angry
with. Not really. "I fought the idea," he went on. "The
entire plan was an abomination. And many others of
my kind did as well, but we were not the majority. We
couldn't overrule those who believed we finally had a
chance to possess the world that was denied us.

World that was denied us. He had said that to
me, once upon a time, but hadn't elaborated. Now I
thought I finally had the opportunity to get some
clarification.

"What does that even mean?" I asked. "If we're
getting all biblical here, I thought God created the
world for mankind."

A weary smile. "The djinn were here first, but then
God made man, and thought mankind His greatest
creation. The djinn were told to bow down to man,
as the angels did. But my people had been given free
will, and they refused to bend to a thing they saw as
lesser than themselves. And so the djinn were banished
from this world, and lived on planes of existence the
human mind could only dimly comprehend. Even that

banishment did not keep us away completely, but we could not make our permanent home here, not as a unified people."

If that really was what had happened, then I supposed I could see why the djinn would be so upset and might want to scheme to take back something they thought should have been theirs. But to do so by exterminating the entire human race...it was beyond appalling. Even now, after months had passed, I still hadn't completely absorbed what that meant. I'd been so tied up in what was happening in the immediate world around me that I hadn't forced my brain to really process that all those people were gone, that beyond our little corner here in New Mexico, there might be hundreds and thousands of square miles of nothing.

I wasn't sure how much it would help, but I figured a couple of large swallows of wine right then were better than nothing. Those swallows emptied my wine glass; wordlessly, Jace picked up the bottle and replaced what I'd just drunk, and then some.

My voice was barely a whisper. For some reason, getting out the words hurt, but I had to know. "So what was the plan?"

Frowning, Jace said, "I told you the plan. To rid the world of mankind."

"No. Not that. Afterward. What happens...after?"

After they're all *gone,* I thought. *After the djinn have scoured every trace of humanity from the face of*

*the planet, except for these small havens where the One
Thousand live with their Chosen. And even those might
soon be gone if the rogue djinn have their way.*

Jace was very still, watching me. The firelight awak-
ened those warm little gleams in his hair that I loved so
much, but I felt no warmth within me. Something at
my center seemed to have gone cold.

He said, "The djinn will establish their homesteads
and courts and compounds here. There are not that
many of them, not compared to mankind's billions,
and so they will all have as much land as they require.
The air will clear, as there will be nothing to pollute it,
and slowly the vines and the trees will grow, and in a
hundred years, there will be nothing left to show that
man once held dominion over this world."

The words were simple enough, but I could almost
see it in my mind's eye—the vast forests and grasslands
that had once covered this continent coming back,
taking over and hiding the gas stations and skyscrapers
and mini-malls and everything else we'd left behind.
Blue above, green below. And here and there djinn, in
their houses or castles or whatever the heck it was that
they called home.

I finally found my voice. "And you, Jace? How
much land do you require?"

He did get up then, and moved around to my side
of the table. To my surprise, he knelt beside me. "Only

as much as the walls of our house in Santa Fe contain. That is all I need. Our home, and you."

I'd been wrong to think that my center had gone cold. Or if it had, it melted then, in a warm rush, and I put my arms out and drew him to me, feeling the strength of his body, the brush of his lips against my cheek. I wanted the whole world to be this—just him and me, the warmth of the fire, the sleeping dog by the hearth. That was all I needed. I wanted to will the rest of it away.

But the world, as it often did, had its own way of intruding.

A pounding at the door woke us up. Jace and I had been asleep in one another's arms, where we'd collapsed after making frenzied, urgent love. I couldn't even say which one of us had initiated it, only that we both felt compelled to reassure ourselves with our lover's touch. It was as if I needed to let Jace know that I still loved him, despite everything he'd told me, just as he needed to reaffirm his connection with me after hearing of Julia's treatment at the hands of Richard Margolis.

Jace was out of bed first, making a short detour to the bathroom so he could grab one of the terrycloth robes that hung on their hooks behind the door. I sat up, clutching the sheet to my bare breasts. No one had ever knocked like this in our time there, no matter what the emergency, so I couldn't think what might be happening now. Had the rogue djinn discovered some new way to attack us?

The door opened, showing a rectangle of faint yellowish light from the corridor outside. To save power, the sconces there had been converted to hold pillar candles, and I guessed that was the illumination I was seeing now.

Zahrias stood outside. As I stared at him, wondering what the hell he was doing, pounding on our door in the middle of the night, he said to Jace, "They have gone. Well, two of them. Rafi was not so lucky."

That news made me sit up straighter and blink the rest of the sleep out of my eyes. I thought I knew who he meant by "they." The three djinn who had come to argue with Zahrias about escaping Taos, getting outside the field generated by Miles's device so they could try to get some help from the other, more neutral djinn.

But what had Zahrias meant when he said that Rafi was not so lucky?

Since the two men were occupied with one another at the door, I slid out from under the covers and grabbed my discarded clothes from where they still lay on the floor, then hurriedly began putting them on.

Jace asked, "What happened?"

"I don't know for certain," Zahrias replied. "That is, I knew they would make the attempt soon. They were far too impatient to do otherwise, and I knew that nothing I said would change their minds." He paused then; I could tell from his silhouette in the doorway that he leaned heavily on his cane. He must have expended a good deal of energy in rushing over to our suite. "Alif and Nizar got away, but Rafi...did not. They left enough of him that he was able to stagger back over the boundary—as a warning, I would guess—but he will not live the night."

My hand went to my mouth. I wouldn't say that Rafi was one of my favorites among the djinn, since he seemed possessive of Lindsay to a fault, but he certainly didn't deserve to be set upon by some of his own kind and then left for dead.

Zahrias seemed to catch a glimpse of my movement, because he shifted and directed his next words to me, "Jessica, you are friends with Lindsay. I came to ask that you would go to her and bring her to see Rafi. He's been laid on one of the couches in the reception area, since I could carry him no further."

Those words startled me. If asked, I would never have said that I thought the djinn leader capable of such exertion. Maybe he'd called up hidden reserves of strength to bring Rafi someplace where he could be laid down with dignity. As to why he'd come to Jace and me, rather than Dani and Lauren, well, it was true that Lindsay and I had gotten somewhat close, just because of the time I'd spent down in the lab with her.

"Of course I'll go get her," I said. It was not an errand I looked forward to; now I had an inkling of what those officers in the military must have felt like, the men and women who'd had to bring news of loved ones' deaths in combat to family members. But it was something that needed to be done.

I slipped my feet into some flats I had kicked off next to the bed and hurried to the door. Jace reached out and gave my hand a squeeze just before I slipped out. Our eyes met, and I could only hope he might see something of what I was feeling—how glad I was that he hadn't done something foolish to endanger himself, how dear he was to me, and how devastated I would be if anything should happen to him.

Something appeared to communicate itself to him, because he nodded slightly, just as Zahrias said quietly, "Thank you, Jessica."

Before that point, I hadn't done much wandering around in the corridors at night. There hadn't been any real need, after all. Now I couldn't help thinking how creepy it felt, hurrying along, my way lit only by candles, with no other sound or movement in the resort. The djinn were sleeping more and more now, so it wasn't surprising that I hadn't run into any of them. And apparently their human companions weren't leaving their sides.

Lindsay's suite wasn't that far away, down another corridor that branched off from the one where Jace and I currently made our home. In a way, I wished her rooms were on the other side of the resort, just so I would have more time to rehearse what I was going to say. But she had to have known this was a risk, right? Rafi had said that he and the other two djinn had spoken with their Chosen, so this horrible news shouldn't catch her completely off guard.

Even so....

I stopped outside her door, pulled in a breath, and then knocked. Not pounding like Zahrias had done, but two short, quick raps.

She must have been expecting something, because Lindsay opened the door almost immediately. And I saw that she was fully dressed, as if she'd been anticipating receiving bad news. Or maybe she simply hadn't wanted to go to sleep yet, perhaps thinking that Rafi and his compatriots would be quickly successful, and would come back with help.

Her eyes widened when she saw me, but then I saw her square her shoulders, as if she had just realized what my presence must mean.

"Zahrias sent me," I said hurriedly. "It's—" Now that the time had come, it was harder than I'd thought to get the words out.

"It's Rafi," she interjected, her tone almost too calm. "Something's happened."

I nodded. "I'm so sorry, Lindsay. I'm supposed to take you to him."

She inhaled deeply, obviously steeling herself. "Okay. Show me."

"He's—he's in the lobby."

That seemed to be enough, because she began walking in short, brisk steps toward the front of the resort. All I could do was trail along, wishing I could think of something to say that would hit exactly the right note of being sympathetic but not too much so— Lindsay was not the sentimental type. I had no doubt that she cared deeply about her djinn partner, but she wasn't the kind of girl who would show it.

When we reached the lobby, Jace and Zahrias were already there, as was Miguel. I supposed Zahrias had called him in to see what he could do to help, even though it had sounded as if Rafi was past any sort of assistance, human or otherwise.

And when I looked at him, I could see that Zahrias' assessment had been correct. Lindsay's partner lay on one of the couches, bandages wrapped around his throat, his chest, his—well, from what I could see, there didn't seem to be any part of his body that hadn't been injured in some way. Although normally he had a warm olive complexion, now he looked pasty and drained, blood-smeared hair plastered to his forehead.

Lindsay rushed forward, then dropped to her knees and took his hand in hers. "R-Rafi?"

It was probably the first time I'd ever heard any real hesitation in her voice. But now her usual brisk, no-nonsense veneer had been stripped away, and I could see how scared, how vulnerable she was.

He didn't move. I thought I saw his fingers tighten on hers, though, just as he whispered, "They'll be here soon."

"I know, Rafi. Just—try to stay so you can meet them when they get here, okay?"

"Take care of you. That's all…I wanted. Take care of you."

Those words seemed to be the last he had the strength to utter, because his hand fell away from hers, and he went completely still.

"R-Rafi? Rafi!" A shudder went through her as she seemed to realize he was gone. "No! No!"

Jace and Miguel both stepped forward, but then Jace hesitated, as if realizing that perhaps one of her own kind should be the one comforting Lindsay now. Bending down, Miguel wrapped his arms around her and pulled her up.

"It's okay," he said. "It's okay."

"No, it's not!" she raged. "It is not okay! Rafi's gone, and those animals killed him!"

"And we will have our vengeance," Zahrias said quietly, his deep baritone cutting through her words.

Something about his voice seemed to calm her, and she went limp then, allowing Miguel to guide her away from the body of her djinn lover. A nod from Zahrias, and Miguel kept walking with her, obviously taking her back to her suite.

"I'll go with her," I offered.

"Thank you, Jessica," Jace told me, while Zahrias' gaze shifted away from the two of us to where Rafi lay, his blood staining the pale tan leather of the couch.

Something in his grim face made me stop, though. I stared at him, thoughts churning away at Rafi's final words. Finally I asked, "Do you really think help will be here soon?"

His eyes wouldn't meet mine. Then, heavily, "I don't know."

CHAPTER TWELVE

I ENDED UP SITTING WITH LINDSAY FOR SEVERAL hours, until she at last cried herself to sleep. By then my body was practically screaming with exhaustion—first hearing Julia's story, and then going through this with Lindsay had sapped all my reserves—but I made myself wait until a soft knock came at the door. Lauren was outside, offering to spell for me.

"Get some rest," she whispered. "I'll stay with her for the rest of the night."

"Are you sure?" I glanced back at Lindsay, who was huddled into a ball, one of the pillows hugged against her chest, as if she was clinging to it in a desperate attempt to pretend that Rafi was still with her.

"Yes. I can tell you're about dead on your feet." There wasn't much perky about Lauren at the moment; her eyes were wide and scared, and I thought I even saw some tears glistening in them. "This is awful. If I'd only known—"

"If you're trying to beat yourself up for not talking them out of this, just stop."

"I didn't have the chance. Zahrias didn't say anything to anyone. Even Dani didn't know until Rafi—well, until that happened."

I was so tired that I didn't have the energy to put a filter on my words. "Probably because he didn't want anyone else trying something so crazy." Right then I yawned, the kind you can't stop, the kind that feels like it's about to crack your face open. "Sorry."

"Don't apologize." She reached out and patted me on the arm. "Go to bed. We'll take turns staying with her as needed."

I didn't have any energy left for arguments. Shooting Lauren a grateful smile, I slipped past her and left the door open so she could go inside the suite. The door shut quietly behind her, and I took that as my signal to head for home.

By then I had no idea what time it actually was. Two in the morning? Three? I had to hope that Julia was resting peacefully in her own suite on the opposite side of the resort, because there was no way in hell I had the strength to go and check on her. She must be completely dead to the world; after an ordeal like the one she'd just survived, I probably would have slept for days.

Despite the late hour, Jace was still awake and waiting for me when I got back to my own rooms. The only illumination was the dying fire, which sent odd little shadows into the corners of the room and seemed to throw into deep relief the contours of his cheekbones, the pools of darkness beneath his eyes.

As soon as I entered the suite, he rose and came to me, folding me into his arms. Feeling him, I almost wanted to begin crying. I couldn't even say why, except that maybe I was just so glad he was safe, that he was here with me. Back in Los Alamos, I'd come perilously close to experiencing the same kind of loss Lindsay was suffering now, and seeing her tragedy made me realize once again how much I needed Jace, how I didn't think I could live without him.

"Some of the Chosen came to help move Rafi to a more secluded place," he said quietly. "And in the morning, we'll have to let everyone know—and also let them know what those three were attempting. Zahrias did not want the word to get out, just because false hope can be a very dangerous thing when a group of people walk on a cliff edge as they do now. But it is a secret that can't be kept any longer."

"Is it really false hope?" I asked, lifting my head so I could stare up into his eyes and try to see the truth in them.

"It is very long odds," he replied. His gaze met mine directly. I could tell he thought he owed me the truth, not some pretty platitudes he might use to dance around the issue. "First, to escape this world at all—as Rafi was unable to do, in the end—and then to search out those in our world who might come to offer help...the chances of success were not good. It is hard to explain, but our world is not the same as yours. Palaces float on the air, and no one may necessarily be found in any one fixed location. So even though Alif and Nizar know they must go to the elders to appeal to them for assistance, they will have to be found first. And that may not be an easy thing."

I shivered. "Your world doesn't sound very welcoming."

"It has its own beauties. But it is very different from yours, and yes, we djinn prefer it here. Else we would not have had all this ugliness, because the djinn would have had nothing they coveted."

Yes, this world was a beautiful one. I thought of a family trip we'd taken to the Grand Canyon once, and how I'd watched the sun rise over the South Rim. At the time I hadn't thought there could be anything more beautiful, the kind of beauty that awoke an ache deep within you. I could see why the djinn would want the earth and all its wonders.

"So," he went on, "while it is possible they might be successful, it's nothing we can depend on, or wait for. We have our own resource here in Miles Odekirk, and although he hasn't found a solution yet, I believe it's more likely he will come up with something to help us, rather than the cavalry galloping in from the djinn world."

I nodded, yawning again. At once Jace pulled me over to the bed, his fingers working at the buttons on my shirt. It was a testament to my current exhaustion that I wasn't even aroused by the thought of him taking my clothes off. I knew he was only doing that to help me, since I was so tired I could barely slip out of my shoes.

The jeans came next, and then Jace was pushing me into bed while I still wore my bra. The last thing I remembered was him pulling the covers over me, and then everything slipped away into darkness.

When I awoke, I was alone. Well, not completely alone—Dutchie came over as soon as I stirred, and stuck her cold, wet nose into my hand, which was hanging down over the side of the bed. She didn't seem particularly urgent, though, which meant Jace had probably already fed and walked her.

"Morning, girl," I mumbled.

A tail thump, and then she went back to her favorite spot by the fireplace. The room smelled good, of wood smoke and coffee and cinnamon. I discovered the reason for the latter two scents when I focused on the little table by the window. Sitting there were a carafe of coffee and a plate with a couple of muffins. Jace must have left them for me before he went out.

And it was late—I retrieved my watch and saw that nine o'clock was long gone, and ten almost here. I could understand why Jace had let me sleep, but at the same time I worried that I hadn't been there for Julia when she woke up. All I could do was hope that Lauren had sent someone to check on her. If Lauren was even awake, either. She might have been up until dawn, keeping watch over Lindsay.

Since I knew I wouldn't be very functional until I had my coffee, I went over to the table and poured myself a cup. It had cooled enough that I could drink it right away, so I took several large swallows, then broke off a piece of the muffin, which turned out to be apple spice. I couldn't help wondering right then how long all this luxury would last—we were only feeding some hundred-odd people, so it would take a while to work through all the supplies in Taos. Sooner or later, though, we'd have to start focusing on becoming more self-sustaining rather than using up all the resources in the immediate vicinity.

That sort of strategy would have to wait for another day. For now, I wanted to focus on getting enough caffeine and carbs into my system that I'd be up to facing what was left of the morning. Next, a shower.

I hurried through that, then blotted my hair dry. Blowing it out would take too long and use up too much precious electricity, so I just ran a comb through it and called it a day. Clothes, shoes, tinted lip balm. That was enough to make me more or less presentable.

Still no sign of Jace even after all that. Frowning, I let myself out of the room. *Jace?* I ventured.

You're awake.

Thank you for not saying "finally."

A chuckle. *I certainly wouldn't begrudge you some much-needed rest. I'm with Zahrias and the others.*

Is Julia there?

No, I haven't seen her yet this morning.

I'd been debating whether to go see Julia or Lindsay first, but that seemed to decide things. Lindsay had suffered a hideous loss, but at least she had people around who knew her, whereas Julia was more or less surrounded by strangers. Well, all right, she knew Miles Odekirk, but his wasn't exactly the most comforting of presences. Besides, he spent so much time holed up in the lab, I didn't know whether he'd even heard that Julia was here...or what had happened to Rafi. I pictured Miles complaining to himself about Lindsay being late once again, with no actual idea of what had caused her to avoid the lab this morning, and shook my head.

The hallways were deserted, although I thought I detected voices coming from the dining area. That made sense; it was usually in that spot where Zahrias made his announcements. I wished I could be there, but Jace could fill me in later. For now, I thought it was more important to see Julia.

She replied, "Come in," to my knock, so I opened the door and let myself into her room. The bed was made, and she was sitting in the chair by the window, where the curtains were drawn to allow the morning sun to pour in. She'd traded the yoga pants and long-sleeved T-shirt she'd worn to sleep in for a pair of jeans and a dark blue sweater.

I found myself reflecting that I didn't think I would look that good after walking sixty-plus miles, dehydrated and hungry. "Sorry I didn't get here sooner," I said. "I overslept."

"It's all right." Her expression darkened. "Jace stopped by earlier and brought me some breakfast. He told me what happened last night."

"Oh." There was only the one chair, so I came over to her and perched uncertainly on the edge of the bed. "Yes, it was pretty bad. The djinn aren't really used to losing one of their own."

"No, I suppose they wouldn't be." She hesitated, then asked, "Jessica, where's Evony? I'd sort of thought she might have stopped by to see me."

Oh, shit. I swallowed past the lump in my throat. The pain of Evony's loss had started to smooth itself out over the past few weeks, but now that Julia had asked about her, it almost felt as if I'd just seen her die the day before. "She—she died defending us from the rogue djinn on our way back from taking Miles Odekirk."

Blue-gray eyes widened. With a shaking hand, Julia reached for the half-drunk cup of coffee sitting on the table before her and gulped it down. "That's...terrible."

"I know. But...." I hesitated, uncertain of how to say the words without sounding uncaring. Then I realized that Julia had been there, and had seen how Evony had reacted to Natila's death. "She took it really hard, losing her djinn. Maybe with time she would have bounced back, but I can't help thinking that Evony went out in her own personal blaze of glory because she just didn't want to be here anymore."

"Damn him," Julia murmured, and I looked at her in question. Mouth hardening, she said, "Margolis. Damn Margolis. That bastard has left a horrible trail of destruction behind him. And no one in Los Alamos will question his judgment, or ask whether he's finally gone too far, because he's keeping them safe." She spat the last word as if it tasted foul on her tongue.

I didn't argue. I agreed with her. If the residents of Los Alamos would only stand up to their resident bully, then maybe they'd have a chance. Or maybe not. The problem was that the decent people, the ones who only wanted to start over after the Dying had changed the world forever, probably didn't have the courage it required to face down someone like Margolis, who had his own personal hit squad made up of goons like Mitch Kosky and Butch MacElroy.

Unfortunately, it wasn't as if Jace and I could lead an army to go rescue the community at Los Alamos from their own private dictator. We had our own problems to deal with, and at the moment, those seemed far more pressing.

Thinking it might be better to change the subject, I asked, "Has anyone except Jace come to see you?"

Julia shook her head. "There was some more stuff outside my door this morning—more toiletries and clothes, but I don't know who dropped it off. And then Jace came by a little before nine to bring me some breakfast, but that's all."

So maybe Miles really didn't know she was here. Or didn't care.

"I thought I'd better sit tight until you came by," she continued. "Jace obviously had pressing business to take care of, and I didn't know if it was kosher for me to be wandering around by myself."

"Oh, it's fine," I reassured her. "It's not as if we're keeping any state secrets here or anything. It might have felt strange for you to be around so many djinn, but because they can't access their powers right now...."

"It's not as if they can turn me into a newt." She was smiling a little as she made the remark, so I guessed she hadn't meant it seriously.

I didn't know if that was a power the djinn even possessed. Control of the elements, the ability to pop in and out of this plane of existence as it pleased them… those were things I'd witnessed for myself. How much more they could do was still a mystery, and also a moot point, if Miles couldn't manage to modify his device.

"Would you like to see Miles?" I asked then, albeit rather hesitantly. The two of them knew each other, but I had no idea whether Julia had much of an opinion of Miles or not. After all, he'd participated in some fairly dubious behavior while working with Richard Margolis, and she'd made her opinion of the commander pretty clear.

But she nodded. "He—well, I think he tried to come my defense. Whether it was out of misplaced chivalry or because his scientific mind was offended by the lack of empirical evidence proving my guilt, I don't know for sure. But I heard him arguing with Margolis once. They were standing in the hallway just past the detention area, and the door hadn't closed all the way. So I guess I would like to see him, if only to say thank you."

For some reason, I was relieved to hear that. After what had happened to Natila, I'd had the worst opinion possible of Miles Odekirk. And though his actions over the past weeks seemed to indicate he'd had a change of heart, I wasn't sure if I believed it. Not really. That he'd tried to defend Julia, though, raised my estimation of him several notches.

"Then I'll take you to the lab," I said. "And show you around a little on the way. It'll probably feel good to get out and stretch your legs."

"My legs had plenty of stretching over the past few days, but you're right." She got up from her chair and went to the mirror, grimacing as she inspected the bruise on her jaw. It seemed to have faded a little more, but it still stood out against her skin, which looked as if it had picked up a bit of a tan during her long walk to Taos. Unfortunately, even the tan couldn't hide the mark Margolis had left on her. "I hate this. I can try to pretend it didn't happen, but every time I look in the mirror, it's like I've got this big red letter 'A' written on my face."

Right then I wished I had a gun in my hand and Richard Margolis standing in front of me. I would have drilled a hole in his diseased brain without batting an eyelash. But he wasn't there, so I said gently, "Julia, only Jace and I know what happened, and neither of us would ever say anything to anyone about it. If anyone asks, you got roughed up while they were questioning you. No one's going to think anything strange about that."

She sighed. "You're right. It would probably help if I stopped looking in the mirror. But I keep checking, hoping that it'll be gone the next time I look."

My heart ached for her. All I could do was pray that she'd allow herself to get past this, and that sooner rather than later she'd realize she'd done nothing wrong and that no one could possibly hold her responsible for Margolis' actions. The problem was, Julia had been an abused woman before the Heat had done her the favor of killing off her asshole fiancé, and so she already had a tendency to assign blame to herself when it wasn't warranted.

Getting out would do her some good. I said, "Let's go down to the lab. Miles hates getting interrupted, but maybe he'll make an exception when he sees it's you."

She gave a half-hearted chuckle. "I kind of doubt it. But we'll see."

We left the room. I purposely took the long way around so I could lead her out into the courtyard area, where the wind could ruffle her hair and the sun could shine on her. It did seem to help; she paused on the bridge and breathed in deeply.

"It must be absolutely gorgeous here in the spring," she said, looking around. "I mean, it's still beautiful now, but once the trees leaf out and the irises start blooming? It'll be stunning."

"Hopefully, that won't be too far off," I replied. "I'm not sure, though. I've heard that winter can last a long time here in Taos, but I'm an Albuquerque girl. I don't have much frame of reference."

"Neither do I." Her hair was blowing around her head in a torrent of dark gold. I'd always been perfectly fine with being a brunette, but I had to admit there was something glorious about that mane of Julia's.

Even though the day was fine, the air still had a bite to it. Neither of us were wearing jackets, so she didn't protest when I said we should head on to the lab. By then it past eleven, and so I doubted we'd be interrupting Miles's beauty sleep or anything.

That was definitely not the case. The door stood open, so Julia and I went ahead and entered the basement workshop. Miles sat on a stool next to the workbench, but he wasn't tinkering with the device. Instead, he was typing away on the laptop we'd brought from his Los Alamos lab, his back to us. Because the laptop's screen was angled toward us, I could see what he was working on.

Correction—I could see the numbers and symbols flowing across the screen, and what looked like 3D models of strange vortex-appearing objects spinning up and then collapsing. But just because I could see it didn't mean I was able to make heads or tails of it.

He must have heard us approach, because he swiveled on the stool, brows creasing. The frown seemed to increase as he took in the two of us. "Oh. I thought you were Lindsay. Where is she? She's not always the most conscientious about her hours here, but—"

If it had been anyone else, I might have been surprised by his lack of reaction to Julia's presence. But because it was Miles, I put that aside for now. "No one's been down to tell you?"

"Tell me what?" he snapped.

"Several of our djinn went outside the barrier and attempted to reach their own world. One of them didn't make it. That was Rafi."

Miles stared at me, expression so blank that I felt compelled to add,

"Lindsay was his Chosen. She's pretty upset, as you might guess. So I'm not really sure when she's going to feel up to returning to work here."

Still that stare. Then Miles frowned and said, "That was foolish of them. After so many weeks of having their powers blocked, they wouldn't have been able to summon the energy quickly enough to open the portal they required."

I really hadn't expected him to offer any words of condolence, but calling the three djinn "foolish" so soon after Rafi's death seemed awfully cold to me. Voice hardening, I replied, "Maybe not as foolish as you think. Two of them did actually manage to get away."

"Hmm." Miles seemed to finally register Julia's presence, since he gave her a faint nod. "It's rather surprising to see you here, Julia."

She must have been a lot more used to his foibles than I, because she smiled at him and said, "Well, I'd say it was surprising to see you here, too, except

I had a suspicion this is where you went when you disappeared."

"Was kidnapped," he corrected her.

"You look well," she responded, apparently not wanting to address the whole kidnapping issue. After surveying the lab, she added, "It doesn't look like you've slowed down too much."

"They brought some of my equipment. And the young woman who's been assisting me has a surprisingly quick mind."

That was a comment I hadn't been expecting. Most of the time, Miles seemed to only tolerate Lindsay's presence. Was he attempting to be kind now because of her recent loss? Trying to figure out his thought processes was beyond me most of the time.

But since Julia didn't know anything about the history between Miles and Lindsay, she only nodded. "I'm glad you have someone working with you. And hopefully she'll want to resume her work soon, if only to have something to keep her mind occupied."

For some reason, that remark made Miles appear distinctly uncomfortable. He shifted on his stool and turned his attention back to the laptop's screen. Without looking up at either of us, he said, "When she feels she's ready."

Julia appeared to have a better grip on Miles's reactions than I did, because she said, "Well, we don't want to keep you from your work. I just wanted to stop by and let you know that I'm grateful to you for sticking up for me with Margolis."

He still didn't glance away from the laptop. "He was only going on a hunch, with no real evidence. While I realize that we don't have a true judicial system in place any longer, I still believe we should do our best to present evidence as to someone's guilt before pronouncing any kind of sentence."

"True...but you knew I was guilty, didn't you, Miles?" There was the slightest sly note in Julia's voice as she asked the question, as if she was inquiring mainly because she wanted to see how he would react.

"Yes, but I didn't have any real evidence, either." This time he did finally look up; the familiar abstracted frown was pulling at his brows, deepening the line in between them. "And besides...."

"Besides what?"

"Margolis was wrong. I was wrong."

Julia and I exchanged a bewildered glance.

"Wrong about what?" she asked softly.

"About the djinn. About Natila." His face twisted, and I saw his hands clench on the edges of the stool where he sat, knuckles turning white. "I wanted to stop him, but I knew he wouldn't listen to me. So I stood there and watched. And then afterward, when he wanted me to cut her up, I did. It was wrong."

I didn't dare breathe, and beside me, Julia also held herself still. The horror of seeing Natila die had only been compounded by the knowledge that she was being dissected afterward, like some kind of science experiment. At the time, I sure as hell hadn't seen any remorse or hesitation in Miles Odekirk.

Maybe he'd hidden it because he, like pretty much everyone else in Los Alamos, was scared shitless of going up against Richard Margolis.

"And you know what was ironic about that?" Miles went on, almost appearing to address the air, since he wouldn't look directly at either Julia or me. "There was absolutely nothing anomalous about her, except that she was in perfect physical condition. Nothing to distinguish her from a human being. Margolis didn't like that at all."

No, he probably didn't. He'd wanted evidence that the djinn were completely other, despite their appearance.

"I wanted to bury her. Margolis had no use for her any longer, since there was nothing he could point to as being obviously different from the rest of us *homo sapiens.* But the ground was too cold. So I used the crematorium in the funeral home, and I placed her ashes in one of the urns I found in the display case. And then I put her on the mantel in the sitting room there, since I didn't know what else to do."

He sounded completely lost, so very un-Miles-like, that I didn't know what I should do, either. Julia, however, roused herself and went to him, taking one of his hands in hers.

"It's okay, Miles," she said. "I know you did what you could."

"But I didn't. I should have tried to stop him—"

"You couldn't have," she cut in, but gently. "You would've just ended up in jail like me—or worse—if you'd tried to interfere."

For a long moment, he only stared at her, eyes wide and haunted behind the rimless glasses. Then she did something I knew I would never have had the courage to do—she let go of his hands and put her arms around him, hugging him wordlessly. I could almost see him stiffen in shock, but then he sighed and allowed himself to relax into the embrace. They stayed that way for some time. At last she let go of him and backed away, but she still held his gaze.

"If you need to talk, I'm here."

He nodded, but then seemed to realize I'd been watching that moment of supposed weakness. His back went stiff, and he returned to typing on the laptop.

"Let's go," Julia murmured, and we both turned away from Miles and headed out of the lab, pausing only to shut the door behind us.

When we were almost to the stairs, I stopped and said, "How could you do that?"

"Do what?" Her expression was genuinely curious, as if she couldn't quite figure out what I was driving at.

"I don't know—comfort him like that, after everything he's done?"

The corners of her mouth lifted slightly, but it wasn't precisely a smile. Her eyes were too sad for that. "He's sorry. It won't change what happened, but...it's obvious he didn't really want to do it. He's not evil. Margolis—now, I won't argue with you if you want to call *him* evil." She was silent for a second, then went on, "There's nothing wrong with offering someone a little grace. If we can't manage that, how does that make us any different from the bad djinn?"

I stared at her, and had no answer.

CHAPTER THIRTEEN

By the time we got back to the main floor and had wandered toward the dining area, it was empty. Obviously, whatever announcement Zahrias had gathered everyone to hear was long over. Just as well, probably. I didn't know whether Julia was up to facing that many strangers at once. It would probably be better if she met them gradually, rather than in one big group.

I was explaining to her how we'd marked off the perimeter of the safe zone, making it easy to come and go within its boundaries—and also making it easy to go down to the plaza and "shop" for clothes and shoes and jewelry—when we ran into Jace and Zahrias, who had just turned a corner in the corridor that led to Julia's room.

"How are you faring today, Ms. Innes?" Zahrias asked politely. He had the cane with him but didn't seem to require it at the moment, since it was looped over one arm.

"Julia," she said quickly. I couldn't help noticing the way her gaze swiftly tracked from the bare muscled chest revealed by his robes, then up to his face, as if she was embarrassed to be caught staring.

No worries, Julia, I thought. *If I weren't with Jace, I'd probably be staring, too.*

Zahrias didn't appear to detect anything odd about her response. He said, "It seems as if you're recovering very rapidly."

"I am," she replied. "Thank you so much for the care you've given me, and for taking me in."

"It's the least we could do. You rendered a very great service to Jasreel and Jessica, and so we must repay the debt as best we can." He glanced over at me. "Everyone has been informed about Rafi. The farewell will be tomorrow morning."

"How did they take it?" I asked.

A grim smile touched Zahrias' lips, and I saw the way he and Jace exchanged a single charged glance, one that seemed to say, *This isn't over yet.*

But the djinn leader only replied, "As well as can be expected. At least, after what happened to Rafi, none of them are demanding that we send more of our people for assistance."

No, I supposed they wouldn't. Nothing like seeing one of your own die horribly to turn you off from wanting to attempt the same thing.

There wasn't any way to turn the conversation toward lighter topics, not really. But I figured I might as well try. "Miles was grumbling about not having Lindsay to assist him."

"She's in no shape for that," Jace said. I could tell from the downward droop of his mouth that he was very worried about her, possibly because he'd seen how Evony had reacted when she lost her djinn lover. "And she'll decide when she's ready, and not have Miles pushing her into something she's not emotionally equipped for."

"I don't think that's what Jessica meant," Julia said, coming to my rescue. Or maybe it was a little of Miles's rescue, too. He'd seemed irritated that he wouldn't have Lindsay to assist him, but at least he hadn't made any noises about putting pressure on her to come back to the lab right away. "It sounded like Lindsay was valuable in his research, that's all."

"I know." Zahrias' tone was heavy, and although he didn't look precisely worried, he was probably trying to calculate how much Lindsay's absence would delay the work being done in the lab. "She seems to be a strong young woman, so let us all hope that she finds herself able to resume her work sooner rather than later."

Jace nodded, but I could tell he wasn't all that hopeful. Maybe he had more evidence on which to base that assessment—after all, I hadn't seen Lindsay yet today, so I had no idea how she was bearing up.

Then Zahrias turned to Julia. "You've come to us at a difficult time, a time of grief. I am sorry for that. Perhaps you will sit down to dinner with the three of us this evening?"

I had to keep my mouth from dropping open. Never—and I mean *never*—had I seen Zahrias joining the community for the evening meal...or any meal, for that matter. It seemed that he always took a tray in his rooms. Why, I wasn't sure, except that everyone ate with their partners, and seeing all that togetherness when he himself was alone might be too much to take. Once or twice I'd considered asking Jace about it, but I had a feeling he didn't know for sure, either. Or maybe he had his suspicions, and didn't feel comfortable sharing them with me.

At any rate, I just stood there as Julia smiled and said, "Thank you, Zahrias. That's very thoughtful of you."

A nod. "We usually dine at seven. But I think Jasreel and Jessica will come and show you where to go."

It wasn't a question. And it was a subtle message— *join me for dinner, but don't expect me to come pick you up at your room. This isn't a date.*

All right, I was pretty sure Zahrias had never gone on a "date" in his life, but that still seemed to be the emotional vibe I was getting.

"We'd be honored," Jace said. At the same time, his dark gaze flickered toward me, just for a second. It seemed I wasn't the only one picking up on a little bit of something here.

Not that I'd be one to judge. Julia was drop-dead beautiful, and Zahrias had been alone for a long, long time.

And now you're being a crazy matchmaker, I scolded myself. *Just because he extended an offer of dinner doesn't mean he intended anything else by it except trying to make Julia feel at home here.*

Very true. Still, this was one dinner I very much looked forward to.

But there was the rest of the day to get through before that. I saw Julia back to her room, although we stopped briefly on the way to make a detour at the resort's gift shop, which had a collection of paperback books that we'd turned into a sort of lending library.

"I don't know if there's anything here you'd like, but it's something to pass the time," I told her.

"'Pass the time,'" she repeated in musing tones. "It's been a long while since I had an empty afternoon to fill up. Being able to just sit and read sounds like heaven."

"I guess it depends on what you like," I said. If she preferred highbrow literary fiction, I feared she'd find pretty slim pickings among what we had to offer, since most of what was on hand was vacation reading sort of stuff—mysteries and thrillers and romances.

She plucked one of the mysteries off the rack. "This should keep me occupied."

I should have guessed that she wasn't exactly the bodice-ripper type. Then I shivered. No, Julia had experienced her own real-life bodice ripping. I doubted she'd want to be reading about it. Anyway, that term was kind of unfair. Back when I'd had time, I liked to read romances, interspersed with a variety of other genres, and the true bodice-rippery stuff had pretty much gone out of vogue.

"Jace and I'll come get you a little before seven," I promised her as I dropped her off at her room.

"Looking forward to it," she replied, then thanked me and shut the door.

So was she looking forward to it on general principles...or because of the company she'd be sharing?

I had a feeling I was letting my mind play with an attraction that probably didn't even exist because it helped to distract me from everything else that was going on. After that I went back to my suite, where Jace was waiting for me.

"Zahrias giving you a spare moment to breathe?" I teased, even as I went to him and wrapped my arms around his waist.

"One or two," he replied. His lips touched the top of my head, and a little thrill went through me. I wished we could sink down on the bed and lose ourselves in one another for an hour or two. That wouldn't happen, though. We needed to go check on Lindsay, and expending Jace's fragile energy reserves for a little bit of afternoon delight probably wasn't the best idea.

He seemed to pick up on what I was thinking, because he let out a breath and then stepped away from me, although he held on to my hands. "Ah, Jessica, it's times like these when that damned device seems almost to be doing more harm than good."

"You don't really mean that. We need it. And it isn't as if you've been neglecting me...it's okay if we have to scale things back to once a day for a while." Anyway, when I stopped to think about it, I realized that we'd mostly fallen into a pattern of lovemaking only one time each day back at the Santa Fe house. We'd simply been too exhausted by all the work that needed to be done. Or rather, I'd been too exhausted. At the time, there hadn't been a device hampering his vitality, forcing Jace to conserve his strength, but he'd had to act like any other regular mortal who'd get tired by a day spent looking after the animals and tending the plants in the greenhouse and helping out with whatever else needed to get done around the place.

He took my hands and lifted first one to his mouth, and then the other. A shiver went through me at the

touch of his lips against my skin, and I began to wonder if I should rethink my position on no afternoon
lovemaking.

But then he let go of me, saying, "You're right, of
course. Let's go see Lindsay."

I forced aside the disappointment that wanted to
flood through me. Instead, I nodded. "Yes...maybe
she's tired of visitors by now, but I don't want her to
think I've completely bailed on her."

As we walked left the suite and headed toward
Lindsay's rooms, my feeling of uneasiness began ratcheting back up. She'd never been the overly emotional
type, from what I could tell, but I didn't know if she'd
ever suffered a loss like this before. Of course, she had
to have lost family and friends in the Dying, but losing
a lover, especially one who had vowed to spend what
could literally be eternity with you...that had to be an
extra level of pain you couldn't actually prepare yourself for. Certainly Evony hadn't been able to deal with
it. Not really.

When we got to Lindsay's suite, though, she
sounded composed enough as she called out, "Come in."

Jace and I looked at each other, and then I steeled
myself as we let ourselves into her rooms.

They were large, also done in a Southwest style like
the suite Jace and I shared, with a kiva-style fireplace
and tile floors and shades of tan and terra-cotta and
turquoise blue. A fire was crackling in the hearth.

Lindsay sat at the table by the window. A notebook, its pages covered in the same sort of cryptic symbols and diagrams that I'd seen on Miles Odekirk's laptop, was open on the tabletop in front of her. She didn't seem to be looking at it right then, though; a pen lay across the right-hand page, and instead she was staring out the window at the fluffy white clouds racing across the blue sky, driven by a wind that meant we could have some weather again tonight.

She might have spent most of the night crying—her eyes looked puffy, the lids reddened—but otherwise she seemed composed enough. Certainly she wasn't crying now.

"You can sit down on the bed," she said, again in that almost too-calm voice. "There aren't enough chairs."

Jace and I complied. At least the bed was made, so sitting there didn't feel too intrusive.

"How—how are you doing, Lindsay?" I asked, since I could tell Jace was waiting for me to speak.

A shrug. The afternoon light cast a halo around her hair, and she continued to stare out the window without turning toward the two of us. "I'm okay. I keep telling everyone that. It's—I told him it was stupid. I told him not to go, but he did anyway. He was like that, you know. Always wanting his own way. We butted heads a lot, but I still loved him." She hesitated then, and I could see the way the muscles in her jaw tightened, as if she was fighting back tears. "That is, I *think* I loved him. I'd never been in love with anyone before, except a couple of stupid high school crushes that didn't really count. I didn't have time for that sort of thing. So... now he's gone, and I'm trying to remember what it felt like to be with him, and...I can't."

I wished I knew her well enough to go to her and put my arms around her, give her a hug. Unfortunately, Lindsay had never really been the type for physical displays of affection. Every time I'd seen her with Rafi, they hadn't been touching. It wasn't as if any of the djinn seemed all that inclined toward physical displays of affection, but I'd still seen them holding hands from time to time, leaning in for a kiss when they thought no one was watching.

"It's all right, Lindsay," Jace said soothingly. "You're probably still trying to work through what happened."

"That's what everyone says." With an impatient gesture, she flung back her hair and then got up, walking over to the hearth so she could spread out her hands and feel the fire's warmth. "And I think I miss him, but we'd spent so much time apart lately that I can't even tell that for sure." At last she turned around and faced us, her back to the fireplace. "But anyway, I'm not going to be a total mess. I'm not like Evony."

"What's that supposed to mean?" I asked, realizing after the words left my mouth that they'd come out a bit sharper than I'd intended.

"Oh, come on, Jessica. You saw the way Evony acted after she lost Natila. She totally lost it. I mean, it's all right to grieve, but she went sort of overboard. It wasn't as if she and Natila were this couple who'd been together for years and years and had never known anything else. They'd only been with each other for a few months."

I didn't exactly bite my tongue, but I reminded myself that Lindsay had just suffered a huge loss and probably wasn't thinking clearly. To my utter relief, Jace stepped into the awkward silence that followed Lindsay's last pronouncement.

"Everyone grieves in their own way," he said, and although his tone was gentle enough, there was an underlying note of steel in it that said he'd prefer if Lindsay didn't make any more disparaging remarks about Evony.

Since Lindsay was a smart girl, she got it. I saw her swallow, and then she said, sounding chastened, "Sorry. I didn't—I guess I'm sort of angry with myself. It's as if I keep thinking I should be screaming and crying and wearing sackcloth or whatever, but I'm just...numb."

"You should be doing what works best for you," I told her, my anger ebbing as quickly as it had come.

"No one should tell you the right way to grieve…not even yourself."

She nodded, and for the first time I saw the glitter of tears in her eyes. They didn't fall, though.

"Um…Miles sends his condolences," I offered. It was an utter lie, but she didn't need to know that."

Surprisingly, her mouth quirked a little. "He does? And I suppose in his next breath he was asking when I'd be back to work?"

That hit a little too close to the mark. "Well…."

The faint twitch of her lips turned into a full-blown smile. "It's all right. I'd be worried if he hadn't. And you know—I want to. Just sitting around here in my room isn't going to change anything. If I'm working in the lab, at least I'm doing something."

"I'm not sure if you should rush into that," Jace began, but she held up a hand.

"I'm not rushing into anything. But I think it'll feel good, getting back to work. And I plan to, after the farewell tomorrow. So you can tell Miles that if you see him."

I opened my mouth to tell her that the only guarantee of my seeing Miles was if I went directly to the lab, since he never ventured out on his own, but then I stopped myself and just said, "Sure. I'm sure he'll be happy to hear that."

"I don't know if Miles is ever 'happy' about anything, but the news might make him slightly less cranky."

It had to have been tough, working next to him day after day when he was more or less in a perpetual state of annoyance. But then I remembered the way his voice had broken when he spoke of Natila. I doubted Lindsay had ever seen any such signs of doubt or guilt in him. She probably would have had far different opinion of Miles Odekirk if she had.

That had been a private scene, one I wasn't sure I would share even with Jace. I did know it would color all my future dealings with Miles, since I'd seen a side of him I doubted many people had.

"Well, here's hoping," I said.

Lindsay shook her head. "I wouldn't hold my breath. But I don't think I'd even mind his crankiness. At least I wouldn't get this feeling that I was walking on eggshells around him." I watched as she paused for a moment, clearly trying to work out the best way to phrase the words she had rolling around in her mind. "And—thanks for coming by. Really. I appreciate it. But I think I need to be alone for a while. Everyone's been coming over, and I know they're trying to be kind, but...."

"But your thoughts need space to breathe," Jace said, and her reddened eyes brightened a little.

"Yes, that. Exactly that. Thank you, Jace."

He rose from the bed, and I followed a second later. "If you need anything—" I began.

"I'll let you know," she broke in. "Thank you again. And if you see anyone heading down the hallway in this direction, could you please head them off at the pass for me?"

"Consider it done," Jace said.

She offered us another smile, and we let ourselves out. By then it was almost five. Time for Dutchie's walk. I was glad of that, because it would give Jace and me the chance to get out of the resort, breathe some fresh air.

We had it down to a ritual by then, so we were able to go back to the suite and get the dog saddled up—so to speak—while remaining in our own thoughts. I had to wonder what Jace thought about Lindsay's reaction to Rafi's death. Would he consider it disrespectful that she wasn't openly mourning? I didn't think so, but....

"Sometimes the strongest people suffer the worst," he told me as we walked down Kit Carson Boulevard, Dutchie at the farthest end of her retractable leash while she sniffed happily at the sidewalk. What she was smelling, I wasn't sure, as I hadn't seen any sign of other dogs since coming here. Back when all this started, Jace had reassured me about all the ownerless pets, saying the animals would be taken care of, but what did that mean, exactly?

Just another question I'd have to ask when the world wasn't constantly shifting around me.

I shot him an inquiring look, and he went on,

"Lindsay is a tough girl. I've seen that in her. But now she feels she can't open herself up to any weakness."

"Grieving isn't weakness."

"You know that. I know that as well, but what we don't know is what might have happened in Lindsay's past that's informing her reactions now. All we can do is be there for her when she needs us."

"*If* she needs us," I pointed out in gloomy tones, tightening my grip on the leash when Dutchie spied a large crow sitting on a fence post and began to charge.

"She will." At another time, he might have taken the leash from me, since the dog was clearly feeling her oats on this brisk March afternoon, but with his strength sapped the way it was, he knew I could probably handle Dutchie better. He added, watching as I hauled the dog back to a more manageable distance, "Or, at the very least, she'll need someone."

I nodded. At the same time, I couldn't help wondering who that "someone" might be.

We went to fetch Julia at a little before seven. For some reason, I was feeling almost nervous, which I tried to tell myself was silly. I understood trying to distract myself and everything, but surely I had better things to do with my time and mental energy than create attractions where there were none.

When she came out to meet us, though, I felt my eyes widen. Yes, I'd brushed my hair, put on some lip gloss, changed into a nicer sweater, but I'd never done much more than that in the past to prepare for dinner. If I'd sent the primping into overdrive this evening, Jace might have asked what prompted the extra attention. "Because we're on a double date" didn't seem like a very good answer.

But Julia was wearing a long flowy skirt and a snug-fitting knit top, with some expensive-looking turquoise jewelry at her throat and on her wrists. Her warm honey-colored hair flowed over her shoulders, and although she wasn't wearing any makeup besides mascara and gloss, she still looked polished in a way I wasn't sure I ever had.

"Wow," I said.

She brushed a hand over her skirt. "I hope it isn't too much. Lauren came by this afternoon and asked me if I wanted to go down to the plaza with her so I could pick out a few more things. It was...fun."

Well, I wouldn't argue with that. Julia Innes was definitely a person who needed some more fun in her life. And if a few hours of going through the boutiques in downtown Taos and choosing things she probably wouldn't have been able to afford in her old life was how she needed to get her fun, then bless her. And bless Lauren for thinking of it. I was a little surprised that Zahrias had let her go this afternoon.

Or maybe the whole thing had been Zahrias' idea....

"No, it's perfect," I said hastily. "A lot of the djinn women have pretty fancy clothes, so I wouldn't say it's too much."

"You look lovely, Julia," Jace put in. A wicked glint entered his eyes, and he added, "Perhaps you could give Jessica a few hints. I don't think I've seen her in a skirt since Thanksgiving."

Which was only the truth. I teased, "Gee, honey, I'm sorry I wasn't wearing a pencil skirt and four-inch stilettos when I went out to milk the goats."

He laughed then and planted a kiss on my cheek. "My darling, you are perfect no matter what you wear. But now we should go, or we'll be late."

"Can't have that," I said lightly, but it was true enough. I didn't want Zahrias to think we were running late because of something Julia had done.

Even so, he was already there when we got to the dining area. Because he was Zahrias, he'd taken one of the choice tables, the ones half-hidden by the trees growing in planters off to one side, giving the diners sitting there much more privacy.

He stood when we approached. "It's very good to see you...Julia."

From the way he'd tacked her first name on there at the end, I guessed that he'd almost slipped and called her "Ms. Innes." She appeared not to notice, however, and smiled before saying, "This is a lovely dining area."

"Well, if you have to hole up somewhere to ride out the apocalypse, best to choose a five-star resort," I remarked as Jace pulled out a chair for me so I could sit down. I decided not to comment on the way Zahrias had barely greeted the two of us, his attention clearly on Julia instead.

Even though I'd thought I was being circumspect, Zahrias' expression turned almost sour at my comment. Apparently noting how Jace had helped me into my seat, the djinn leader began to do the same for Julia. Almost at once she demurred, saying,

"Thank you, Zahrias, but I know what Miles's device does to a djinn's strength. Please, sit down."

He didn't protest, but instead said smoothly, "If you wish. I will confess that it's something of a relief not to have to explain my...condition...to you."

She didn't seem to know how to respond to that, so she offered Zahrias a hesitant smile before seating herself. Jace and I busied ourselves getting settled, and while I was putting my napkin on my lap, Zahrias picked up the open bottle of wine from the table and poured some into Julia's glass. It was a red; I hoped she wouldn't mind that, since I'd only seen her drink white wine back in Los Alamos.

But she thanked him, and he handed the bottle to Jace so he could pour wine for himself and me. After that, we seemed to be more or less set. I wondered, as Zahrias picked up his own glass, whether he would offer some kind of toast, and what it would be. Apparently he'd decided that wouldn't be appropriate, for whatever reason, so after a brief nod, he took a sip of wine, with the rest of us immediately following suit.

"Although this used to be a restaurant, it no longer truly functions like one," he told Julia, who seemed to be enjoying the red wine just fine. Or maybe it was the company that had brought the faint curve to her lips. "We are lucky enough that one of our Chosen used to be a chef, so he creates a fixed meal each evening. Tonight it is a dish he called barbacoa."

I felt a little pang when I heard what we were eating, then reassured myself that at least our own goats were safe in Los Alamos. Where Phillip, our resident chef, had gotten his hands on the ones that had become our dinner, I didn't know. But it was surprising what you could scrounge within the half-mile radius allowed by the device's field of effect.

"Sounds wonderful," Julia said. Her eyes seemed to scan the former restaurant, taking in the Chosen and their djinn. Except for a few cases, they mostly sat together as couples. I did notice Lindsay sitting with Dani and Lauren, and a little stir of relief went through me. It seemed like a bit of progress for Lindsay to be out and about, and I was impressed that Lauren had coaxed her into it. Or maybe that had been Dani's doing. In his own way, he was just as persuasive as she was. "You seem to have a smooth-running setup here."

A shadow passed over Zahrias' face. He was probably thinking it had been a lot smoother before some of his own kind went rogue and we had to use Miles's device to protect ourselves. However, he only said, "We do what we can. And of course our community is much smaller than the one at Los Alamos. How many do you have there now?"

If I hadn't known better, I would have thought he was merely making polite dinner conversation. Jace and I had made our own reports after we returned to Taos, but of course Julia had access to far more detailed information than we did.

And of course she was far from stupid. She knew what he was asking. A brief hesitation, as if weighing her possible responses, and then she said calmly, "It was just over a thousand at our last census. I doubt it has grown any since then, with the way your people are hunting down the few survivors who are left."

Zahrias' brows drew together, but his voice was level enough as he replied, "I have no control over their actions, Ms. Innes."

I doubted he had used that form of address by accident, and I shifted in my seat, wondering how she was going to react.

Her expression didn't change, however. "I know you don't," she said. But even as she spoke, her words sounded tinged with disappointment, as if she'd half-way hoped he would have been able to do something to prevent the djinn from carrying out their own final solution.

I wished it were that easy. If Zahrias had been in charge of all the djinn, then things would have turned out very differently. Unfortunately, he held the same minority opinion as the rest of his people here in Taos. And now, without access to his powers...I supposed I should just be glad that most of the djinn in his community saw no reason to rebel against his decrees.

Beside me, Jace stirred. "Julia, every day we think of that tragedy, and hate that we can't do anything to prevent it. But we have to think of our own survival now."

She nodded, then sipped at her wine. "Yes, those other djinn have broken their pact, haven't they? That is, it sounded to me, from what I heard, that the Chosen were supposed to be left alone."

"They were," Jace said. He drank as well, although I could tell he didn't expect the wine to banish any of his memories of the djinn who had attacked us on the road back to Taos, who had killed Evony and Ethan. "And we still know nothing of our Chosen who volunteered to go to Los Alamos to see why it was suddenly blocked from our vision."

"They never got there," she told him. Her gaze flicked to Zahrias, who had been listening to them, brows knitted in a frown. He looked quite fearsome when he did that, but she didn't seem to notice. "I'm sure I would have heard of it if Margolis had captured any human survivors. That was"—she stopped then, and I thought I saw a brief shiver go through her— "that was back when he still trusted me. I would have known."

I glanced upward, although it wasn't the ceiling of wood beams and skylights I was really looking at. "It had to have been *them*."

"We don't know that for sure," Jace began, but Zahrias interrupted,

"No, we don't know, but I think it is the most likely possibility. And after what happened to Clay and Martine and Aidan...." He let the words die away. Most likely he didn't see any need to go into detail. The memories were horrific enough.

But Julia didn't have those memories. Head tilting to one side, she began, "Clay and Martine—"

"And Aidan," I finished for her. My eyes roved the crowd until I spotted Lilias and her consort, barely visible through the ficus trees that shielded us from the main part of the dining room. "Over there, to the left. The dark-haired djinn woman and the man with the scars on his face."

Julia followed my gaze. I saw her eyes widen and guessed that she'd just spotted Aidan, had noted the wounds that would forever disfigure him. "They—the rogue djinn—did that?"

"And killed Clay, and took Martine," Zahrias said. Right then he sounded very tired. Up to this point, he'd done a very good job of concealing the exhaustion that must haunt his every waking moment, but maybe having to revisit the horror of what had happened to three of his people had done its work in sapping his energy. "They were not here when the djinn attacked and Jessica triggered the device, so they were unprotected. You see what that bought them."

"My God."

At that inopportune moment, Phillip stepped out into the dining room to announce that the food was ready.

"We eat buffet-style here," I explained. "Phillip has a few helpers in the kitchen, but no one really wants to wait tables all night. It's easier this way."

She nodded, even as her gaze drifted to Zahrias. "Would you—would you like me to get a plate for you? I know that exertion can be...difficult."

A long pause, as he watched her carefully. I didn't know about Jace, but I was almost holding my breath.

But then Zahrias nodded, saying, "That would be most gracious of you."

Jace and I looked at each other. Although I'd learned that it was considered somewhat rude for a djinn and his Chosen—or two djinn who were currently bonded—to engage in mental conversation in front of company, I couldn't help myself.

Jace, are you thinking what I'm thinking?

Beloved, I am thinking that whatever you're thinking is entirely premature.

I flashed a grin at him, then stood up. "Come on, Julia. Let's get the menfolk some vittles."

And then we both began to laugh as Jace and Zahrias exchanged a look of utter puzzlement.

The next day was the farewell for Rafi. Since the ground had thawed slightly, we were able to bury him, earth elemental that he was, in a cemetery that luckily was located within the safe zone. Although we'd all shared a remarkably relaxed dinner the night before, this morning Zahrias seemed to take little notice of Julia as she stood with Jace and me. Then again, he was having to say farewell to a member of his community, one of his own.

He'd positioned himself next to Lindsay, and Lauren and Dani were on her other side. Standing a little ways off from the crowd was Miles Odekirk. The bright sun glinted off his glasses, so it was hard to read his expression. Had he come merely because he'd thought it was expected? Or had he thought he might be able to get a read from Lindsay as to when she'd be ready to go back to work?

As it turned out, that was sooner than anyone had expected. The morning after Rafi's farewell, she headed straight to the lab. I wouldn't have even known for a while, except that Julia had been there talking to Miles when Lindsay showed up.

"She went right up to Miles and said, 'I'm ready,'" Julia told me over lunch. The "menfolk" were having some sort of convo with Phillip, and so I'd been left to my own devices. We'd taken our food back to my suite, since neither of us really felt like eating in the main dining room.

"And what did he do?"

A grimace. "It's Miles. What do you think he did?"

Not knowing Miles as well as Julia did, I could only shrug.

"He barely looked up from his laptop. Then he told her, 'Good. I have some calculations I want you to run through the simulator.'" She shook her head and picked up her sandwich. "Which could be Miles's equivalent of a bear hug. But I think he seemed marginally glad to see her."

I couldn't help chuckling a little. "Well, here's hoping his utter emotional cluelessness is exactly what she needs to get through all this."

Julia was laughing as well, reaching for her iced tea, when an unearthly hooting sound began to fill the building. She paused, frowning. "What's that? The fire alarm?"

It took me a moment, just because I'd only heard that sound once before. Miles had set it up only a few days after he came to Taos, saying that we needed some kind of warning system, just in case.

Warning system....

"Oh, my God."

Julia stared at me. "What is it? Jessica!"

It was hard to form the words. I could actually feel the ice of fear working its way along my veins, seeming to prevent me from replying. But I made myself force the words out, even though saying them aloud seemed only to make the fear that much more real.

"It's the alarm for Miles's device," I told her, and watched as comprehension began to grow in Julia's big blue-gray eyes.

"It's failed. It's not protecting us anymore."

CHAPTER FOURTEEN

I HEARD RUNNING FEET IN THE HALLWAY OUTSIDE, and then Jace burst into the suite. "Jessica—"

"I know," I told him. "What are we going to do?"

"Protect ourselves," he said. His gaze flicked to Julia and then back to me. "At least all of us djinn are now in possession of our powers, so we are not completely helpless."

"But they take time to come back all the way!"

His mouth tightened. I could tell he didn't care to be reminded of that fact. "Still, it is better than nothing. And our Chosen are also arming themselves."

"With what?" Julia asked, voice jangling with fear. "Guns? What good is that going to do against djinn?"

"More than you'd think," I replied. "I saw it myself when our caravan was attacked on the way back from

Los Alamos. Bullets can't kill them, but they do slow them down. And if they're hit enough times, they have to blink out of here to go back where they came from and heal."

"Precisely," Jace said. "Zahrias wants us all together in the dining hall. We'll make our stand there."

I nodded. My own pistol was sitting on the top shelf of the closet, so I went to retrieve it, along with as much spare ammo as I could shove in my pockets.

"I don't know how to shoot," Julia said in a small voice that didn't sound like hers.

Jace managed a smile. "That's all right. Plenty of other people here do. You'll be protected."

She didn't look precisely encouraged. However, all she did was nod. I called to Dutchie—maybe she would have been safer staying in the suite, but no way was I leaving her behind—and we all hurried out into the corridor and into the dining area where the rest of the Taos contingent was congregating.

As we joined the group, I kept shooting wary glances up at the ceiling, wondering if the djinn were going to attack by breaking through the skylights like something out of a superhero movie. Everything seemed intact so far, though.

I wasn't the only one doing that, either—I saw other Chosen darting those same suspicious looks upward, even as they clutched the rifles and shotguns and pistols they'd brought with them. And the djinn—well, they looked worried, but also more robust than I'd seen them in weeks, color returned to cheeks, flames dancing around the fire elementals among them, an unseen wind fluttering the hair of the air elementals.

And Zahrias, face dark with anger as Miles and a white-faced Lindsay hurried into the restaurant area. They were still at least ten feet away when he thundered, "What foolishness is this?"

Lindsay flinched, and Miles reached up to push his glasses farther back on his nose. Without blinking, he said, "I told you from the beginning that this work was a calculated risk. We took all the necessary precautions, but there was always a chance that once we began to modify the field projected by the device, it could fail."

"It was my fault," Lindsay blurted. Even from where I stood, I could see the way her slender form was shaking in terror, although I couldn't be sure whether her trembling was caused by the prospect of an incipient djinn attack or having to face down a furious Zahrias. "I thought Miles asked me to make a correction of .05, but it was actually .005. And...the machine just blinked and turned off."

"Lindsay," Miles broke in, his tone remarkably even, considering the circumstances, "I am the lead on our team. It was my responsibility to check your work."

Zahrias didn't appear all that impressed by Miles's improbable grace under pressure. "How very noble of

you, Dr. Odekirk. But now that the device is broken...
how soon can you fix it?"

The scientist faltered a bit then. It probably didn't
help that Zahrias was such a formidable specimen
compared to him, especially now that the djinn leader's powers had returned and he wasn't slumping over
a cane. "Difficult to say. An entire assembly has been
shorted out, and I don't have an adequate replacement."

"Do what you must," Zahrias rasped. "But fix
it. Your life depends on it just as much as the lives of
everyone around you."

A hurried nod, and then Miles murmured a few
words in an undertone to Lindsay. It must have been
something along the lines of "let's get back to the lab,"
because she nodded, and immediately afterward, they
hurried out of the room.

I could hear the angry murmurs following them,
but no one attempted any pursuit. Instead, everyone's
attention was fixed on Zahrias, waiting for him to give
the directions that would save them all from destruction at the hands of the rogue djinn.

For a few seconds, he said nothing, only watched
the waiting crowd. At my side, Jace was tense, but silent.
Dutchie seemed to pick up something of the mood,
since she pressed herself again my leg and looked up at
me with her mismatched eyes, as if asking me what the
problem was.

You'll be all right, I thought then. *The djinn have always left the animals alone. As for the rest of us....*

I shivered, and Jace reached out to take my hand. On my other side, Julia appeared still, but I felt rather than saw the tremor that went through her. I could tell she was just as scared shitless as I was.

Zahrias spoke. "While it is true that our primary means of defense is currently disabled, that does not mean we are completely defenseless. We have our powers, and we have the guns of our Chosen. If those djinn who have decided to defy the covenant all our people agreed upon come to attack us now, we will be ready."

Murmurs of assent, and I saw people nodding, djinn eyes glittering. And hands tightening on the guns they held. These people were ready to fight.

And was I? My heart pounded in my chest and my stomach tightened with fear, but somehow, with Jace beside me, I couldn't help thinking we would make it out of this somehow, even when the odds were so stacked against us.

Then an enormous pressure crushed against my ears, as if I'd suddenly climbed a thousand feet in altitude in a single second, and a roaring sound reverberated against my aching eardrums. All the glass in the bar, which was located directly behind the restaurant itself, shattered like a spray of ice, including the mirror behind the bar itself. I threw up my hands to protect my face, although I should have been far enough away from the wreckage that none of the debris could hit me.

Despite that precaution, I felt little slivers of broken glass peppering my hands and showering down around me. Dutchie whined, and I immediately bent to brush away with my free hand any glass that had landed on her.

When I straightened up, I saw what had caused the destruction. A group of at least forty djinn stood in what used to be the bar. Smoke curled away from them, although I couldn't see anything actually on fire. And in front of them was the black-haired, cruel-faced djinn who had led the group that attacked our caravan, and killed Evony and Ethan.

Khalim.

Through all of this, Jace had retained an iron grip on my right hand. That grip only tightened now, and I immediately saw the reason why. To Khalim's left, and only a foot or so behind him, was Aldair. His blue eyes blazed through the smoke, an angry, burning glare that settled on me.

Although my every instinct was to look away, I forced myself to stay where I was, to return that stare as if it mattered nothing to me.

Jace caught it, too, and I felt him shift next to me, as if he intended to move toward his old adversary. Now it was my turn to tighten my grip on his fingers.

No, beloved, I told him. *Wait to see what Zahrias does.*

A very faint nod. Behind me and off to one side, I heard the unmistakable sound of someone taking the safety off their pistol. I didn't dare turn to see who it was. All I could do was hope they wouldn't shoot first. We didn't need a reenactment of Fort Sumter here.

Zahrias had turned as well. I stood close enough to him that I could see a muscle twitch in his cheek, although otherwise his face was deadly still.

"You have no business here, oath-breakers."

An ironic lift of Khalim's brows. "Indeed? I would say our business is everywhere, since we djinn now have dominion over this world."

"Not among us," Zahrias replied. I wondered how he managed to keep his voice so calm, so steady. I knew I would have been shaking like an aspen leaf in a gale. "It was agreed that this community—and others like it around the world—would be kept safe. What, have you so tired of hunting Immune that you must come here to molest us?"

These last words were delivered with an almost condescending flip at the end, as if the djinn leader didn't consider Khalim and his group of thugs to be much of a threat. I noticed there wasn't a female djinn among them. Were their women less warlike than the men, or had they simply declined to join this particular raiding party?

"Not at all," Khalim said. The flames around him wavered for a few seconds, then burned higher, licking almost to his waist. If he'd been a mortal man, he would have been screaming in agony by now. Or were the flames even real? Were they simply a form of supernatural theater? I'd never gotten quite close enough to Zahrias to find out. "It is more that you have taken up residence in a region we have decided to claim for our own. All we are doing is...cleansing...the area."

I darted a quick glance up at Jace, puzzled by Khalim's words. This was the first real confirmation I'd heard of the other djinn coming here to colonize the now mostly empty planet, although Jace had spoken as if it would happen eventually. After all, wasn't that the whole point of the Heat, to depopulate the world so it would finally be theirs? But Jace was frowning, attention fixed, not on Khalim, but on Aldair, whose sharp blue gaze seemed to pierce through the crowd.

"The world is wide," Zahrias said. "You have no need of this tiny corner of it."

"Ah, but we have taken a fancy to this place." Khalim waved a hand, as if to indicate the resort around us. "Not quite the palace I am used to, but it should suit my people very well."

For a few seconds, Zahrias was silent, appearing to consider Khalim's statement. If Taos was really all they wanted, then I had to think it would be far easier for us to simply pick up and go someplace else, like back to

Santa Fe. Surely there were enough empty hotels and condos and casitas there to accommodate everyone. And with the threat of the rogue djinn removed from the equation, we wouldn't even have to worry about whether Miles fixed his device or not.

"That is all you want?" Zahrias asked then. It seemed as if his thoughts had run along more or less the same lines as mine, because I could see just the tiniest lessening of the tension in his jaw, although otherwise he hadn't moved.

"Not precisely."

Well, that couldn't be good. Jace's fingers were clamping down on mine so tightly that in other circumstances I would have made some sound of protest. Now, though, I just gritted my teeth and endured the discomfort.

Aldair stepped forward then. "I would take the woman Jessica Monroe as well."

The crushing pressure on my fingers suddenly released as Jace's hands knotted into fists and he took several steps forward. "Never."

Lips pulling into a sneer, Aldair replied, "How like you, Jasreel, to put your own needs before those of everyone else around you. Would it not be far more noble to sacrifice one mortal woman rather than risk the lives of the others in this community, human and djinn alike?"

"We are not slavers, to traffic in human flesh," Zahrias rasped, and Jace subsided somewhat, although he remained in his current position, one clearly intended as a barrier if Aldair should decide to move toward us. Through all of this, Zahrias hadn't spared one glance at me, but instead held his gaze fixed on Khalim. There were some murmurs in the watching crowd, although I couldn't say whether they were in protest at Aldair's outrageous suggestions…or possibly agreeing with him.

"Indeed?" Khalim replied. "What is this woman's importance, that you would put her ahead of all others? For let me tell you, Zahrias al-Harith, our offer is a generous one. Your people would be safe. Only leave, and go south, and leave the woman to Aldair."

Zahrias' next question surprised me. "Why this place? For I would think there is far more in some of the other settlements left behind—Santa Fe, Albuquerque—that might be of use to you."

"No." The flat delivery of that one syllable left no room for doubt. "We want this place. There is power here—power in the river gorge to the north and west, power in the mountain lakes. We have already had a taste of it, and we want more."

That didn't sound good. I had no idea what sort of power Khalim was talking about, but giving someone like that access to anything that might increase his

ability to dominate the area had to be an extraordi-
narily bad idea.

Once again, it seemed as if Zahrias and I were of the
same mind. His brows drew together, and the flames
flickering near him turned a dark, dark orange, angry,
brooding. From the way he was looking at Khalim
and the djinn clustered around him, I got the impression that he was measuring their strength, calculating
whether we had a chance at all. In numbers, we were
roughly even, but half our contingent was human, and
not all of them carried guns. And I'd seen how many
blasts it had taken to drive back even a few djinn. Now
we faced forty.

At last he said, his tone heavy, "We will give you
this place, if that is your will. But Aldair must with-
draw his claim on Jessica Monroe."

"You are in no position to bargain, Zahrias," Aldair
said, stepping forward.

With one lifted hand, Khalim held him back.
"Peace, Aldair." His dark gaze flickered back toward
Zahrias. "It is such a small thing to be fighting over.
One mortal woman. What does her life matter, against
the lives of all those in your charge?"

A heavy silence fell. I could almost feel everyone
staring at me, although I knew that wasn't the case. Not
really. At least as many of them—mostly Chosen—
were glaring at the two djinn who were making such

insane demands. And beside me, Julia stood stock still, her expression aghast.

I should have been reassured that Zahrias seemed prepared to make a stand on my behalf. But I wasn't, because I could feel the tension ratcheting up in the space, see the way people's hands were tightening on their guns. It would take so very little to set them off, and what might happen then?

People would die.

I'd seen enough death.

My heart was hammering so hard in my chest that I wondered how everyone around me couldn't hear it. The scene looked like a still from a movie...or maybe that was only how I perceived it. Time slowing down to this one moment, this one instant where I knew I had the power to fix this, if I could only summon the courage.

Jace was in profile to me. How beautiful he was, every sculpted line of his jaw and nose and mouth, the spill of night-black hair over his shoulders. I wanted to go to him and hold him, tell him how much I loved him. But of course if I did that, he'd know what I intended to do next, and he would try to stop me.

Of course he would, because he loved me.

Maybe one day he would forgive me. I had to do this, though. Zahrias had said he didn't barter in human flesh, and I admired him for that, admired him for the way he stood up for me, when he could have easily brushed me aside, a mortal woman of no real importance. In that moment, I loved him, too. Not the way I loved Jace—I could never love anyone the way I loved Jace—but as the older brother I'd never had and secretly wished for, someone who could be counted on to do the right thing and be the person I could look up to.

Throat tight, I bent down and patted Dutchie on the head. Then I whispered to Julia, "Look after Dutchie for me."

"Look...." she began, and then let the words trail off as she seemed to realize what I was up to. "Jessica, no!"

But I'd already begun to stride forward, pushing past Jace as quickly as I could so he couldn't reach out to stop me. Despite that, he was moving, too, only a pace or so behind and gaining fast. It would be so easy to slow down, to let him catch me by the arm, keep me from pursuing my insane plan.

No. I wouldn't do that. This was horrible, the hardest thing I'd ever done, but I wouldn't allow anyone else to die. Not when I could do something to prevent it.

I burst through the crowd and stopped a few feet away from where Khalim and Aldair stood in the destruction that once been the El Monte Sagrado's bar. "I will go with you, Aldair," I said loudly. "If you swear that you will leave all of Zahrias' people alone."

Aldair's blue eyes flashed in triumph. At the same time, Jace came up beside me and spun me around to face him. "Jessica, you cannot do this! You don't know what you're promising!"

There would be no pleading with him, I knew. In that moment, he truly thought I was more important than all of the Taos community. If our situations had been reversed, maybe I would have felt the same way. But this was my choice, my decision.

No more blood on my hands.

Zahrias was surging through the crowd as well, which parted to let him pass. A veritable halo of flames surrounded him as he stopped on my other side.

So they aren't real flames, I thought then, incongruously. *They only look like it...or maybe they are real, but he does something so they can't hurt you.*

Distracting myself again.

He said, his voice barely above a murmur, "Jessica, are you sure?"

I nodded. The choking sensation in my throat was so overwhelming that I knew I wouldn't be able to force any words past it.

A brief hesitation, while Khalim looked at us with a strange combination of amusement and triumph. And Aldair—I saw triumph in his expression as well, but also impatience, as if he intended to interrupt us if we took too long with our business.

Zahrias released a breath slowly. "Very well. I will have him swear an oath that no harm will come to any of us if you accept their bargain and go with Aldair."

"An oath?" Jace demanded, not bothering to lower his voice. "I think Khalim and Aldair and their followers have shown all too well that they care nothing for oaths, and will break any promises made whenever it suits them."

I thought for sure that remark would anger Khalim, but he only flashed us a lazy smile and said, "I will gladly swear any oath you require, Zahrias. This one should be easy enough to keep. If only we had been allowed to select our own place in this world before you and your Chosen took it for yourselves, all this unpleasantness might have been avoided."

Unpleasantness? I raged at the way this man—this creature—had disfigured Aidan, killed Clay. And what had happened to Martine?

Most likely, that oldie but goodie, a "fate worse than death," which was probably going to be my fate as well. My stomach churned, and I swallowed the bile that began to burn at the back of my throat. If I was going to sacrifice myself, then I'd do it with some dignity, damn it.

Jace said, desperation clear in every plane and angle of his face, every note in his voice, "Jessica, I beg you. There must be some other solution. You can't do this."

"Can you think of one?" I asked, gaze flicking toward the djinn who stood behind Khalim, all of them big and beefy and probably possessed of some very nasty talents, and then toward the watching crowd of our own djinn and their Chosen. "We'd never win in a fight. You know that. They'd do their best, and I'm not saying they wouldn't succeed in hurting a few of the other djinn, but in the end, they couldn't win. And how many of them would die, Jace? I'm not willing to take that on myself. I won't. Not when I can stop it."

He shook his head. At the same time, Zahrias turned toward Khalim. "She is determined." A baleful glance in Aldair's direction. "And you most certainly do not deserve her. But we'll leave that aside for now."

As he drew himself up, I realized that Zahrias was an inch or so taller than Khalim...a discrepancy I didn't think was lost on the leader of the rogue djinn, who scowled.

Grim-faced, Zahrias told him, "For now, you will swear on this earth that God created, and on the ranks of angels who watch over it, and on the stars that shine down upon it, that you will leave the people in my care alone, now and forever, knowing that we have agreed to the terms of your bargain and will leave this town and the countryside around it to you and your followers. And that Jessica Monroe, Chosen of Jasreel al-Ankara, will go with Aldair al-Ankara to be his, fulfilling the final term of our compact. Do you so swear?"

"I swear," Khalim said, and then, as an echo, all the watching djinn behind him murmured "I swear" as well.

I glanced up at Aldair. He was smiling, but oddly, his gaze didn't appear to be directed at me, but rather toward Jace. Still with that hateful smile pulling at his mouth, he said, "I swear."

"It is done." Zahrias turned toward me. "No one will forget your sacrifice."

"Sacrifice?" Aldair repeated, brows lifting. "I am sure that within a day or so, once she has enjoyed my touch, she will have forgotten all about Jasreel."

Jace surged forward then, eyes blazing, but Zahrias caught him by the arm. "No, Jasreel. The oath has been made. She is not yours anymore."

The look of despair that crossed Jace's features in that moment might as well have been a punch to my gut. I felt it there, as if someone had hit me hard enough to knock all the air out of me. Oh, God, what had I done?

Saved them, my mind told me. *It's what you had to do.*

Cold comfort, when weighed against the agony in the face of the man I loved. At last tears began to run down my cheeks. "I'm sorry, Jace. I'm so sorry. I love you. I'll always love you."

All he could do was stand there and stare at me, features contorting, hands clenched into fists at his side.

Apparently ignoring our shared torment, Khalim told Zahrias, "You have two days. After that...."

He didn't complete the sentence. He didn't need to. If all the djinn and their Chosen weren't gone from Taos within the allotted time, then no doubt Khalim would return with his followers to remove them. He would be able to do so with impunity, since at that point Zahrias would have broken the strictures of his own oath.

"We will be gone tomorrow," he said coldly.

Another of those lazy smiles. I'd already begun to hate them. Then Khalim looked out into the crowd, his gaze stopping as he seemed to spot Lilias, an enraged-looking Aidan next to her. "Would you like to come with me, Lilias?" the djinn asked. "For surely by now you have tired of looking at that scarred monster beside you."

Her dark eyes flashed. "I left the only monster I knew long ago."

Khalim's smile faded slightly, and then he shrugged. "As you will. You always were a woman of odd notions." After shifting back toward Aldair, he went on, "We are done here, I think. Claim your prize, and let us be gone."

Before I could move or react, Aldair came forward and took me by the arm, pulling me toward him. At the same time, Jace lunged in my direction. Zahrias caught him just before his hand closed on my wrist.

"No, Jasreel," Zahrias said sadly. "You must let her go."

"I can't!"

Then I was pulled against Aldair's bare chest, his arms encircling me like bands of steel. "Rage all you want, Jasreel," he said. "She is mine now."

It was as if every wind on the planet swirled up and around us, howling in my ears. The last thing I saw was Jace reaching out to me, hand outstretched, negation in every feature.

And then he was gone.

CHAPTER FIFTEEN

It probably would have been better if I could have passed out. Unfortunately, I was awake and aware when we came to rest...someplace. I was also aware that Aldair's arms were still wrapped around me. Shuddering, I pushed myself away, and to my surprise, he actually let me go.

"Welcome home," he said. "Or at least home for the next few days. Then I shall take you back to Taos."

He was practically gloating as he spoke. But at least he wasn't touching me, so that was a start.

"Where are we?" I asked, surveying the space. I didn't know exactly what I'd been expecting—something out of the Arabian Nights, maybe, with a touch of Disney—but this place looked like typical New Mexico architecture, with heavy white stucco walls and a ceiling of dark wood vigas, or beams. A variety of mismatched couches lined the wall, and a close-weave beige carpet covered the floor.

"A place your people called Ghost Ranch," Aldair said. "Its remoteness suited our purposes, but we would prefer something slightly more comfortable for any long-term use."

I'd vaguely heard of the Ghost Ranch; Georgia O'Keeffe used to paint around here, and the facility had been set up for artist retreats and that sort of thing. Just another place my family had talked about visiting but had never actually made it to. If it had been used for retreats and such back before the Dying, then I supposed it would have sufficient space for the rogue djinn contingent to hang out in, so to speak.

Crossing my arms, I remarked, "I'm surprised you bothered with a base of operations here at all. I mean, can't you just pop in and out of this plane of existence without any problem? What's the point of staying here?"

Aldair smiled. I'd thought Richard Margolis had the market cornered on flesh-crawling smiles, but this djinn was doing a pretty good job of making my skin feel like it very much wanted to creep away someplace else, out of sight of his smug face.

"Because your kind can't exist in the djinns' world."

"My kind?"

"Come." He reached out a hand, and I drew back. I couldn't help it. Yes, I'd agreed to come with him, but the very thought of feeling his skin touching mine was enough to make me sick all over again.

Those dagger-sharp eyes seemed to bore into me. "Would you break your oath so soon?"

I swallowed. Obviously, my cooperation was key to the continued survival of my friends and loved ones back in Taos. Footsteps dragging, I went back over to Aldair.

His hand closed around mine. Like all djinn, his flesh was warm, almost uncomfortably so, and I had to force myself not to flinch, to let my fingers rest lightly in his palm. I'd thought maybe he was going to blink us out of the room where we stood, but he only led me out of the building and onto a narrow path that wound its way between a series of cottages. Or at least they looked like cottages. I guessed they were the rooms formerly used by guests at the ranch.

We came to a larger structure, probably some sort of common area. Still holding my hand, Aldair led me inside. The space was clearly a library—or at least used to be, as stacks of books still lined the walls. However, it seemed as if these djinn were using it more as a social space, since I saw several of them standing there, holding heavy blown-glass goblets of wine and talking and laughing.

Among them was Khalim. He had his arm around a slender dark-haired girl—not a djinn—who leaned into him, her head snugged up against his shoulder. As he bent to pick up a wine bottle sitting on a table near him and refill his glass, she turned slightly, and I could finally see her face.

It was Martine Leroux, the girl who'd been stolen from the hunting party.

I stared at her in consternation. It wasn't that I knew her well—we'd maybe exchanged twenty words the whole time I was in Taos before she was taken—but my memory told me that she'd been a strong, out-doorsy type, tough, able to hold her own with the guys despite her porcelain-doll prettiness. Now, though, she only stood there placidly, a vacant smile on her face as Khalim poured her some wine as well. And I didn't think she was drunk. She looked more like she'd been drugged.

"What have you done to her?" I asked in a fierce whisper.

Aldair appeared supremely unconcerned. "My dear, we've done nothing. Doesn't she look happy?"

"She looks like she's high on E or something."

"'E'?" he echoed, one eyebrow arching.

"Drugs."

"I assure you, she has been given no drugs. Unless you would call wine a drug."

Well, no, I normally wouldn't. But there was no denying that Martine did not look like herself.

As I searched for a suitable reply, he went on,

"Khalim claimed her. She is quite happy here, I assure you."

Yeah, like the way someone in a cult is brain-washed into being happy, I thought.

Aldair continued, "Martine is not the only one of your kind with us. See, there are several more. You should all be friends, I think."

I looked toward the far side of the room, where he'd gestured. Standing there were two young women around my age, both beautiful, one with rich chest-nut-brown hair and the other probably Native American, with her shining jet-black tresses and high cheekbones. With the girls were two more djinn, arms draped around their companions.

"Where did they come from?" I asked, ignoring his remark about being friends. None of those girls looked lucid enough to make their own decisions about who they would or wouldn't be friends with.

"They were in the group that went to Los Alamos, attempting to ferret out its secrets," Aldair replied.

Well, that was one suspicion confirmed. But then I recalled how Zahrias had told me that Aldair's Chosen was one of the girls who'd disappeared, and I frowned. "Which one is your Chosen?" I asked, hoping my question would arouse even the tiniest bit of guilt in him.

Unfortunately, he just gave me another of those greasy smiles. "Katelyn? She was never truly my Chosen. I took her so I could still be a part of Zahrias' community, learn more of what they were doing. She is with Qadim now."

The cavalier note in his voice sent a shiver down my spine. He must have been intimate with that girl, maybe even told her that he loved her, and now he spoke of her the way a child might talk about a toy he'd played with once or twice, then discarded. I wished I could do something to help her, but I had no idea if I could even help myself.

Voice hard, I asked, "What happened to the men who were with them?"

A negligent lift of the shoulders. "We had no need of them, so they were disposed of."

"Killed, you mean."

"Semantics. Now, come along."

He didn't quite drag me over to the group that included Khalim and Martine. I supposed I should have been glad that he hadn't immediately taken me to whichever cabin was his and assaulted me right away, but I couldn't help getting the impression that he was dragging all this out so as to torture me a bit more. To tell the truth, I didn't mind. I preferred that the evil moment be postponed for as long as possible.

"Aldair!" Khalim called out as we approached. "So good to see that you're introducing Jessica to our retreat here."

Funny choice of words. I sort of doubted the people who used to run Ghost Ranch would have appreciated the term "retreat" being applied to a group of rampaging djinn and the women they'd decided to ravish.

I resolved to ignore Khalim and instead focused my attention on Martine. She was smiling at me in a sort of watery way, as if she halfway recognized me but couldn't exactly figure out how.

"Hi, Martine," I said.

She nodded, then sent an inquiring glance up at Khalim.

"Martine, this is Jessica. Remember her? From Taos?"

"Oh, hey," she said vaguely. "So you're here now? Cool."

Girl be trippin', I thought. Or something. I wanted to grab her and shake her, see if I could snap her out of her current languid state, which was completely unlike the Martine Leroux I'd known back in Taos. That Martine had fished and gone hunting with the guys. This Martine looked like someone who'd spent her entire high school career on the little knoll that we'd affectionately referred to at my school as "Stoners' Hill."

But I had Aldair standing uncomfortably close to me, and Khalim just on the other side—not to mention a couple of heavies whose names I hadn't yet caught—and I knew if I did anything out of line, I'd be stopped immediately.

And punished.

A shiver went through me, and Aldair said, "Cold? Some wine should warm you up." From nowhere a glass appeared in his hand, and the wine bottle lifted of its own accord to fill the glass halfway.

"Showing off again, I see," remarked one of the other djinn, a burly man with black hair in a ponytail and arms roughly the size of tree trunks.

Aldair sent him a foul look, then gave me the glass.

I had to take it, of course. But was there any way to avoid drinking that wine? Sure, he'd said Martine wasn't drugged. On the other hand, I trusted Aldair not even as much as I could throw him, which wasn't very far.

He must have noticed my hesitation, because he gave me an oily smile, then said, "Nothing to fear, my dear," before lifting the glass to his lips and taking a healthy swallow. Then he handed the wine to me.

With the other djinn looking on, their eyes dancing with cruel amusement, there wasn't much else I could do. I drank as well, as small a sip as I could manage without it being too obvious. It tasted fine, of course. Then again, if they really were drugging their wine, I doubted they'd use anything that could be easily detected.

"Very good," Aldair said, his voice almost a purr. He was enjoying this immensely, I could tell. A veritable cat toying with a mouse.

Well, mice have claws, too, I thought, *even if their claws might not be as big as yours.*

"So, Martine," I said, ignoring Aldair for the moment. "How do you like it here?"

She glanced up at Khalim again, as if for reassurance. When he nodded, she replied, "Oh, it's great. There are horses, and we go riding, and the food's wonderful, and...other things."

Judging by the way Khalim's mouth turned up at that last pronouncement, I had a good idea what she meant by those "other things." My mouth tasted sour, the wine turning to vinegar on my tongue.

Still, I managed to keep my tone bright as I asked, "And you don't miss Samhal?" Samhal, or "Sam," was her partner back in Taos. An earth elemental, he'd taken her disappearance in stoic silence, but you could tell from the way you'd find him staring into space, or not answering right away when spoken to, that he missed her very much.

"Who?" she asked, dark brows drawing together.

Khalim frowned at the same time as well, although probably in irritation, rather than confusion. His black gaze passed over my head and focused on Aldair. "And so you were saying you would be dining alone with Jessica this evening?"

"Yes," Aldair replied immediately. His own expression was fairly annoyed as well, and I knew I'd stepped way over my boundaries.

Not that anyone had actually told me what those were. Anyway, I wouldn't have cared, even if they had informed me of what I was and wasn't allowed to do or say.

He continued, "In fact, I think I'll take her back to my room now. You're famished, aren't you, Jessica?"

Food was pretty much the last thing on my mind. However, the wine was sitting uneasily in my stomach, and it would probably be a good idea to eat something to soak up the alcohol. Assuming the food wasn't drugged as well.

"Um, sure," I said.

That lackluster response appeared to be all he needed. This time he did "blink" us away, to a different place from the room where we'd first appeared. When I opened my eyes, I saw that I was in a smallish chamber, but one far more luxuriously furnished than either of the rooms I'd been in so far at the Ghost Ranch. I could still see the "bones" of the space, the wood-beamed ceilings, the white stucco walls, but carved screens stood in the corners, and silks in various shades of blue and green and purple had been draped across the armchairs and the bed as well.

Looking at the bed probably wasn't a good idea. I turned away from it and toward Aldair, who had just waved his hand, coaxing the glowing coals in the fireplace to more brilliant life. Flames began to lick up along the wood stacked inside, sending the aromatic scent of burning applewood throughout the room.

I'd more or less forced myself not to think about Jace up to that point, since I knew that would destroy my fragile composure more quickly than anything else, but the wood smoke made me think of him, the way his clothes had smelled that first time he'd held me in his arms. Only as a friend back then—and barely that, since we'd only just met—and yet even in that moment, I'd known somehow that he was destined to be much more. What was he doing now? Were Zahrias and Julia doing their best to calm him down? Maybe they were all occupied in gathering their belongings for the move to Santa Fe. Surely it would be easier now that they had their powers back. For all I knew, the djinn would merely blink themselves down to what used to be our state capital and set up house from there. No muss, no fuss.

And would they let Miles go? But then, I doubted he would want to go back to Los Alamos. Not with Margolis in charge.

I wanted to distract myself with thinking about such things because that way I wouldn't have to think about why I was here. Who I was with.

But pretending to inspect the furnishings would only last me for so long. Aldair seemed content to stand there and watch me, which in itself was creepy enough. What would happen when he decided he'd had enough of merely watching?

I turned back toward him. Those blue eyes met mine, and it took a physical effort for me not to look away. He had the upper hand here; we both knew it. That didn't mean I intended to act like a victim.

"Dinner?" he said, still with that half-smile playing around his mouth. A wave of his hand, and the table placed up against the far wall and draped with a dark blue silk cloth was suddenly heaped with food—what looked like a roasted goose, although I'd never had goose before, and bowls of rice and vegetables and a basket of bread. There was also a decanter made of what looked like gold encrusted with lapis and turquoise.

If I'd been sitting down to this meal with Jace, I would have been enchanted. As it was....

"Oh, you didn't have to go to all this trouble just for little old me," I said.

His lips pressed together, and I could see his eyes narrow. Then he said, tone almost too even, "It was no trouble. Sit."

It wasn't a request. Since I didn't want the situation to flare into open confrontation this early in the game, I did as he said and pulled out the chair closer to the fire, then sat down. He followed a few seconds later, taking the chair opposite me.

At first I was glad he'd chosen that seat. Better to have him across the table from me than right by my side. On the other hand, now he was able to stare directly into my face.

"So where did all this come from?" I asked. "Do you djinn have some sort of eternal take-out place where you can just blink in anything you need?"

"No." He picked up the decanter of wine and poured a good deal into the goblet that sat next to my place setting. Like the decanter, that goblet appeared to be gold, with lapis and turquoise inset in the base. I probably could have hocked one of those things and used it to pay for my entire college education. "We imagine what we want, and it simply…manifests itself."

"Handy. So why didn't the djinn back in Taos do the same thing?"

"You would have to ask Zahrias that. He is a great lover of order." A curl of the lip, and Aldair added, "Perhaps he thought the practice too chaotic."

I supposed I could see that. With everyone magicking into existence whatever they wanted at the time, it might have gotten a little crazy. But maybe that was why, at least at the beginning, Zahrias hadn't been too concerned about using up their stores of food. Why would he, when he and the other djinn could quietly zap a few sides of beef into the resort's freezers whenever things were getting low?

As logistically interesting as all that might have been, it didn't do much to solve my current predicament. I picked up my goblet and allowed myself a sip. Maybe it was drugged...and maybe it wasn't. For some reason, I got the impression that Aldair wanted me awake and aware for all this.

The wine was good. Faintly spicy, which made me think it was probably a shiraz. I supposed if you were going to blink in wine from nowhere, you might as well make it a decent vintage.

Aldair drank as well, still watching me. Feeling sort of like a butterfly pinned on a pad, I asked, "Are you going to tell me why now?"

One eyebrow went up. "Why what?"

I doubted he was being deliberately obtuse. No, this was just more of his toying with me. "Why me? I'm no one in particular. There were plenty of girls there in Taos prettier than I am, if all you wanted to do was deprive some djinn of his Chosen."

He didn't answer at once. Instead, he drank some wine, then sat back in his chair, goblet in his hand as he languidly swirled the liquid within. "It's true. I didn't want you because of you. I wanted you because Jasreel wanted you."

Some women might have found such a statement insulting. Since I didn't give a good crap what Aldair thought of me, it was almost a relief to know that he hadn't chased after me because of some insane otherworldly lust. I leaned forward and set down my goblet. "Why do you hate him so much?"

I honestly wanted to know the answer. Jace was one of the warmest, most generous people I'd ever met, human or djinn. What he possibly could have done— real or imagined—to have engendered such animosity in Aldair, I couldn't begin to imagine.

A single blink. Then he said, "You are a direct little thing, aren't you?"

It was my turn to lift an eyebrow. At five foot eight and a bit, I really wasn't used to being referred to as a "little thing." "I don't see the point in beating around the bush. So again...why?"

"He's my brother."

If I'd had a mouth full of wine, I probably would have spat it out. As it was, I still felt as if someone had just kicked me right in the stomach. "Your...*what?*"

"Half-brother, actually." Aldair sat up straighter and then set down his goblet. Tone off-hand, he said, "You should have some of this. It's going to get cold."

He picked up a bone-handled carving knife and two-pronged meat fork, then began working away at the goose. A large chunk of breast meat landed on my plate, and he then put more or less the same amount on the plate in front of him.

Whether he was delaying the conversation on purpose, I didn't know, but I supposed he was right about one thing—this was some beautiful food in front of me, and I really should eat some of it, if for no other reason than to keep up my strength. And while it was quite possible that I shouldn't be feeling overly relieved—for all I knew, Aldair still planned on taking me to bed out of spite if not actual desire—I found I couldn't quite prevent myself from relaxing a little. It didn't seem as if he intended to drag me over to the bed by my hair, which I feared was more or less exactly what had happened with Martine and Khalim.

I ate a few bites of goose, which was rich and strange and delicious, followed by some wonderful rice dish spiced with cinnamon and accented with nuts and golden raisins. Figuring that should satisfy Aldair for the moment, I asked, "Half-brother? Same mother?"

"Hardly." He poured himself more wine. From what I could tell, the djinn had a far greater capacity for alcohol than us weak humans, but even so, I worried what he would be like if he kept drinking at that pace. "Same father."

At the time, I'd been so frightened and distracted that I hadn't been paying much attention, but now I recalled the words of the oath that Zahrias had made Khalim swear. In that oath, he'd called out the names of the interested parties, and Jace and Aldair had seemed to have the same surname. Maybe I'd brushed it off, thinking "al-Ankara" was the djinn equivalent of "Smith" or something.

Aldair continued, his tone so studiously casual that I knew it was anything but, "His mother was a mortal."

Good thing I'd just set down my fork, or I might have dropped it right in my lap. "He's half *human?*"

"Yes." The cruel smile was back, just before he swallowed some more wine. "Ah, it appears he neglected to mention that particular detail to you."

He sure had. All I could do was sit there, mind spinning. And then I remembered that conversation I had overheard in the courtyard, when Rafi and the two other djinn who wanted to make a break for it had confronted Zahrias. When referring to Jace, Rafi had said that he was "not precisely one of us." At the time, the remark had mystified me, and then so many other things had happened immediately afterward that it had completely slipped my mind.

But now I understood. Jace was other because he was half human.

As I stared at Aldair, not sure what to say, he went on, "But that is our Jasreel, isn't it? He withholds information as he deems fit. It seems he even lied to you, his Chosen, the woman he has sworn that he loves above all others. Surely you can see that he isn't quite the paragon you believe him to be."

That remark was enough to spur me to speech. "Not telling someone something isn't the same as lying to them."

"Oh, it isn't?" At last Aldair speared some goose on his fork and ate a hearty mouthful, staring at me the whole time.

I supposed I should be glad he was sending some food down to soak up the wine he'd drunk, but right then I was too flaring with righteous indignation to bother. "No, it's not. I'm sure he would have told me when the time was right. We had very little time together after I learned he was a djinn, because the Los Alamos people came along with their stupid device. And even once he'd been rescued, we had so many things to deal with—"

"You are very good at defending him, Jessica," Aldair cut in. To my dismay, he poured himself yet more wine. So far he wasn't showing any signs of being particularly intoxicated, but, as they say, the night was still young.

"I'm not defending him," I began, then stopped myself. Actually, I was. To me, the reasons why Jace might not have revealed that particular tidbit about his past may have sounded valid enough. Aldair, on the other hand, was a much tougher crowd. At any rate, I didn't see the point in arguing that one particular detail. I wanted to know more of why such animosity existed between the two brothers.

Blue eyes gleamed knowingly, but he didn't speak. It seemed obvious enough that he thought he'd scored a point there.

Maybe he had. I wasn't about to waste my energy on playing games. I wanted the truth, or at least Aldair's version of it.

"So Jace's mother was a mortal," I said. "That still doesn't explain why you're out to get him. What, did your father dump your mother for a human?"

His dark brows drew together. Right then, although otherwise they didn't look at all alike, I thought I could see the faintest hint of a resemblance between Aldair and Jace. Voice hard, Aldair replied, "No. My mother and father had been apart for many years before my father settled his attentions on a mortal woman."

Some trace of surprise must have showed on my face, because he smiled thinly and said,

"We djinn are not like mortals in this respect. Our lives are so long that we know we won't spend the entirety of them with any one partner. My mother and father had their time together, and went their own ways when I was a young man, just into my majority."

So Aldair was the elder of the two. It would have been hard to tell for certain, as apparently once the djinn reached adulthood, their aging processes were so slow as to be nonexistent. Both Jace and Aldair appeared to be in their late twenties, or early thirties at the very most.

"But then my father must have this mortal woman he spied, and he took her and had a child with her. I had very little to do with any of that, as I was an adult and living my own life."

"So what was the problem?" I asked as I picked up a piece of bread and broke off a piece. There was no butter, instead a dish of olive oil for dipping. "I mean, if you were off somewhere else, what difference did it make if your father had a child with a new woman?" I didn't say "wife," since in none of these revelations had Aldair mentioned wives and husbands. Those conventions seemed to be a bit looser in djinn society.

Aldair's face darkened with anger, and once again he picked up his goblet and took a large swallow of wine. Of course I couldn't tell him to slow down. And one would have thought that decanter might be getting low by now, but I had a sinking feeling that it would keep refilling itself at the djinn's whim.

"Our father," he said, the "our" dripping with distaste, "took a fancy to his little half-breed. Bestowed property upon him that should have been mine, showed him favor that I'd never had myself. And why? Merely because the brat took after him, whereas I had always favored my mother."

"Well, that's hardly Jace's fault," I pointed out in a reasonable tone. "Sounds like your beef should be with your father."

At that remark, Aldair shot me a look of such ill-disguised ire that I shifted backward in my seat. Not that putting a little more space between us would do anything to help me in the long run. I was pretty sure that even if I got up and ran out of the cabin right then, he'd blink himself in front of me before I even had a chance to, well, blink.

"He should never have been born," he snarled. "And even when such abominations do happen to be conceived, they should be left to rot here in the mortal world, and die without ever knowing their birthright. But because my father cherished his half-breed son, and made sure that his djinn blood and powers came to the forefront, he lived in our society, and took from me that which should have been mine."

"And so you decided to take something of his from him," I said slowly.

Eyes glittering like shards of sapphire, Aldair nodded.

"Problem is," I continued, "I'm not Jace's. I'm not a piece of property. I'm with him because I love him. I'd love him no matter who or what he was. Because he's *Jace*. So even if you think you've won...you really haven't."

As soon as I'd made the comment, I wished I could take it back. Not because I didn't believe it with all my heart, but because my words only served to enrage Aldair further. Pushing back his chair, he got to his feet, then took two steps to be by my side. Before I could flinch or pull away, he grasped me by the arm and hauled me upright so my face was only mere inches from his.

"'Love'?" he rasped. "You may dress it up however you like, but what you feel is not love, but only a glamour he has placed on you. It is entirely false."

"That's not true!" I shot back. My world might have teetered on its foundations multiple times over the last six months, but through it all, my love for Jace was the one thing that had never faltered. "You have no idea what you're talking about."

"Oh, but I do." Aldair didn't quite sneer, although a corner of his mouth lifted in something very close to a smirk. At the same time, he loosened his grip on my arm—not enough that I could pull entirely away, but at least enough that I wasn't directly in his face. "You are no better than Martine or the other girls here with us. Granted, Khalim cast his glamour a little too heavily, and so Martine is not quite herself, but believe me, when a djinn comes to a mortal woman, he is sure to make himself irresistible. Have you never heard of the legend of the incubus?"

Well, I had, but only because of my studies in English lit, and not because I believed there really was such a thing as demons who appeared in the night, merely to have sex with human women. Actually, back before the Dying, there probably had been a number of people who believed such entities were aliens, rather than demons.

But Aldair was saying they were neither. They were djinn.

"Maybe I've heard of them," I said. "And I'll agree with you that Martine got too big a dose of whatever Khalim was dishing out. But that is not what happened with Jace and me. We didn't even—"

I'd been about to say that we hadn't even slept together until we'd lived under the same roof for more than a month. That information, though, was far more personal than anything I wanted to share.

My discretion didn't appear to have helped me, though, because Aldair tilted his head slightly, blue eyes bright with malice. "You were not intimate until some time had passed? That does not surprise me. Jasreel was always one for the long game."

Don't listen to him, I told myself. *He's more full of shit than an outhouse.*

"You can have your opinion," I said. "My mother used to say everyone was entitled to their own opinion. Then again, my father also liked to say that opinions are like assholes. Everyone has them, and they mostly stink."

"Pithy," Aldair returned with a thin smile. "How sad that the world should be deprived of such penetrating insights."

Right then I wished I could hit him. How dare he sneer at my parents, at people who were dead because of djinn like him? Then I stopped, confused. Aldair had been a member of the original community in Taos, which meant he'd been part of the One Thousand, the conscientious objectors. From what he'd said earlier about Katelyn, his Chosen, that had all been a front. But I wanted to make sure.

"Why Taos?" I asked. "You don't seem to have much use for us piddly mortals. So why through your lot in with the human-lovers?"

"I should think that would be obvious."

"Well, it's not obvious to my puny human brain."

His fingers tightened on my arm again, and I wanted to wince but wouldn't. "He cheated his way to you the first time. I had no choice but to select someone who would allow me to stay nearby. I knew the opportunity would come up again at some point, if I were patient enough. But then Jasreel asked Zahrias if he might stay down in Santa Fe, away from the community that had been established in Taos, and I feared I would have to wait for some time. The Immune from Los Alamos took care of that problem, though, in removing Jace from your side. Zahrias even agreed to petition you on my behalf. But you believed yourself in love, and would have nothing of me."

He pulled me toward him again, his face scant inches from mine. This close, I could smell the wine on his breath, feel the heat radiating from him. In Jace that warmth had always been comforting, but now it seemed oppressive, as if I would soon be buried within it.

Which was probably Aldair's plan.

Now he held me by both arms, and was pulling me against him, his mouth on mine. I squirmed and turned my head, doing anything I could to keep him away from me, but he was too strong. His tongue forced its way between my lips, and I nearly gagged. Despairingly, I realized it didn't matter that he only wanted to do this to hurt Jace, and not because of any particular desire for me. He'd still force me into his bed, claim my body.

But not my mind, I thought fiercely. *No matter what you do to me, Aldair, my thoughts and my heart and my soul will be mine. And Jace's.*

Even as I struggled in Aldair's grasp, however, the room flared with light so bright that it seared into my retinas. I blinked and ducked my head, pulling my mouth away from my attacker.

"Aldair al-Ankara!" an unfamiliar voice thundered, and he let go of me, turning to face the intruders.

I did so as well, shocked and breathless from my unexpected reprieve. Standing between us and the bed were five djinn, three male and two female. Although at first glance they appeared just as ageless as all the djinn I'd encountered so far, something in the gleam of their eyes and the set of their mouths told me they must be older than Aldair, possibly older than any of the Taos contingent.

"You will release this mortal, oath-breaker," said the djinn in the middle, who actually had a few streaks of gray in his hair, although his face was free of lines, save for around the eyes.

"I am no oath-breaker," Aldair protested. "I swore a pact with Zahrias al-Harith to leave his people alone, if they would but quit the place they have claimed as their own, and if they would give this woman to me. She is here of her own free will. Are you not, Jessica Monroe?"

Everything in me wanted to lie, to say that he'd forced me to be here, but that wasn't the truth. I had volunteered to come with him, although only to save the people I cared about back in Taos. And I had a feeling these djinn with their too-old eyes would catch a lie before I was even halfway done speaking it.

I pulled in a breath. "I am here voluntarily. I agreed to this bargain to save the people of Taos from further attack by Aldair and Khalim and their little band of thugs here."

Improbably, the leader of the strange djinn smiled. "'Little band of thugs.' I like that." His expression grew stern, though, as he stared at Aldair. "But it is not that pact of which I speak. I refer to the original oath we all swore, that those of the One Thousand and their Chosen should be left alone to live as they saw fit. That is the oath you have broken, Aldair al-Ankara, for I have word from Nizar al-Naqda and Alif al-Masur that you participated in an attack on the Taos community. Such an attack directly violates the compact we have all agreed to abide by."

At first I didn't recognize those names, and then I realized they must be the two djinn who, along with Rafi, had attempted to flee this plane so they could find help. And they'd been successful.

Against all odds, the cavalry had arrived.

CHAPTER SIXTEEN

ALDAIR BEGAN TO SPLUTTER, "YOU HAVE NO PROOF," but, emboldened by the presence of these apparent elders, I broke in,

"And you killed Rafi, too. Or at least one of your gang did."

One of the female djinn, with hair like rippling copper, spoke for the first time. "Is this true, Aldair? Alif and Nizar said they were beset, but they were unable to identify who had attacked them."

"It's true," I said quietly. "We buried Rafi yesterday."

"An oath-breaker and a murderer," the lead djinn intoned. "You have much to answer for, Aldair, as do Khalim and the rest of his followers."

"Who are being attended to as we speak," another djinn added. "So do not think that help will come to you, Aldair."

His eyes were glittering, and I could see the way his bare chest rose and fell. Cornered, but wild animals were often at their most dangerous when cornered. "You will take their side, those who would debase their djinn heritage by lying down with mortals?"

"What, you mean like what you were about to do with me?" I snapped, and the djinn elders almost looked as if they were fighting back smiles.

"I would watch your words, if I were you, Aldair," the copper-haired female djinn said. "True, there are not many of us with mortal blood, but those who possess it and have been recognized by their parents are just as much a part of our world as you are. Or rather," she added, distaste clear in her fine features, "more so, because at least none of them have cast themselves into darkness by ignoring oaths that all of us swore to uphold."

His hands knotted into fists. Clearly, he could tell he was outmatched, but even with all that, he refused to surrender. Maybe that was because he knew he had no real alternatives. What did the djinn do with oath-breakers, anyway? Based on what Jace had told me about the djinn not being all that organized politically, I somehow doubted there was "djinn jail" someplace where Aldair and the rest of his cronies could be locked up.

"I claim the right of combat with Jasreel al-Ankara," Aldair said then, his eyes seeming to bore into those of the leader of the djinn elders.

"You have no such right," said another of the djinn, one who hadn't spoken yet. He was dark, like Jace and Zahrias, and I wondered if he might be some sort of distant relative. "You forfeited such rights when you allied yourself with Khalim and the rest of his band."

"Not so," Aldair replied. Now the slightest of smiles touched his mouth, and I wondered what he was playing at. I just didn't know enough about how djinn society and its laws—or lack thereof—to know what sort of angle he was trying to manipulate now. "That is, we have two oaths at work here. While you may think it incontestable that I have broken the one, on the other, I have the compact Jessica Monroe made with me. She is not free to go until I release her, or Jasreel stakes his own claim by besting me."

"Which he has already done before," said the redheaded djinn woman. Her voice sounded almost amused, but then she went on, in sharper tones, "So I am not sure what you think you will accomplish by all this."

"I will accomplish maintaining my claim on this woman," Aldair told her, the set of his jaw seeming to indicate that he would never back down on that particular point.

"To what end?" the leader of the djinn present demanded. "As an oath-breaker, you have already doomed yourself to exile in the outer circles. You cannot take this woman with you. She will surely die."

At those words, my heart seemed to stop in my chest. So there was some sort of jail for djinn after all... and apparently one that no mere human could possibly survive.

"What care I for that, as long as Jasreel does not have her?" Aldair said.

A long silence. The redheaded djinn woman murmured something to their leader, and he slowly nodded.

"You shall have your combat, Aldair al-Ankara," the elder djinn said slowly. "And if you lose, you forfeit all claim to this mortal woman."

"But if I win—"

"If you win"—the djinn sent a pitying glance in my direction, but his voice never faltered—"if you win, she will be yours, even into the outer circles."

"Yes," Aldair said, and this time his eyes were focused on me, hateful, piercing. I wanted to look away, to avoid that terrible gaze, but I made myself stare back at him, chin up. He couldn't see how terrified I was. I wouldn't allow it. "She will be mine...even unto death."

There must have been a good deal of mopping-up taking place on the grounds of the Ghost Ranch, but I didn't see any of it. Instead, the redheaded djinn woman took me by the hand, while two of the other djinn, both male, flanked Aldair. In that next instant, we were blinked out of the room where we'd been standing, only to appear in the dining room of the El Monte Sagrado resort.

The shattered glass from the rogue djinns' entrance appeared to have been cleaned up, although I noticed no one had bothered to repair the bar. Bags and suitcases and crates were stacked in neat piles near the entrance. I assumed that was because of the preparations to move to Santa Fe. Maybe it was easier for the djinn to send everything whizzing across the miles if it had all been neatly packed first.

I didn't have time for further speculation, however, because in that moment Lauren and Dani began hurrying past...and then came to a skidding halt when they saw the contingent of unfamiliar djinn, Aldair clearly their captive, standing in the dining area. By then the djinn woman had let go of my hand, but the two male djinn who held Aldair by the arms didn't seem to have any intention of letting him go.

"Jessica?" Lauren blurted, even as Dani bowed very deeply, his hands pressed together before him.

"Honored ones," he said.

They seemed pleased that he had shown them the proper respect. The eldest djinn smiled and said, "Greetings, Danilar al-Harith. We would have speech with your brother, and with Jasreel al-Ankara."

"Of course," Dani said, then disappeared.

It appeared that the Taos djinn were now more or less in possession of their full powers. Was Miles packing up his equipment, since it was no longer needed? Despite my predicament, I couldn't help wondering where he would go now, what he would do. Richard Margolis wasn't exactly forgiving of those he thought had failed him.

Lauren remained there, staring at us as if she expected the entire group to blink out of existence the same way we'd appeared here. Her gaze flicked to Aldair, and she shivered. Not looking at him, she said, "Nizar and Alif came back a few hours ago. They told us they'd reached someone who could help, but...."

"But you did not believe them?" the redheaded djinn elder inquired. She smiled. "I suppose I can see why you would wonder if assistance was truly on its way. After all, we had left you more or less alone until now."

"I—" Faltering, Lauren glanced over at me. It was clear enough that she felt out of her depth, but I didn't have any words of reassurance for her. Not when I had the specter of this "combat" and its possible consequences hanging over me...and Jace.

He appeared then, with Zahrias only a split-second behind. At once he rushed over to me and took my hands in his. Oh, the wonder of his flesh against mine, when I'd been sure I'd never see him, let alone touch him, ever again. But I couldn't allow him to be too joyful. This reunion might be horribly short-lived if Aldair had his way.

"Jessica, are you all right?"

"Yes, Jace." I hesitated, then added so only he could hear, *He didn't touch me. Not really.* I decided it was better not to mention that one kiss, and I didn't feel comfortable sharing any more subvocal speech than those few words in the presence of the djinn elders.

Despite the lack of detail I'd provided, Jace appeared to relax almost visibly. Lord knows what horrible visions he'd been torturing himself with.

But then the lead djinn said to Zahrias, "We have put a stop to the activities of Khalim al-Usar and his followers. Your people need not fear any further harm from them, as they are already being sent into exile. However, Aldair claims that a compact still exists between him and Jessica Monroe, and he will not give her up voluntarily. To prevent her from being sent to the outer circles with him, Jasreel must face him in combat."

Zahrias scowled at that revelation, but Jace only turned from me so he could level a glare at Aldair.

"I welcome the chance to show him once and for all that he has no hope of defeating me," Jace said. The light in his eyes was almost eager. It could be that he intended to finish Aldair for real this time. I had no idea how a djinn battle even worked. Was it to the death, or to first blood? Or some rule I couldn't even imagine?

"We shall see," Aldair said. "You may not find it so easy to cheat this time, now that I know the tricks you employ when you think no one is watching."

"I have never cheated—" Jace began, and Zahrias held up a hand.

"You will have the opportunity to prove yourself soon enough, Jasreel. Let us make the preparations—if, Jasreel, Aldair, you feel you are ready."

"I am ready," both men said, almost at the same time, and then glared at one another.

It was still hard for me to believe they were brothers, except for something very subtle around the brow. By then Lauren had sidled up beside me. "How do djinn even fight?" she asked in an undertone.

I could only shrug. "I don't know," I replied. "But I have a feeling we're about to find out."

No one seemed to care that it was nighttime, the sky black as pitch, with no moon. Almost at once I realized that was no impediment, not when you had fire elementals among you. A ring of dancing flames encircled the open area on the resort's grounds where Jace and Aldair faced one another. I wouldn't say it was bright as day, not with such a baleful orange-yellow glow lighting the fighting grounds, but it did allow us to see clearly what was happening.

Before we'd gotten here, I'd—well, I hadn't exactly pleaded with Jace, since I knew the only way to avoid certain death was for him to fight and win. But I had tried to get him to tell me what to expect, and he'd only shaken his head and dropped a kiss on my cheek. Against Aldair's protests, the elders had granted me a few minutes alone with the man I loved.

"Jessica," he'd said, "what good is it for me to say things that will only worry you? You've returned to me, and that is a miracle. And I have beaten Aldair before, and I will do so this time, and over and over as many times are necessary until he is no longer a threat. I will not risk losing you again."

"All right," I'd replied. I could tell he was going to be intractable on this, and for all I knew, it was for my own good. Not once had Jace ever done something that wasn't intended to keep us safe and together. "But... why does Aldair keep going on about you cheating? I don't believe him, but...."

Jace had taken me by the hands and pulled me to him, kissing me. I wanted to lose myself in that kiss. I wanted him to keep on kissing me, awakening the fire of desire in my veins, because maybe then I might stop worrying about what was about to come next. And if he kissed me enough, it might erase the memory of Aldair's lips on mine, the way he'd violated my mouth with his tongue.

"Beloved," Jace said, "the answer is so very simple. He contends that I cheated, since otherwise he would have to admit that I bested him. In his mind, I am so beneath him that it is impossible that I might have beaten him fairly."

"Beneath him because you're half mortal."

Dark eyes searched my face then, and Jace nodded slowly. "So he told you that."

"Yes." A second went by, then another, as my heart thudded in my chest and I searched for the words to ask the question. But, as my mother always said, the simplest way was usually the best. "Jace...why didn't you tell me?"

His fingers threaded through mine. "In all honesty, I find it difficult to say for certain. There was such a long time when you didn't know what I was at all, and then afterward...the opportunity never seemed to present itself. And perhaps—perhaps I wasn't sure if I wanted to know whether you would love me more, or less, because I had mortal blood in me."

I knew I needed to clear up that misconception right away. "Jace, I love you because you're *you*. Whether you're all djinn, half djinn, part sea monkey...I just don't care."

To my relief, he smiled. "Alas, no sea monkeys. Only divided straight down the middle, djinn and mortal."

"I can handle that." Right then, I recalled something else Aldair had said. As much as I really didn't want to bring him into the conversation, I wanted to know what he'd meant. And also, Zahrias and the elders had given Jace and me this time together, our little calm before the storm. Could anyone blame me for stretching it out as long as possible in an attempt to delay the inevitable confrontation between the man I loved and the man who hated him?

"Jace...."

"What is it, beloved?"

Oh, how I loved hearing him call me that. I wished we could stand here together forever, tucked into a little alcove off one of the conference rooms. But even as I tried to extend it, I knew this time we shared was borrowed. Soon, Aldair would be coming to collect on his debt.

"Aldair said something I didn't quite understand."

At the mention of his brother's name, Jace's brows drew together, but his tone was even enough as he asked, "What was it?"

"Right after he told me you were half mortal, he said something that made it sound as if having djinn powers wasn't necessarily automatic. As if, had you been born here, you wouldn't have even necessarily known you weren't completely human."

"It is complicated, and I don't have time to explain it all right now." I tilted my head at him, indicating with a raised eyebrow that I didn't much care for that reply, and he went on, "I promise you that once I have defeated Aldair again, I will tell you anything you wish to know. But it is true that those children who are sired

by djinn but left with their human mothers don't necessarily exhibit djinn powers. They might have their
own gifts—many of those who possessed true psychic
talents had a djinn strain in their blood—but they
would never be able to tap into their elemental powers the way they could if they were raised in the djinn
world."

I still didn't completely understand, but I knew I'd
have to leave it at that for the moment. It was strange
enough to think that there might really have been psychics and people with other special gifts in the world
before the Heat came along. I'd never believed in any
of that stuff, after all. Then again, if I was willing to
believe in djinn and angels and a God who was apparently so annoyed by what man had done to the planet
that he'd allowed his creation to be wiped out of existence—well, after all that, a few psychics should be
fairly easy to accept.

I said, "But your powers developed because you
were raised in the djinn world by your father."

"Yes."

"So...where is he? Why hasn't he intervened in
some way, told Aldair to back off?"

A long pause. I could see the way Jace's lips pressed
together, how a flicker of pain passed over his eyes.
When he spoke, he sounded tired. "It is not the djinn
way, to interfere in the doings of one's children once
they have reached their majority. We live for so very

long, you see, and to have parents meddling that entire time...." The words trailed off, and he shrugged. Voice too casual, he continued, "I am not sure whether my father has even admitted to himself how his favoritism caused such enmity between Aldair and me. Also, we quarreled when I told him that I intended to take a Chosen and throw in my lot with the One Thousand. I think he was not that pleased that Aldair had apparently chosen the same path, but he'd held his tongue. But when I told my father of my own plans, he lost his temper, and told me that he didn't want to see me make the same mistake that he did."

Maybe it wasn't the best time to be probing, but I couldn't let Jace make a statement like that without asking, "So what did happen to your mother?"

His face darkened, and he shook his head. "Those were different times, and long ago. It was better that my father took me in."

Once again I wondered exactly how old Jace was. Very, very old, if that off-hand comment about Helen of Troy was to be taken at face value. I'd have to let it go for now, though. The last thing I should be doing was upsetting him with memories of his mother when he was about to face an opponent who had nothing to lose.

I went on my tiptoes to kiss his cheek. "We'll talk more afterward. I mean, we'll have all of eternity to learn more about each other, right?"

A light came into his eyes, which before had been shadowed, troubled. He reached out with one hand to brush the hair away from my face, then said, "Yes, beloved. We will have all of time."

I remembered those words as I stood in the cold night air, Dani and Lauren on one side of me, Zahrias and Julia on the other. Although Dani and Lauren were snuggled up against each other, Lauren clearly glad of the warmth Dani provided, I didn't see any such closeness between Julia and Zahrias. Not that I'd really expected to. Maybe some kind of attraction did exist there, or maybe I'd manufactured the whole thing, reading more into stray glances and hesitations than I should have. I had a feeling that Zahrias had asked Julia to stand next to me as my friend, and he needed to be nearby since, as the leader of the Taos community, he was responsible for making sure I had a good vantage point.

Right then I wasn't sure if I wanted to see. Jace and Aldair faced one another in the open area Zahrias had designated as the fighting grounds. Their chests were bare, as were their feet, but they didn't seem to notice the cold. But why would they? They were djinn after all, impervious to the effects of the elements.

The elders had remained to watch the battle. Maybe that was because they wanted to make sure everything would be on the up and up, or maybe because they simply needed to be on hand to spirit Aldair away as soon as the fight was over. Because either way, he was going into exile in the outer circles, whatever those might be.

And if Jace lost, I'd be going into exile, too. A temporary one, since apparently I wouldn't be able to survive in the djinn world for more than an hour at best, but....

"Begin," the leader of the elders said.

Out of nowhere, a howling wind descended on the two men. It buffeted them both, but they remained on their feet, glaring at each other. I couldn't even tell who had conjured it, since it seemed to be affecting them both equally. As I'd imagined, this was how two air elementals would fight, by using the very thing that was part of their nature as a weapon against one another.

Oddly, that wind seemed to be confined to the open space they occupied. I couldn't even feel a breath of a breeze against my skin or touching my hair. Were the other air elementals in the group doing something to keep the spectators protected, or was this one of the rules of the game, that whatever the two combatants did to each other had to leave their watching audience untouched?

Something else I'd have to ask Jace...assuming he emerged the victor. I had a feeling Aldair wouldn't be too interested in answering any of my questions, even if I had time enough to pose them before I was snatched away to suffocate or die of heat stroke or whatever it was that would end up killing me in the djinn world.

And then it seemed as if the wind began to take shape, curling into what appeared to be two small tornadoes, one a dusty bronzy shade, the other grayish-blue. The tornadoes wrapped around one another, twisting and twining like two snakes attempting to choke the life out of each other. I couldn't really tell which was Jace's and which Aldair's, although I guessed Aldair's must be the bluish one, simply because of those blazing blue eyes he had.

If my guess was right, then it seemed as if the gray-blue tornado—for lack of a better word—was gaining on the other one, seeming almost to be swallowing the bronze-hued whirlwind, which shrank more and more as I watched. I looked over at Jace then, saw the muscles of his jaw and neck taut with effort. Aldair's blue eyes flashed in triumph as the bronze tornado shrank further, and I swallowed, willing myself to not show any reaction. It couldn't be over this quickly, could it?

Cool fingers slipped into mine, and I started, then glanced over to see Julia give me a single nod, as if to reassure me that everything would be all right. I didn't know if I believed that, but I appreciated the gesture nonetheless. Beyond her, Zahrias was watching the battle of wills, face impassive. If Jace and Aldair were half-brothers, then that meant Aldair must be Zahrias' cousin as well, since I was almost positive they must be connected on Jace's father's side. Was Zahrias at all conflicted because of his family connection with

Aldair, or did that not matter to him, considering the traitor and oath-breaker Aldair had turned out to be?

Yet another question whose answer I might never know.

But even as I looked on, heart pounding, I saw the bronze-toned tornado that had to be Jace's drop to the ground and spread out, seeming to disappear. Aldair grinned in triumph—only to have that grin turn to a rictus of pain as the whirlwind reappeared in the shape of a golden rope that dropped around his neck and began to pull. His fingers tore at it, but that was like trying to wrestle with the wind. Unable to gain a purchase, he dropped to his knees, gasping.

Julia's fingers tightened on mine. I didn't dare glance over at her, though. I couldn't risk looking away for a single second. Good thing, because then I saw Aldair fall over on his side...but not in defeat. Even though all of us watching were somehow protected from the effects of this unearthly combat, I could almost feel my ears begin to ring as an enormous gust exploded outward from where Aldair lay on the ground, catching Jace off guard and sending him to his knees.

Despite Julia's grip on my hand, I began to move forward, instinctively wanting to go to my lover's side. I hadn't gone a foot, though, before I collided with some sort of invisible barrier that blocked my way. It wasn't as hard and unyielding as an actual wall, but it served more or less the same purpose. From across the way, the redheaded djinn caught my eye and shook her head slowly, just once.

Clearly, I wouldn't be able to help Jace in any way... not that I was sure I could, even if I had been able to get to him.

As Jace was hunched over, trying to catch his breath, Aldair approached, a nasty smile on his face. But he apparently didn't want to waste any air on a mocking speech. Instead, he raised his hands, and a gust of wind came forth, one so strong that it knocked Jace flat. His fingers scrabbled at the hard earth, but he couldn't gain enough purchase to raise himself.

It was worse than torture, having to stand there and watch and know that I could do nothing to save him. In that moment, my own fate mattered very little. What mattered was that Aldair seemed intent on killing the man I loved. And all I could do was watch as the breath was slowly being crushed out of him.

"Do something!" I hissed at Zahrias, but he merely shook his head.

"I am sorry, Jessica," he murmured. "This is between the two of them. No matter what my personal feelings might be, I can do nothing that would interfere with their combat."

I hadn't expected anything else, really, but even so, Zahrias' words only added to the crushing sensation of despair that seemed to overtake me then, smothering my hopes just as surely as Aldair was smothering Jace. A quick glance around the ring of spectators told me that I could expect no help from any of the djinn—their faces were tense, but stoic, and their Chosen equally tense, yet helpless, as if they chafed at these alien laws that kept them from assisting someone they now viewed as one of their own.

Cursing, I let go of Julia's fingers and pushed against the barriers with both my hands. I knew that wouldn't solve anything, and yet I couldn't simply stand there and do nothing. Palms flat against the force field—or whatever it was—I watched as Jace lay pinned on the ground, his breaths appearing to grow more and more labored. While I looked on, my own throat grew more and more tight, as if I were suffocating right along with him. That would be the final cruel irony, wouldn't it? Perhaps I would die along with Jace, and Aldair would be deprived of his revenge.

I didn't want to die...but I also didn't want to live in a world without Jace.

Somehow he managed to move slightly, shifting so he was able to raise himself an inch or so off the earth, black hair spilling over his shoulders. In that moment, his eyes met mine. To my surprise, he didn't look worried or frightened at all. One corner of his mouth lifted slightly.

Are you ready, beloved?

Ready for what? I returned, shocked that he'd been able to reach out to me beyond the invisible barrier the elders had erected.

You'll see.

And then—it wasn't a gust of wind, or a tornado. It was a shockwave, bursting outward from where Jace lay. And when it hit the barrier, I felt the resistance against the palms of my hand disappear, even as my hair blew backward from my face and I heard everyone around me cry out.

Aldair staggered but somehow managed to retain his footing. Jace's gaze was still fixed on me, that small smile playing around his mouth.

Now, beloved.

I didn't stop to think. I knew what Jace needed, what had to be done.

Together, we were far, far stronger than Aldair had counted on.

My feet propelled me forward, onto the fighting ground. The rogue djinn's back was to me, and I hurtled into him with every ounce of strength I possessed, gathering my anger, my worry for Jace, all the pain and doubt and struggle of the last twelve hours, and used them to lash out, to kick his feet out from under him the way my father had trained me.

Aldair went down like the proverbial ton of bricks, hitting the ground with a crack! that made me wince, even though I really didn't care how much pain he might be in. At the same time, Jace pushed himself up to a crouching position and then knelt on his half-brother's back while another of those bronze-colored winds came from nowhere, knotting itself into a rope and wrapping itself around Aldair's throat.

"You are beaten," Jace said then, his voice remarkably calm and unruffled, considering that he'd been the one to be almost smothered to death just a minute or two earlier.

A snarling sound of negation emerged from Aldair, who didn't seem capable of actual speech in that moment. At the same time, the elders came forth to stand in a semicircle around us. The lead djinn did not look particularly pleased by the turn of events, possibly because of the way Jace had knocked down their barrier as if it were nothing. Next to him, however, the red-haired djinn woman appeared to be having some difficulty keeping a smile from her lips.

"Let him speak," the lead djinn told Jace, who then got up off his half-brother...although the wind-rope remained knotted around the other man's neck.

A few hoarse gasps, and then Aldair said, "You see? A cheat. Declare my victory now."

Shit. I wasn't familiar enough with the rules regarding these sorts of confrontations to know whether Aldair was correct or not. I glanced over at Jace, but for once he wasn't looking at me, his gaze instead fixed on the elders.

"I think not," the redhead said. She seemed to have given up fighting back a smile, as she now wore one quite prominently. "There is no rule against knocking down our barrier." A sidelong flicker of her eyes toward the lead elder, who still wore a disapproving expression on his face. "Although that may change in the future."

"He brought in his whore to help him!" Aldair protested, and Jace let out a snarl of his own, the rope tightening still more around the other djinn's neck.

"Peace, Jasreel," said the female elder. "You have won, so there is no need to torture your brother further. As for Jessica, Aldair, she is your brother's Chosen. As such, they are one. She had every right to come to his aid. True, we had not thought you would be able to bring her to your side to assist you, Jasreel, but I must commend you for your original thinking."

"Original—" Aldair began, but he didn't get any further than that. The lead elder nodded at the others in his group, and two of them came up to flank the rogue djinn.

"I cannot say I approve of your methods, Jasreel," the elder said. "But as they did not violate our rules for these battles, I will declare you the victor here. Aldair's claim on Jessica Monroe is negated for all time, and he will be taken from this place to an exile from whence he will not return."

After making this pronouncement, the elder djinn bowed toward me, then inclined his head toward the rest of the group.

"No—"

That was the last we heard of Aldair, because in the next instant, all of them vanished, the red-haired djinn last. I could have sworn she winked at me before disappearing, but it could have been my imagination.

What wasn't my imagination was Jace's arms going around me, and his lips on mine as he swept me into his arms. And all around was cheering and congratulations, the flames generated by the fire elementals leaping into the sky, as if from sheer joy.

We had won.

CHAPTER SEVENTEEN

Zahrias was the first to approach us, Julia standing diffidently a few paces away, as if she wasn't quite sure what she should do.

"Clever," he said, although there was a faint note of disapproval in his voice, as if he wasn't sure he would have employed such rule-bending methods if he'd been in the same situation.

"Desperate, actually," Jace replied, but he was grinning despite his words.

"I suppose that is what these situations sometimes require." Zahrias' gaze moved from Jace to me, and he actually smiled. "You two do make quite the formidable team."

Together, we are stronger.

Yes, Jace had been right about that. And now...now that the enemy had been vanquished, the dragon slain?

Zahrias seemed to pick up something of my thoughts, or maybe the question had been clear enough on my face. He glanced back toward the resort, where some of the people in the crowd now appeared to be headed. Well, why wouldn't they? The show was over, and the night cold. Better to be inside.

"Now," he said simply, "we go to Santa Fe."

I didn't pretend to understand all of it, but it seemed that when the elders spoke, the rest of the djinn listened. If they didn't want us in Taos, even now that Khalim and the rest of his followers couldn't lay claim to it, then we'd move. Apparently the elders had decided that no djinn should call Taos home, now that they had been here themselves and felt whatever "power" existed in the Rio Grande river gorge and the mountain lakes the people of the pueblo had once called their own sacred places.

Part of me was really hoping that Jace and I could go back to the house outside town, but when I asked, he shook his head sadly. "It's not safe."

"Why?" I demanded, even as I shoved the last of my things into my duffle bag. Off to one side, Dutchie was watching the proceedings with a resigned air, as if she knew we were about to change our base of operations once again. "We don't have to worry about the renegade djinn anymore."

"True, but Richard Margolis and his followers are still out there, and they're still in possession of two of Miles's devices."

Crap. I'd almost let the entire conundrum of the Los Alamos community slip from my mind. Jace's words brought them to the forefront, unfortunately. The good part was that Miles was with us—for now, anyway—and so my nightmarish visions of Margolis being able to wield dozens of the damn djinn-neutralizing things would never come to pass. That didn't mean the commander and his followers might not put the ones they still had to bad use, however.

Interpreting my silence correctly, Jace went on, "I doubt they'll come after a group as large as ours, especially if we stay more or less in and around the city center. But our house back in the canyon is too remote. We would be easy prey there, especially since Margolis already knows where it's located. And if he brought a device to block my powers, I would not be able to call out for help."

"I could help," I grumbled. "I'd meet him at the door with a machine gun and tell him to say hello to my little friend."

Apparently *Scarface* wasn't in Jace's pop-culture database, because he frowned slightly and said, "Beloved, I admire your bravery, but he brought seven men with him last time, and most likely would bring even more the next. It's simply not worth the risk."

He was right. It wasn't worth the risk, and it wasn't worth arguing about. I went over to him and put my arms around his waist, then laid my head on his chest. As his arms wrapped around me, I told him, "I know. And it doesn't matter where we are, as long as we're together."

A light kiss brushed against the top of my head. "Exactly. Besides, I think Zahrias will do his best to accommodate us. After all, Santa Fe appeared to be a lovely town, from what I saw of it. There are actually far more options for housing there than here."

I couldn't argue with that. I told myself to give Zahrias some credit, and wait and see where we'd end up.

Well, I doubted anyone had the nerve to accuse Zahrias of playing favorites, but I also doubted it was coincidence that Jace and I ended up in a quaint little five-bedroom pueblo-style mansion only a few blocks off the square, with Zahrias in an even larger house just down the street. The rest of the Taos community weren't all that far away, in an area probably just a little bigger than the mile-radius safe zone we'd been allowed back in Taos.

I couldn't blame everyone for still being a little spooked, even though the rogue djinn had been safely hauled off and exiled to the outer circles. After we were more or less settled in our house, and I'd carefully gathered up any personal belongings from the former owners—there weren't many, which led me to believe this enormous place had been a second or even a third home—I asked Jace, "Just what *are* the outer circles, anyway?"

He'd been silent for a moment, apparently considering his reply. Then he said, "Picture the place your people called Death Valley, but with the atmosphere of Venus."

Ouch. No wonder we mere mortals wouldn't last more than a few minutes there. And having to spend all of eternity in such a place....

No, I wouldn't feel sorry for Khalim and Aldair and the rest, since they didn't deserve my pity. At the same time, the mental image of the outer circles that Jace's words conjured made me wince. Those djinn must have really hated us humans to have taken such an enormous risk.

Or maybe they'd thought the elders just wouldn't care, and wouldn't act against them. Thank God they'd been wrong.

But our community had obviously decided there was strength in numbers, and since there wasn't any shortage of housing near the center of town, everyone seemed to get more or less situated in a place that suited them. Martine was returned to her djinn lover and seemed to be slowly recovering from her ordeal, while the other girl rescued from Khalim's band of rogue djinn, Emma, also went back to the partner who thought he had lost her forever. Aldair's erstwhile Chosen, Katelyn, moved into a casita on the grounds of Dani's and Lauren's place, where they did their best to look after the shell-shocked young woman. She still didn't seem to recall exactly what had happened to her, which was probably for the best.

And Julia took a townhouse only a block or two from the Plaza, explaining, "I'd feel silly in anything bigger. It's just me, after all."

I didn't press her. If that was where she felt comfortable, fine. And if things happened to change in the not-too-distant future, well, I'd be more than happy to help her move her things. Not that there was any sign of something like that going on. Once we were in Santa Fe, Zahrias seemed content to settle into his enormous home and direct things from there. Lauren and Dani were just down the street, so she could still act as Zahrias' de facto secretary.

"Not that I plan to do that forever," she told me one day, a little more than a week after we'd migrated the colony from Taos. Dani had gone over to Zahrias' house, and Lauren and I were having a little "girl" time, shopping in one of the stores on the main square, the kind of place neither of us probably could have afforded to frequent back before the Dying made consumer culture more or less irrelevant. "I'm hoping Julia might take over, if she's willing."

"Really?" I asked, surprised. From what I could tell, Lauren seemed to enjoy acting as Zahrias' right-hand woman.

"Yes." She hesitated, and then I saw her hand go to her stomach. It looked completely flat to me, but....

"Wait—you and Dani?"

"In November sometime, I think." Another pause, and then she glanced around, even though we were the only two people in the store. "We haven't told anyone else yet, since it's pretty early, but...."

I recalled how Jace had said it could be difficult for djinn and humans to conceive children. Apparently not as difficult as he had thought. "Congratulations!" I said, hoping I sounded enthusiastic enough. "That's great news."

"Thanks." Lauren was smiling, but her expression grew serious a moment later. "It's kind of frightening, though. I mean, it's not as if I'll be able to see an ob-gyn or get an epidural when the time comes, or whatever."

"You'll do fine," I told her. "We have Miguel, and EMTs get training in delivering babies. Besides, women were having babies for thousands of years before anyone invented epidurals."

"Yes, but I have a feeling they didn't enjoy it."

I stared at her for a second, and then we both burst out laughing. True, those women who'd had to endure natural childbirth back in the day probably hadn't enjoyed it, but they'd still survived, which was the important thing. I knew Lauren would do fine. Hers would be the first baby born to our little group here, but it wouldn't be the last. Slowly, the community would grow, mortals and djinn mingling their blood, creating a new line of people to inhabit the earth.

Was that the intention all along...that this separation between the two races would slowly crumble away, until there came a time when no one could remember when only man was the ruler of this world?

Well, some would remember. Just because a few djinn were having offspring with humans didn't mean there wouldn't still be plenty of pure-blood elementals around to recall the days when they'd been exiled from the planet they coveted so much.

Still, it was a step. One in the right direction, I hoped. And maybe someday Jace and I would have a child of our own. Would there be play dates in this future I imagined, helicopter parents, other carry-overs from the paranoid time before?

God, I hoped not. This world was ours, and safe enough for now. Sooner or later we'd have to deal with Margolis, though. I couldn't imagine Zahrias allowing the current state of affairs to continue indefinitely. That would be like living with a brush fire on the horizon at all times. It might look out of range for the moment, but you'd never know when a sudden wind could fan the flames and send it raging right in your direction.

For the moment, though, I was willing to let it go. We'd earned our small measure of peace.

To my infinite surprise, Lindsay and Miles had taken up residence in a house on Canyon Road, at the outer edge of the area where we'd all settled. Not to say they were shacked up together or anything, but, according to Lindsay, so they could continue their work together.

"It's built with the bedrooms in two separate wings," she explained quickly, since my eyebrows began shooting up into my hairline when she stopped by to tell me where she was living. "He has his, and I have mine. But the important thing is that the place has a huge five-car garage with a workshop area, so it makes a great lab space. The cars weren't there when we moved in, though. I think it was someone's vacation house."

Like the one I was living in. Intellectually, I knew there had been people who could afford to have million-dollar-plus houses scattered in strategic vacation spots around the globe, but my brain still boggled a bit at the idea. And that wasn't the only thing it was boggling at. "You and Miles, living together," I said flatly.

"In *separate wings*," she repeated, although I couldn't help noticing the way her gaze wouldn't quite meet mine. She lifted her chin and went on, "It just made more sense to be there together. Most of the time I don't even see him until we go out to work in the garage. The lab, I mean."

"Okay," I replied. *Methinks the lady doth protest too much* passed through my mind, but I sure as hell wasn't going to push it. And it was entirely possible the whole thing was innocent...living arrangements of convenience, as it were. At least on Miles's end. I sort of got the impression it had only barely registered with him that Lindsay was even female.

Changing the subject, I asked, "Why is Miles even still pushing the research? I mean, we don't have to worry about protecting ourselves from the rogue djinn any more."

A lift of the shoulders, followed by a smile I thought was a little too indulgent. "I think he'd go nuts if he wasn't investigating some scientific mystery. Anyway, he says he thinks he might be on to something—my screw-up actually may have had some benefit, because it has him going in a different direction, trying to see if a certain series of adjustments may be the key to blocking the powers of only the djinn outside its radius, not the ones within it."

Several days earlier, I would have rejoiced at hearing that news. Now, though, I couldn't help thinking Miles's research was an exercise in futility. The rebel factions in the djinn world seemed to have been quashed, and I was pretty sure the elders wouldn't allow any more of that kind of nonsense, no matter how loosely they might govern otherwise.

But pursuing his research did keep Miles off the street, so to speak, and who knows—tweaking the device might have some use in the future. "I'm sure Zahrias will be interested to hear that," I told Lindsay. "Have you said anything to him about it?"

"Not yet," she replied. "Miles has been seeing some interesting results, but he's not ready for field tests. For one thing, he's not sure any of the djinn would even consent to them."

That didn't surprise me. I wasn't a djinn, but even I could relate to wanting to avoid any further interruption of my powers after I'd finally gotten them back. "Well, maybe not right away. But after things have calmed down a little...."

I let the words trail off. Had they calmed down, really? It seemed that way, and yet I still couldn't shake the feeling that we weren't quite as safe as we thought we were. What if another group of djinn decided Khalim & Co. had had the right idea? Would we always have to be on our guard against another attack? If that sort of thing kept up for any length of time, maybe the elders would finally decide they were tired of fighting our battles for us and would let things run their course.

Lindsay wasn't looking all that hopeful, so it seemed as if her thoughts ran along more or less the same lines as mine. All she said, though, was, "It's possible. Anyway, we're a little ways out from that yet."

We'd been sitting on the patio, enjoying a rare day of temperatures that reached into the upper 60s. She got up from her chair then, adding,

"I should get back. I just wanted to drop by and let you know what I was up to. It seems like the djinn have some way to communicate with one another, but we mortals stuck out there on the edge have to resort to the old-fashioned ways of getting the word out."

I hadn't thought of that, but she was right. It did appear that the djinn could silently relay messages to each other when necessary, even if that communication wasn't as detailed or intimate as what they shared with their Chosen. But people like Lindsay and Julia could only drop by to talk, since of course there was no phone service, no email, no texting…and probably never would be again, unless Miles decided to move on to telecommunications once he was done with refining the djinn-repelling devices.

Maybe I should have left it alone, but I found myself compelled to ask as I got up from my own chair, "Lindsay, do you know what you're doing?"

A shrug. "Do any of us?"

Good question. I didn't have an answer for her, so I only offered her my own lift of the shoulders.

"That's what I thought." She hesitated, head raised to watch the breeze move the branches of the still-bare trees. That same breeze touched a few loose tendrils of her hair and waved them around her face, although most of it was pulled back in a ponytail. "I've been thinking a lot, the past few days. About Rafi and me, I mean."

"It must be hard for you."

She smiled, but the expression wasn't one of fond remembrance. Instead, it looked almost bitter. "That's the problem. It really isn't. I keep feeling like I should miss him more than I do. When he was around, I felt...I can't really describe it. As if I was the most important thing in his world, and so he should be the most important thing in mine. Sometimes it was hard to concentrate. In a way, I felt relieved when I had to pitch in and really use some of my training and talents to get things done. It was almost as if a fog had lifted from my brain or something."

Her words sent a little chill through me. I couldn't help recalling Aldair's words, although his was not a voice I particularly wanted echoing around in my head.

When a djinn comes to a mortal woman, he is sure to make himself irresistible.

So had Rafi cast a glamour on Lindsay as well, to ensure her cooperation? It was beginning to sound that way.

I couldn't tell her of my suspicions, though. What would be the point? Rafi was gone, and what he might or might not have done was now in the past. Lindsay seemed to be focused on the future, whatever that might turn out to be. If that future included Miles sometime down the road, who was I to judge her? He'd loved someone once; Julia had told me he'd lost a wife and young child to the Heat. It wasn't outside the bounds of possibility that he might someday love again. And after seeing the way he'd broken down in the lab over his guilt at Natila's death, I knew he wasn't quite the robot he wanted us all to think he was.

Somehow I managed to summon what I hoped was a reassuring smile. "It's okay, Lindsay. We all cope in our own ways. It sounds like you've been doing okay."

And I hoped to God she would leave it at that. It was better that she was moving on.

She nodded. "I have been, actually. And I have the work to thank for that. Speaking of which, I really do have to get going. Maybe you can stop by and see what we're working on. I think Miles might like that."

I wasn't so sure, but I didn't bother to contradict her. "Sounds good," I said. "Mind if I bring Jace along?"

"Not at all. I'm really hoping that we'll have made some decent progress in the next day or so. Then Jace will have something good to report to Zahrias."

"I hope so, too."

She smiled and departed soon after that, leaving me thinking. It really did sound to me as if Rafi had put the djinn whammy on her, so to speak. And if that was the case, how many more of the Chosen in our group might have been victims of the same sort of coercion?

That's a serious can of worms, Jessica, I told myself. *You sure you really want to open it?*

Not really, but my parents had imparted to me a pretty strict sense of right and wrong. I didn't think I could let this alone. Jace would have told me the truth—if he had all the facts, and I didn't know if he really did. After all, he'd spent most of his time after the Dying by my side, and had distanced himself from the community at Taos so he wouldn't have to be near Aldair. He probably hadn't been around enough to really analyze the interactions between the djinn and their Chosen.

But Zahrias had.

Since Jace was off with Dani and a few others, scouring the area for livestock, I knew I still had most of the afternoon open. I'd asked him why they were even bothering, since Aldair had made it sound as if the djinn could conjure food out of thin air. At the question, Jace had frowned and said, "No, it has to come from somewhere. We do not have the ability to conjure matter from nothing. True, we could 'blink' a head of cattle here, and use that to supplement our diets. But sometimes it is simpler to have the resources we need here at hand."

That reply made me wonder where exactly Aldair had gotten that goose from, and then I decided I really didn't need to know. It seemed clear to me that our community wanted to be as self-sustaining as possible, and I thought that was probably the smarter choice in the long run.

Now, though, I had an opportunity to speak to Zahrias alone.

I didn't hunt up Lauren and request an audience or anything. No, I just walked down the street to the mansion Zahrias had taken for his own, then went up and knocked on the front door. Lauren might have been there, or maybe not; she tended to spend a good deal of time out and about, talking to people, making sure everyone had what they needed.

When the door opened, Zahrias stood there, not Lauren. His eyebrows lifted slightly, but he sounded civil enough as he asked, "What can I do for you, Jessica?"

"Can I talk to you about something?"

To my relief, he didn't even hesitate. "Of course."

Stepping aside, he let me in. I'd been to his house once or twice before, so by that point I was past staring. Even so, it still required a conscious effort to keep myself from gawking at the art hanging on the walls, the enormous ceilings, the floor of patterned slate. Someone had dumped a ton of money into the house. No wonder Zahrias had taken it for his own.

He led me through the foyer and off into a smaller space most likely intended as a sitting room or study, although it was furnished with only two love seats covered in bone-colored leather. In the art niches on the walls, priceless Russian icons stared at us with blank eyes.

After we'd both sat down, he asked, "What is it?"

Now that the moment had come, I wondered if I'd made a huge mistake in confronting Zahrias with this. Our lives were just settling down into something resembling normal patterns. Did I really want to disrupt that tranquility, just because of my own crazy suspicions?

But then I thought of the Lindsay and how she'd felt as if she was in a fog when she was around Rafi, and I knew I couldn't let it go. "This power of glamour you djinn have," I said abruptly. "How many used it on their Chosen?"

Zahrias didn't even blink. "Some did in the beginning, to ease the transition with their partners. Others, like Jasreel, never needed to. But I can assure you that the ones who utilized that power only did so in a limited fashion. None of them are using it now."

"What about Rafi?"

The djinn leader was far too disciplined to sigh, but he did hesitate for a few seconds. Then he replied, "Rafi...did not choose wisely in his partner."

My eyebrows lifted. "Excuse the hell out of me? Lindsay is amazing!"

Zahrias actually smiled. Well, his mouth lifted. Those dark eyes with their amazing fringe of lashes looked more than a little grim. "I did not intend any slight toward Ms. Adarian by my comment. What I meant was that Rafi desired her for her beauty, and paid little attention to her mind and heart. His mistake, because we've all seen that she has an extraordinary mind. And when she would not bend to his will as he desired, he...ensured that she would."

"By casting a spell on her."

"That is a very crude way of putting it. Djinn do not precisely cast spells. They exert their will on their environment, and those around them, when necessary." Zahrias shifted on the couch then, one of the few signs of unease I'd ever seen in him. "I know that he did not use the glamour consistently, which was why they quarreled from time to time. That was her way of trying to resist, although she had no idea of what she actually was resisting."

I crossed my arms and sent him what I hoped was an intimidating frown. "And you didn't stop him?"

Unfortunately, Zahrias didn't seem at all affected by my scowl. Tone mild, he said, "It was not my place to interfere in Rafi's relationship. I am a steward for this community, true, but that does not extend to meddling in the personal lives of my people and their Chosen. Rafi selected Lindsay, and although I thought his choice a poor one for a number of reasons, I could not interfere."

"Even if he hurt her?"

This time, it was Zahrias' eyebrow lifted that lifted. "Did he?"

The answer was no, he hadn't. At least, Lindsay had never mentioned any kind of abuse, and I'd certainly never seen any signs of it on her. The worst that could be said for Rafi was that he'd been entirely too controlling, on a number of levels.

"Well, no," I muttered.

"So you see." Zahrias placed his hands flat on his knees, smoothing the silky fabric of his dark trousers. "While I understand your concern, believe me when I say that no others of my people are now using their powers to coerce their Chosen in any way. They are all together because they wish to be, just as you wish to be with Jasreel."

"He never used that glamour on me," I said. "Not even in the beginning." And then I held my breath, wondering if Zahrias would contradict me, and what I would do if he did.

But he didn't. "No," he said. "Jasreel chose to let you learn to love him. At the time, several called him a fool."

"Did you?" I inquired, my tone a challenge.

A thin smile. "Let us say that I chose to reserve my judgment. And a good thing, too, since events have amply shown that he was actually very wise in that decision."

I still wasn't used to Zahrias paying me anything close to a compliment. About all I could do was offer a silly little nod. Not quite looking at him, I said, "I hope so."

He began to lift a hand, as if to wave off my false modesty, and then paused, his entire frame going still. The color drained from his face.

"What?" I demanded, looking around wildly, trying to see what had set him off. "What is it?"

Slowly, he stood. His hands were shaking, and he clenched them at his sides as if to quell their trembling. "Someone is using one of Miles Odekirk's devices."

"But—" I shook my head. "Well, I just talked to Lindsay, and she said she and Miles were getting close to a field test. Maybe they went ahead with it."

"No." Moving carefully, he went back out to the foyer, then opened the front door. Mystified, I followed him. What the hell was going on? Lindsay had made it sound as if she and Miles were still several days away from doing any kind of live testing. "I know that Lindsay would have come to me and asked permission before turning the device back on."

"Then what...." The words died away on my lips as a wave of horror washed over me. "No."

"Oh, yes," Zahrias said, watching from the entryway as people began to pour into the streets, emerging from their homes in an attempt to discover exactly what was going on. "I fear that Richard Margolis has brought the fight to us."

CHAPTER EIGHTEEN

THEY MET US IN THE PLAZA. THERE WERE, AS BOTH Jace and Zahrias had once feared, far more than the seven who'd raided my Santa Fe hideaway back in December. Now there had to be at least twenty of them, all armed to the teeth, except Margolis, who seemed to have taken over Miles's job as wielder of the device. He stood in front of his band of marauders, the box clutched in his hands, and wore one of the nastiest smiles I'd ever seen.

I knew why. Because with him, wrists bound behind them, were Jace and Dani and the other djinn and Chosen who'd gone out foraging earlier that day.

The injustice of it made me want to scream. But I was attempting to take my cue from Zahrias, who stood next to me, calm, cold, surveying Margolis and his squad with the sort of respect one might reserve for an invading band of cockroaches.

Jace's eyes met mine. *I am sorry, beloved. They came upon us as we were searching a small ranch at the edge of town.*

No need for apologies, Jace. It's not your fault. We were all hoping that Margolis would leave us alone.

Zahrias spoke first. "What is it you want, Margolis?"

The commander's smile didn't waver. "Simple enough. I want my scientist returned to me, along with any components you stole from my lab. And if she's hiding among you, I want the traitor Julia Innes handed over as well."

"I fear that both Dr. Odekirk and Ms. Innes are masters of their own fates, and so it is up to them to decide whether or not they will come back with you."

Although he still smiled, I thought I could see Margolis' brow crease as he scanned the crowd, obviously looking to see if he could spot either Julia or Miles among the people gathered there. Luckily, Miles was blocks away, and I had no idea where Julia might be. She lived alone, without a djinn partner, so it was entirely possible that she had no idea anything had even gone wrong. For all I knew, she was curled up on her couch, reading a book.

"Wrong answer, if you want these ones to keep on breathing," Margolis said. He ran his hands over the device, and I saw the djinn captives grow pale, their chests rising and falling as they attempted to pull in enough air to prevent themselves from passing out.

Zahrias didn't move, but I could see a shudder go through him. And to either side and behind us, I heard muffled moans and gasps for air. The commander must have compressed the field of effect a good deal to intensify it so much. That would have been a reckless move if everyone in the community hadn't clustered together so tightly. As it was, I doubted if anyone had managed to escape Margolis' net.

"As I told you," Zahrias said, his voice tight with strain, "Julia Innes and Miles Odekirk are not mine to command. They will go with you, or not, on their own determination."

I couldn't imagine either one of them voluntarily returning to Los Alamos. Then again, Julia had already shown herself more than capable of self-sacrifice. She might go back, if it meant saving Jace's and Dani's lives.

"Please!" Lauren burst out, pushing her way through the crowd. "You can't hurt them. Not when"— she hesitated, as if debating with herself, then went on — "not when Dani and I are going to have a child."

Margolis' lip curled in disgust. "You think I care whether you're going to have some misbegotten half-breed with one of these creatures?"

She let out a despairing sob, and I watched as Aidan stepped out of the crowd, then put an arm around her waist and drew her back. Weeping, she stood there as Lilias approached and took her by the hand. It was good to see them so quick to offer comfort, but even so, my rage felt like a physical thing, pounding against my temples.

Just when I'd thought I couldn't hate Margolis any more than I already did....

He raised the box, hands resting on its surface but not moving. The threat seemed clear enough. He'd intensify the field enough that it would incapacitate every djinn in a hundred-foot radius. That wouldn't be everyone, but even those outside the field of effect would be unable to do anything, since the second they got in range to attack, their own powers would be destroyed.

"Two humans," the commander said, his voice growing softer now, insinuating. "What do they matter to you? Not more than your own people, surely?"

"Everyone in my community, whether human or djinn, is of equal worth," Zahrias replied, contempt clear in his tone. His nostrils flared, but I could tell he was attempting to keep a grip on his anger, probably because he didn't have any energy to spare on it at the moment.

"Really? Let's test your convictions, shall we?" Margolis nodded, and Mitch Kosky, who was standing next to him, raised the pistol he held, planting the tip of the barrel directly against Jace's right temple.

Oh, please, God, no....

But then I heard Miles Odekirk's cool, dispassionate voice carrying across the murmurs of the crowd. "You wanted to see me, Richard?"

I whirled to my left and saw the scientist approaching, Lindsay on his right and Julia to his left. She caught my eye and nodded, ever so slightly. I realized then that she must have caught wind of what was going on and had run to fetch Miles.

The next thing I realized was that he held the twin of Margolis' device in his hands.

"I see you've become rather adept at operating these," Miles went on, voice so relaxed that you might have thought he and the commander were having this conversation back at the lab in Los Alamos, rather than out in front of a crowd numbering close to a hundred. "But it seems as if you've forgotten at least half of what I taught you. For example, don't you remember that I'd slaved them all together?"

Miles's hands, with their long, clever fingers, moved with lightning speed over the device he was holding. Almost at once, Zahrias straightened, the strained expression leaving his face. In fact, he began to smile. Then he raised his right hand.

A fireball only a few inches in diameter burst from his outstretched fingers. Its target wasn't Richard Margolis, however, but the thing he held. As soon as the fireball made contact with the box, the plastic began to melt. Letting out a screech of agony, Margolis dropped the device, then watched in horror as it dissolved into a puddle of black, oily-looking liquid.

Almost at once, the squad of men the commander had brought with him lifted their guns. But a bunch of half-trained former middle managers and computer technicians and whatever else they'd been before the Dying was no match for a group of angry djinn. The earth shook beneath them, and a wild wind moved among them, and fire raged out of the air to heat their weapons so all they could do was drop them before their skin was burned right off. In less than a minute, Margolis' men were effectively disarmed and surrounded.

"Enough," Zahrias said. He lifted a finger. This time I didn't see any fireball, but somehow the ropes binding Jace and Dani and the others dropped away, their fibers scorched and smoking.

As soon as he was free, Jace ran to my side, and I saw Dani hurry to Lauren and wrap his arms around her.

"Are you all right?" I whispered to Jace, and he nodded.

"Perhaps a few singe marks, but they'll be gone in a minute or two."

Trust Zahrias to do only what was strictly necessary. Clinging to Jace, I watched as the djinn leader approached Margolis, who looked white as a sheet under his olive skin, but who stood his ground, dark eyes glaring.

"Was it so difficult for you to believe that we would live in peace?" Zahrias asked. "We never offered any threat to you or your people."

"What, besides kidnapping one of them right from under us?"

"Miles has been living among us as an honored guest," Zahrias replied, unruffled.

I thought that was stretching it a bit, but since Miles didn't offer any protest, I knew better than to say anything.

"All of you djinn are a threat." Margolis crossed his arms and locked eyes with Zahrias. "Why else would we need these devices Miles built? To keep you from descending on us and killing every last one of us, down to the children!"

At the mention of the children, Zahrias' lips compressed. Flames flickered around his head and then winked out again, and I heard the captured men murmur amongst themselves. No, they'd never really seen what a djinn in full possession of his powers was like. It had scared the hell out of me the first time.

After a pause, during which he seemed to be measuring his next words, he said, "I do regret what others of my kind have done. But they are not among the One Thousand, those of my people who chose to save what mortals they could. And none of my community has ever lifted a hand against a mortal. In coming after us, you directed your hate against those who were entirely innocent. And now...."

Another hesitation, although I couldn't tell whether it was for effect or simply because Zahrias was unsure what to do next. He seemed to gather himself, asking,

"Who among you will speak for your people? Who is second in command?"

There was a bit of shuffling, and Mitch Kosky began to step forward, only to have someone in the back call out, "Not Mitch! He'll start World War III! Get Brent up there."

Several other people said, "Yeah, Brent!" and an unassuming-looking man in his forties pushed his way through the group. He seemed familiar, and then I remembered he was one of the two men Evony had worked with in the Los Alamos motor pool. Brent Sutherland, the former HVAC technician.

I sent him what I hoped was an encouraging smile. We probably hadn't exchanged more than a dozen words at most, but I knew that Evony had liked him, that he and the other guy from the motor pool, Shawn, had sort of become Evony's adopted big brothers, looking after her, making sure no one gave her too much crap about Natila. If Brent was speaking for the Los Alamos people, they might actually have a fighting chance.

Zahrias inclined his head. "Your name is Brent?"

"Uh, yeah." He held a rifle but didn't appear to be too confident with it. Seeming to realize that it was aimed more or less directly at Zahrias, Brent quickly shuffled it around so the barrel was pointing at the ground.

A muscle twitched in Zahrias' cheek, and I got the impression that he was trying to stop himself from smiling. "Well, Brent, it seems that we have a few matters to discuss."

We all gathered in one of the meeting rooms at the La Fonda Hotel, a cozy space with warm faux-finished walls and red-upholstered chairs clustered around a carved oak table. Why exactly I'd been included in the group, I wasn't sure, except that I'd lived in both Los Alamos and Taos, and could possibly offer some inside information. But I wasn't going to argue when Zahrias included Jace and me in his invitation to decide the fate of Richard Margolis and the rest of his contingent.

The man in question had his hands bound, but Zahrias still gave him a seat at the table. Next to him was Brent Sutherland, who looked more and more worried with every passing moment. They were the only two representing Los Alamos. Both Miles and Julia had sat down on what I thought of as the "djinn" side of the table, along with Zahrias, Jace, Dani, Lauren, Lindsay, and me. Actually, more humans sat there than djinn, a fact I didn't think was lost on Margolis, from the way his lips thinned as he glared at us turncoats.

"Now, then," Zahrias said, "let us attempt to come to some kind of a reasonable settlement."

"Reasonable?" Margolis shot back. "How can we expect reason from a bunch of monsters and traitors like you?"

"Um, Richard, maybe you should back off a little," Brent ventured. It was cool enough in the room, but beads of sweat stood out on his forehead, and he looked like he could use a stiff drink.

"You back off—" Margolis began.

"I'd say you should probably both be quiet and listen to what Zahrias has to say," Julia interposed in her calm, low voice. Her expression was neutral, but I could see the way she kept her gaze fixed on Brent and wouldn't look at the commander. Not that I could blame her. Frankly, I didn't see how she could even bear to be in the same room with him.

Brent slouched in his seat, but the second Julia spoke, Margolis smiled again, a nasty, leering smile. "So that's how it is?" he asked. "I should have known. Once a slut, always—"

"That is enough," Zahrias broke in. His tone remained even, but something about it cracked through the air like a whip. "Ms. Innes is here because she always offers valuable input. Unlike you, Captain Margolis."

Something suspiciously like a snigger cut through the silence following Zahrias' words, but I couldn't tell where it had come from. Maybe Dani; it did seem to have emanated from his general direction. Also, he was probably the only person in attendance who had the nerve to chuckle like that during such a tense scene.

To my surprise, Miles Odekirk was the next to speak. "Richard, you've proven that you're unfit to lead the group in Los Alamos. It's short-sighted and wasteful to wage war on those who've done nothing to you. Even now, you brought the most able-bodied men and the best weapons with you, leaving the people in Los Alamos to defend themselves with only one of my devices and whatever leftovers you saw fit to give them."

Angry red splotches showed on Margolis' cheek-bones as he leaned forward, bound hands knotted on the table in front of him. "Stick to your science experiments, Odekirk. You don't know what you're talking about."

Miles only lifted an eyebrow, although I noted the frustrated pucker to Brent Sutherland's brow and the way he'd nodded at the scientist's remarks. He'd really listened to what Miles had to say, even if Margolis was ready to dismiss those remarks out of hand.

"I fear that Miles is correct," Zahrias said. "No one who truly cared about the people in his charge would leave them so undefended."

"They are not undefended!" Margolis shot back, his expression a peculiar mixture of rage and frustration, as if he wasn't quite sure why everyone had decided to gang up on him, including his own people. "The device is shielding them from any djinn, and they have sufficient weapons to take care of any other invaders."

"So you say," Brent replied. "But we don't have any way of knowing that for sure, do we?" He shifted so he was looking straight at Zahrias. "Sir, the rest of the guys asked me to speak for them, and for Los Alamos. I'm no leader, though. Captain Margolis here, he brought us together, looked out for us. I think everyone will be grateful to him for that. But I'm not sure he's what we need going forward."

"A wise assessment," Zahrias agreed. He steepled his fingers together under his chin. "But if you don't want him to lead you, and you feel that you are not up to the task, who will it be? Someone you left behind in Los Alamos?"

At that question, Brent adjusted his position in his chair once again, then shot a quick glance over at Julia. "No, sir. When she disappeared, most of us knew that our little town had lost its soul. Margolis gave the orders, but she was the one who made sure that things ran smoothly. We need her back, sir. We need Julia Innes."

Almost at once, she began to shake her head. "No, Brent, I don't think that's the best solution."

"It's insane," Margolis growled. "She's a traitor. Have you lost your mind?"

"I think your definition of 'traitor' and mine are a little different, Captain," Brent said. Now that he'd spoken his piece, he looked much more in command of himself.

I allowed myself the briefest sideways glance in Zahrias' direction. I wanted to see how he would react to the prospect of Julia returning to Los Alamos. Maybe the tiny signs I'd thought I'd seen pass between the two of them had been nothing at all, only details I'd manufactured in my mind because I'd thought they would be good for each other.

To my disappointment, Zahrias didn't appear to have reacted at all. Without looking over at Julia, he said, "That is ultimately Ms. Innes' decision...although I think Los Alamos would be lucky to have her back."

Oh, crap. Zahrias had probably just uttered the one thing that would almost guarantee Julia's return to Los Alamos. She'd always been big on duty.

Head up...and also studiously avoiding looking over at Zahrias...she said, "You would have to put it to a vote, at least with the people you brought with you."

Margolis let out a snort of contempt. "Vote to have a woman running things? They'll never agree to it. Better get ready to take over, Sutherland."

Brent paled slightly at that remark. But his voice was steady enough as he said, "Well, I guess there's just one way to find out, isn't there?" Directing his next words to Zahrias, he continued, "And if they say it's okay? What then?"

"Then you go home," Zahrias replied. "I fear you will have to leave the commander here with us, but I promise that he will be given the finest jail cell in Santa Fe."

Something like a growl emerged from Margolis' throat, but he didn't speak. He seemed to have realized that there wasn't much else he could do here, not with the djinn back in possession of their powers.

Now you know what it feels like to be powerless, you son of a bitch, I thought then, recalling how he'd had his men torture Natila and Jace, how he'd forced himself on Julia. I still couldn't quite understand how she could bear to sit across the table from him.

"And I'll return with you, Julia," Miles said. "I've done what I can here, but I really need my lab to continue with the proper research on modifying my device."

Next to him, Lindsay seemed to stiffen, but she didn't say anything.

"And I'd like Lindsay to come with me, if she agrees," he went on. "I think I could make a good deal of progress with her assistance, especially once we have access to the lab and its resources."

She did turn toward him then. "You want me to go with you to Los Alamos?"

"Yes...if you'd like to."

For a second or two, she didn't say anything. Then she nodded. "Sure. Yes. That is, I think I could do more good there."

If Zahrias was at all mystified by this exchange, he didn't show it. "If that is your wish. We will miss you here, but it is true that you and Dr. Odekirk have unique skills that might be better suited to the Los Alamos community. Do you think anyone would mind, Mr. Sutherland?"

Brent startled at being addressed so, but then he shook his head. "No, I think everyone will be relieved to have Miles back. And if he has an assistant, all the better, I guess."

"Well, then," Zahrias said. "Let us pose the issue of Ms. Innes as the new leader of Los Alamos to the rest of your men, and go from there. Shall we?"

He stood, and the rest of us followed suit, Margolis stalking along under Dani's watchful eye. I hung back so Jace and I could exit the room after the rest of them had already left.

"Do you really think they'll go for it?" I asked.

Jace shrugged. "You would know better than I. You lived among them for some weeks."

That was true, but I couldn't begin to guess how the men would react to being asked if they'd have Julia as their leader. They had to have been hand-picked by Margolis, which meant I doubted they'd be very sympathetic to her cause. Then again, the commander had included Brent Sutherland among his team, and so they couldn't all be thugs like Butch and Mitch. If they did decide against Julia, then I supposed the mantle would fall to Brent, as much as he might dislike it. I could tell that Zahrias wanted the matter settled; it wasn't in his nature to allow the men who'd come here under Margolis' command to return to Los Alamos without first settling the conundrum of who should lead them next.

And since Brent and everyone else had gotten a taste of what it was like to confront djinn who weren't being hamstrung by one of Miles's devices, I doubted any of them would protest too loudly.

The group from Los Alamos had been herded into the center of the plaza, next to the obelisk commemorating the Indian Wars, where once upon a time Jace and I had lit candles of remembrance for all the loved ones lost. That felt so long ago now, like something from a different life. Back then, Jace had been Jason Little River to me, not Jasreel, and I doubted I'd ever thought of djinn as anything except fairytale beings out of the Arabian Nights or something.

Now, though, they were my family. Or at least the ones around me were.

Butch and Mitch stood at the front of the group of captives, glaring at the djinn who watched over them. The djinn appeared more amused than anything else. It was all too obvious who had the upper hand here.

"We've come to a decision," Zahrias announced. Several of the captured men exchanged furtive, frightened glances. It seemed fairly clear that they expected to be executed on the spot.

He gestured to Julia, and she stepped forward to stand next to him. I could tell she hated being the center of attention like that...and maybe she hated having to stand next to Zahrias and not show any kind of reaction. I wished I'd had the guts to ask her if she was even the tiniest bit attracted to him. But any conversation along those lines had sounded in my head like being back in junior high and asking a friend, "Do you like him? I mean, *like* like him?"

No way.

Now that opportunity was gone, and I could only stand there, my hand in Jace's as we watched Zahrias address the captives.

"We seek no war with you, no matter what your commander might have told you. It is unfortunate that we cannot govern the actions of the other djinn, but even so, we should not have to take the blame for their depredations. Captain Margolis must stay here as our prisoner, as he has proven himself to be an active threat. The rest of you, however, may return to your homes, as long as you agree to elect a new leader."

"Great," Mitch said, all bravado, although I noticed he wouldn't look directly at Zahrias. "Then I nominate myself."

"Shut up, dumb-ass," Brent retorted. He stood on the other side of Julia, his hands jammed in his pockets. "You couldn't lead a drunk frat boy to a keg. No, who we had in mind was Ms. Innes here."

Startled murmurs erupted at that statement. Julia flushed, although I noticed she kept her head held high.

"But she—" Mitch began, only to have the man standing next to him, a big guy with the blurred outline of a former athlete gone to fat, elbow him in the ribs.

"I think that's a great idea," the man said. "All the food consignments have gone to shit since you left, Julia."

She actually smiled. "Sorry to hear that, Henry. I'll have to look into it."

The murmurs, which before had sounded almost hostile, now became almost approving. I saw a lot of the men nodding, as if putting two and two together and realizing that life had been a lot better before Margolis accused Julia of treason and locked her up.

"She's a goddamn traitor," Butch said loudly. Brent scowled and took a step toward him, but Julia shook her head.

"He's right," she said, her voice clear and strong, carrying over the crowd. As she stood there, the cool breeze playing with the ends of her hair, she reminded me of a painting I'd seen once of the British warrior princess Boudicca. Their features weren't similar; it was the lift of the chin, the proud set of their shoulders, that brought the resemblance to mind. "In Margolis' eyes, I am a traitor. I set Jace and Jessica and Evony free because it was the right thing to do. All Jessica and Evony had done was try to rescue the people they loved. And Jace's only crime was being a djinn. That wasn't enough for me. They were innocent of any wrongdoing. And so Dan"—she stopped then, her throat working, before pushing on—"so Dan and I let them go. Margolis killed Dan for that. Just for doing the right thing. And he locked me up. And he...."

This time she hesitated for so long that I was certain she wouldn't continue, wouldn't dare to say it, not in front of so many people. But her chin went up again, and she said coldly, "He raped me, just because he could. Because he wanted to show me who was in control. That's the man you followed. And you call these djinn here monsters?"

The muttering grew angry again, but now their ire was clearly directed against Margolis, who for the first time appeared almost glad of his djinn escort and the protection it offered. Dani's mouth twisted in distaste, and he called out to Zahrias, "So sure you still want to keep this one captive, brother? He should be put out of his misery, for all our sakes."

Zahrias' features might have been carved from stone. He didn't look at Julia as he said, "No. We have already said he would be our prisoner. Truly, his crimes have earned him a sentence of death, but, as you said, that would put him out of his misery, and I believe he should suffer being himself for some time further."

Butch and Mitch were staring at the ground. I'd always thought of the two as big dumb jerks—and they were—but clearly Julia's declaration had shocked even them.

Brent, white-faced and calm, said, "Does anyone object to having Julia Innes as the new leader in Los Alamos?"

Dead silence. He waited a second, then several more. After that he turned to her and extended his hand. "Looks like you're in charge, ma'am."

And as such matters usually did, everything went way too fast after that. Julia asked me to come back to her townhouse with her—so I could help her pack, she said, but I knew she wanted to talk. In the meantime, the Los Alamos group was guided back to the spot on the western edge of town where they'd left their vehicles.

Just before they departed, Brent Sutherland approached me, expression both worried and puzzled.

"Evony," he said in an undertone. "I haven't seen her anywhere around. Where is she?"

My heart seemed to clench in my chest, but I made myself reply, "I'm so sorry, Brent. She's—she's gone. We lost her when we were bringing Miles back from Los Alamos. A group of rogue djinn attacked our caravan. She—" I forced myself to swallow. The tears were back, like a hard, burning knot in my throat. "She took some of them with her, though."

Brent's eyes were glistening as well. "I'll bet she did. That girl had heart." He paused for a few seconds, obviously gathering himself. "I'll let Shawn know. He had sort of a thing for her, I think. Of course he knew it couldn't go anywhere, because of who Evony was, but...."

That was where he stopped, and I didn't press him to stay anything else. It hurt too much.

Then he was gone, and Julia gesturing for me to come with her. We walked the block or two to her townhouse without speaking. Once we were inside, I said, "That was a brave thing you did."

Her mouth twitched. "Was it?" She moved past me and headed up the stairs, and so I followed her. After that she went into the bedroom and opened the door to the walk-in closet. "I suppose I just wanted them to know the truth so they could decide for themselves. And as awful as it was to say it, once I'd gotten it out, it felt good. I was tired of feeling ashamed. I wasn't the one who did something terrible."

"No, you weren't." I watched as she got out a soft-sided suitcase and a duffle bag, and began folding her clothes into them. She really didn't have that much, so I could tell she'd be done in a minute or two. "And... you're okay with this? Going back to Los Alamos? That is...I mean, I thought...."

The awkward words died away into silence. A sad little smile played around her mouth as she zipped up the suitcase and said, "Maybe I did, for a second or two here and there. Then I realized I was just being stupid. Because if there had been anything, anything at all, well...I would have been his Chosen from the start, wouldn't I?"

I didn't have an answer for her, because deep down I knew she was right. Zahrias would have seen her, and claimed her, back before the Dying, if he'd really wanted her.

"Anyway," she went on briskly, "it's good, I think. We have a chance to make something of Los Alamos, now that Margolis is out of the way. And since Miles is coming back with me, that'll help, too. People will be reassured knowing he's around, doing what needs to be done to protect them from the other djinn." She paused, and then smiled again. This time, though, her expression was almost sly. "And tell me I was hallucinating, because I could swear I saw that pretty assistant of his making googly eyes at him."

I had to smile at the mental image. "I don't know about 'googly eyes,' but I think there's something going on. Or at least she thinks she might want there to be." I wondered how much I should tell Julia and then decided the heck with it. I was going to miss her. In the back of my mind, I'd wanted her to stay around so I could have a friend, a girl friend, to talk to. I loved Jace, and he was the center of my world, but there were some things it was just easier to talk about with a girl-friend. "I don't think she was all that happy with her djinn partner. She mourned him when he was gone, but I think she was also relieved in a way."

Julia nodded, and I realized Lindsay's feelings toward Rafi probably weren't all that far removed from how Julia must have felt about her abusive fiancé, the one she'd lost in the Dying. "How many are like that?" she asked softly. "That is, how many were claimed by djinn, but are nowhere near as happy as you are with Jace?"

If it had happened to Lindsay, it had probably happened to others. But I wasn't sure I wanted to go into all that, and so I only lifted my shoulders and said, "I don't know, Julia. I just don't know."

An hour later, and they were all gone. I could tell nothing from Zahrias' expression as he watched Julia climb into that blasted yellow Hummer next to Brent and then drive away. She didn't look back.

But why would she?

Margolis didn't precisely end up at the local police station. Instead, he was placed in one of the holding cells in the local U.S. Marshals building, a far more state-of-the-art facility. He wasn't too happy about it... not that any of the djinn set to guard him seemed to care.

After that, things quieted down a bit. Jace and I scrounged a ham radio from one of the local electronics supply stores and got in contact with Los Alamos that way. Even though Julia was now in charge and there probably wouldn't be any more craziness from that quarter, I still thought it a good idea for the two communities to stay in touch. If nothing else, maintaining communications might make it less easy for any rogue djinn out there to cause trouble for either group.

And then it was April, and the air began to warm a bit more. The wind still had a bite to it, but the storms brought rain, not snow. And as much as I loved being with Jace no matter where I was, my heart ached for the house in the hills. I wanted to be there with him to watch the first wildflowers begin to grow. It was beautiful here in town, but it would be even better there.

"We would be safe," I told him one morning as we awoke to an achingly clear blue sky beyond the windows of our bedroom. I was lying with my head on his chest, one of his hands lazily stroking my hair. "The Los Alamos community isn't a threat any longer, and it seems as if the elders put the fear into any djinn who might try to mess with the One Thousand and their Chosen. So why can't we go home?"

His hand stilled. After a brief silence, he said, "Beloved, there is no real reason why not. I suppose I had thought you were happy here."

"I am, because I'm with you. But I want to go back to the place where I fell in love. It's not even so very far—fifteen minutes, and we're right back down here with everyone else."

"Less than that," he said, chuckling. "It's not as if we have to drive, after all."

Of course. I'd spent so much time around Jace when he was either hiding his talents from me or they were being blocked that I kept forgetting how much power he truly had to command. "Then what's stopping us?"

"Nothing, my love," he said, pulling me up to him so he could place a lingering kiss on my lips. "Nothing at all."

Zahrias seemed neither pleased nor displeased by our announcement that we'd decided to return to our hidden sanctuary outside town. "If that is what you think of as home, then I suppose that is where you should go," he said calmly.

Yes, Zahrias had been very calm lately...perhaps too calm.

But I was too excited by the prospect of going back to the house to really pay much attention to Zahrias' moods, or lack thereof. We had a few things to pack, and I wondered if Jace planned to "blink" it all over, or whether we'd go the more pedestrian way, in the Land Rover we'd been given for our use, should we need it.

As it turned out, we didn't go home either way. Just as we were finishing up our packing, someone knocked at the front door. Puzzled, I went to answer it. We hadn't really been expecting anyone, but maybe it was Lauren coming over to say goodbye or wish us luck or something.

It wasn't Lauren at the door, however, but Brent Sutherland, accompanied by Shawn Gutierrez. And just beyond them, parked at the curb, was a Grand Cherokee, the one I'd thought I'd left behind forever in Los Alamos.

All I could do was stand there and goggle at it, and at them. "Um...what's this?" I said at last.

"Julia sent it over," Brent said. "We were doing a vehicle inventory, and she found it locked up in the garage at Margolis' house. She thought you might want it back, so she sent us over to deliver it."

"That's—" I didn't find myself at a loss for words all that often, but right then I was fighting to get them out past the tightness in my throat. Up until that moment, I would have said I'd forgotten all about the Cherokee, that it wasn't important, but right then I realized how much I did want that car back, that last physical reminder of the family I'd lost. "That's amazing. Tell Julia thank you."

"We will." Shawn glanced past me to the bags Jace and I had piled in the foyer in preparation for our leave-taking. "Going somewhere?" he asked.

"Yes," I said. "I'm going home."

DUTCHIE RAN AHEAD, TAIL WAGGING. JACE AND I followed at a more sedate pace, the Cherokee idling a few feet behind us. There hadn't been any question of traveling here by djinn methods, not once I had my father's Jeep back.

"Smell like home, girl?" I asked, bending to scratch behind the dog's ears as she happily wuffled around in the fresh grass that had grown up in front of the gate.

Jace came over to stand next to me. His hand rested on the padlock attached to the chain I'd wrapped around the wrought iron of the gate grille. "Do you have the key for this?"

I arched an eyebrow at him. "Do I need a key?"

"No," he replied, flashing me that grin I loved so much. He made a pinching movement with his thumb and forefinger, and the padlock fell away, the metal twisted as if a giant had wrenched it off.

"Handy. But I hope you have something a little less destructive in mind for the front door." Because of course the keys to the home had disappeared long ago, left behind in Los Alamos with the rest of the belongings abandoned in the little house Evony and I had been given to live in. I supposed Margolis must have gotten his hands on the keys and everything else of mine, but I had no idea what he'd done with them. Locked them up somewhere, most likely, which meant Julia would probably come across those items at some point. It seemed as if she was being fairly methodical about going through the erstwhile commander's things and disbursing them as necessary.

Would she take it upon herself to return my belongings to me? It would be a very good excuse to come back to Santa Fe....

"I'll manage," Jace said, interrupting my reverie.

"You always do."

We went back to the Jeep and climbed in. Dutchie, however, decided she'd much rather run up the hill on her own power, and so she trotted a few paces ahead of us as I slowly drove onto the property.

From what I could see, nothing seemed to have changed much. The ground was muddy from a storm we'd had a few nights earlier, and the faintest mist of green was showing on the branches of the aspen trees.

It wouldn't be too long now before they really began to leaf out.

I parked the Cherokee in front of one of the garage bays, then got out. Jace did the same before going around to the back so he could pick up our luggage. It wasn't much—a couple of duffle bags, the backpack that held Dutchie's supplies.

He shouldered the lot of it, then said, "Shall we?"

Now that we were here, I found myself almost nervous. What if someone had broken in, despite all the precautions I'd taken?

Then we'll fix whatever damage they might have done and get on with our lives, I chided myself as I followed Jace to the front door. I did wonder why he'd gone that way, as it would have been closer to let ourselves in through the side entrance off the kitchen.

But then he said, "I wanted us to come here the way you did the first time. Through the front, so we can take it in all over again."

I reached out and took his hand. His fingers were reassuringly warm. Of course, why wouldn't they be? Miles Odekirk and his devices were miles and miles away. There was nothing here that could hurt Jace.

He smiled at me, his hand still wrapped around mine as he reached out with the other one. Just the merest touch on the latch was enough to have the door swing inward, although I knew I'd locked it all up tight when I'd left with Evony, going to Los Alamos to rescue our loved ones.

And she'd never returned.

I swallowed, blinking back tears. I didn't want to cry. I wanted to be happy to be here. Not a day passed when I didn't think about Evony, wonder if there wasn't something I could have done to keep things from turning out the way they did. And I knew I would continue to do so. I just didn't want to do that right now.

Jace's fingers tightened on mine. *It's all right, beloved. Let us go in.*

Nodding, I followed him inside. Dutchie had already pushed past us and was rolling around on the Navajo rug, maybe trying to get her scent on it, or maybe reveling in being surrounded by items that did smell like her. The house was cold, but it didn't smell damp or closed-up. In fact, the air was oddly fragrant.

I realized why when I glanced toward the far corner of the living room. Standing there, yellowed and forlorn, was the Christmas tree Jace had brought me. It hadn't rotted, but merely dried out. That was where the oddly aromatic scent had come from.

The next thing I realized was that it had dropped half its needles on the floor, and it was going to be one ungodly mess to clean up.

Jace unslung the duffle bags and the backpack from his shoulder. "No fear, Jessica—I can take care of that for us."

He made a subtle movement with his free hand, and the next thing I knew, it was as if a small whirlwind had rushed into the room, gathering up all the loose pine needles and bits of dropped popcorn, then swirling around the tree itself until all of it blinked out of existence. The corner was clean, untouched, as if my Christmas tree had never existed.

"Very handy," I said, going up on my tiptoes so I could kiss his cheek. "I think I'll keep you around."

A grin. "That's a relief."

With the tree gone, I could see that the rest of the front room appeared untouched. And as we made our way back toward the kitchen, it became obvious that no one had come here to disturb the house in my absence. Dust lay thick on everything, and I knew I'd have to throw a bunch of stuff out of the refrigerator and scrub it all down, but at least the power had stayed on the whole time, so whatever was in the freezer should be intact.

Truth be told, it didn't smell quite as nice in here. I saw Jace's nose wrinkle, and then he made another movement with his hand. No, the refrigerator door didn't fly open so a parade of spoiled food could emerge, but it did seem as if the air miraculously cleared.

I let go of his hand and went over to the refrigerator, then cautiously opened the door. Inside, all was bare and clean, sparkling in the bright sunshine coming in through the window. "Nice work," I said. "Now all we have to do is fill it again."

"There should still be plenty of food in the cellar." Jace glanced out the window, the sunlight warming his dark eyes to a rich coffee color. "And it looks like a fine day for hunting."

"What, you're not going to magic something right into the fridge for me?"

He didn't smile. "No. I want us to earn what we have, work for it."

"That doesn't sound very djinn-like."

"Maybe it isn't." Only a step separated us; he closed the gap and pulled me against him, but gently, so I could lay my head against his chest and listen to the heart beating within. "After all, I am half human. I want to cherish this world, just as I cherish you. If I make things too easy for us...."

He didn't finish the sentence, but I thought I understood what he meant. We should never take for granted what we had, but give thanks for all of it, for every passing day, for the sun rising in the morning and the moon that would illuminate our nights.

"If it's too easy, then we'll just end up making the same mistakes all over again," I said softly.

There it was, that brush of his lips against my hair, that quiet gesture which told me how much he loved me, almost more than the times our bodies came together in shared passion. Warmth flowed through my limbs. His warmth.

"Beloved, you understand me better than I understand myself." His arms tightened around me. "But you don't believe I am being foolish for thinking this way?"

I began to shake my head, then realized I could only move so far, pillowed against his chest as I was. Going still, I replied, "No. I've been thinking a lot about those few months we had together before everything got so crazy. It was hard work, but there was a rhythm to it, a sort of peace, even though the world—or at least the world I knew—had more or less ended. I think that's why I wanted so badly to come back here. I wanted what we had then. I want the life that Margolis tried to take away from us."

He gently loosened his arms and moved away a few inches, just enough so he could take both my hands in his and gaze down into my face. "I want that, too, Jessica. I want to tend the plants in the greenhouse and take Dutchie hunting in the Polaris."

"And go see if there are any goats and chickens left anywhere around here," I put in.

"Yes, that, and make you coffee in the morning, and lie down beside you every night."

"And wake up next to you every morning." I held his hands, feeling the strength in the bones and flesh. That was only his surface strength, I knew. Far beyond the muscles, or even the power he could wield when necessary, there was Jace. Jasreel, a man of the djinn, and the only man I would ever need or want or love.

It had taken the end of the world for him to come to me, and now that we were together, truly together, I knew we would never be apart.

The End